Timothy Shay Arthur

Heart-Histories and Life-Pictures

Timothy Shay Arthur

Heart-Histories and Life-Pictures

ISBN/EAN: 9783744750554

Printed in Europe, USA, Canada, Australia, Japan

Cover: Foto ©Andreas Hilbeck / pixelio.de

More available books at **www.hansebooks.com**

HEART-HISTORIES

.

AND

LIFE-PICTURES.

BY

T. S. ARTHUR.

PHILADELPHIA:

J. W. BRADLEY, 48 N. FOURTH STREET.

1860.

INTRODUCTION.

So interested are we all in our every-day pursuits; so given up, body and mind, to the attainment of our own ends; so absorbed by our own hopes, joys, fears and disappointments, that we think rarely, if at all, of the heart-histories of others—of the bright and sombre life-pictures their eyes may look upon. And yet, every heart has its history: how sad and painful many of these histories are, let the dreamy eyes, the sober faces, the subdued, often mournful tones, of many that daily cross our paths, testify. An occasional remembrance of these things will cause a more kindly feeling towards others; and this will do us good, in withdrawing our minds from too exclusive thoughts of self.

Whatever tends to awaken our sympathies

towards others, to interest us in humanity, is, therefore, an individual benefit as well as a common good. In all that we have written, we have endeavored to create this sympathy and awaken this interest; and so direct has ever been our purpose, that we have given less thought to those elegancies of style on which a literary reputation is often founded, than to the truthfulness of our many life-pictures. In the preparation of this volume, the same end has been kept in view, and its chief merit will be found, we trust, in its power to do good.

T. S. A.

PHILADELPHIA, *December*, 1852.

CONTENTS.

vi   CONTENTS.

THE BOOK OF MEMORY.

CHAPTER I.

" THERE is a book of record in your mind, Edwin,"
said an old man to his young friend, " a book of
record, in which every act of your life is noted down.
Each morning a blank page is turned, on which the
day's history is written in lines that cannot be effaced.
This book of record is your memory ; and, according
to what it bears, will your future life be happy or
miserable. An act done, is done forever ; for, the time
in which it is done, in passing, passes to return no
more. The history is written and sealed up. Nothing
can ever blot it out. You may repent of evil, and put
away the purpose of evil from your heart ; but you
cannot, by any repentance, bring back the time that is

1*

gone, nor alter the writing on the page of memory Ah ! my young friend, if I could only erase some pages in the book of my memory, that almost daily open themselves before the eyes of my mind, how thankful I would be ! But this I cannot do. There are acts of my life for which repentance only avails as a process of purification and preparation for a better state in the future ; it in no way repairs wrong done to others. Keep the pages of your memory free from blots, Edwin. Guard the hand writing there as you value your best and highest interests !"

Edwin Florence listened, but only half comprehended what was said by his aged friend. An hour afterwards ne was sitting by the side of a maiden, her hand in his, and her eyes looking tenderly upon his face. She was not beautiful in the sense that the world regards beauty. Yet, no one could be with her an hour without perceiving the higher and truer beauty of a pure and lovely spirit. It was this real beauty of character which had attracted Edwin Florence ; and th young girl's heart had gone forth to meet the tender of affection with an impulse of gladness.

" You love me, Edith ?" said Edwin, in a low voice, as he bent nearer, and touched her pure forehead with his lips.

"As my life," replied the maiden, and her eyes were full of love as she spoke.

Again the young man kissed her.

In low voices, leaning towards each other until the breath of each was warm on the other's cheek, they sat conversing for a long time. Then they separated; and both were happy. How sweet were the maiden's dreams that night, for, in every picture that wandering fancy drew, was the image of her lover!

Daily thus they met for a long time. Then there was a change in Edwin Florence. His visits were less frequent, and when he met the young girl, whose very life was bound up in his, his manner had in it a reserve that chilled her heart as if an icy hand had been laid upon it. She asked for no explanation of the change; but, as he grew colder, she shrunk more and more into herself, like a flower folding its withering leaves when touched by autumn's frosty fingers.

One day he called on Edith. He was not as cold as he had been, but he was, from some cause, evidently embarrassed.

"Edith," said he, taking her hand—it was weeks since he had touched her hand except in meeting and parting—"I need not say how highly I regard you. How tenderly I love you, even as I could love a pure and gentle sister. But—"

He paused, for he saw that Edith's face had become very pale ; and that she rather gasped for air than breathed.

"Are you sick ?" he asked, in a voice of anxiety

Edith was recovering herself.

ı "No," she replied, faintly.

A deep silence, lasting for the space of nearly half a minute, followed.   By this time the maiden, through a forced effort, had regained the command of her feelings.   Perceiving this, Edwin resumed—

"As I said, Edith, I love you as I could love a pure and gentle sister.   Will you accept this love ?" Will you be to me a friend—a sister ?".

Again there passed upon the countenance of Edith a deadly palor ; while her lips quivered, and her eyes had a strange expression.   This soon passed away, and again something of its former repose was in her face. At the first few words of Florence, Edith withdrew the hand he had taken.   He now sought it again, but she voided the contact.

"You do not answer me, Edith," said the young man.

"Do you wish an answer ?"   This was uttered in a scarcely audible voice.

"I do, Edith," was the earnest reply.   "Let there be no separation between us.   You are to me what you

have ever been, a dearly prized friend. I never meet
you that my heart does not know an impulse for good
—I never think of you but—"

"Let us be as strangers!" said Edith, rising abruptly,
And turning away, she fled from the room.

Slowly did the young man leave the apartment in
which they were sitting, and without seeing any
member of the family, departed from the house.
There was a record on his memory that time would
have no power to efface. It was engraved too deeply
for the dust of years to obliterate. As he went,
musing away, the pale face of Edith was before him;
and the anguish of her voice, as she said, "Let us be
as strangers," was in his ears. He tried not to see the
one, nor hear the other. But that was impossible.
They had impressed themselves into the very substance
of his mind.

Edwin Florence had an engagement for that very
evening. It was with one of the most brilliant,
beautiful, and fascinating women he had ever met. A
few months before, she had crossed his path, and from
that time he was changed towards Edith. Her name
was Catharine Linmore. The earnest attentions of
Florence pleased her, and as she let the pleasure she
felt be seen, she was not long in winning his heart
entirely from his first love. In this, she was innocent;

for she knew nothing of. the former state of his affections towards Edith.

After parting with Edith, Edwin had no heart to fulfill his engagement with Miss Linmore. He could think of nothing but the maiden he had so cruelly deserted; and more than half repented of what he had done. When the hour for the appointment came, his mind struggled awhile in the effort to obtain a consent to go, and then decided against meeting, at least on that occasion, the woman whose charms had led him to do so great a wrong to a loving and confiding heart. No excuse but that of indisposition could be made, under the circumstances; and, attempting to screen himself, in his own estimation, from falsehood, he assumed, in his own thoughts, a mental indisposition, while, in the billet he dispatched, he gave the idea of bodily indisposition. The night that followed was, perhaps, the most unhappy one the young man had ever spent. Days passed, and he heard nothing from Edith. He could not call to see her, for she had interdicted hat. Henceforth they must be as strangers. The effect produced by his words had been far more painful than was anticipated; and he felt troubled when he thought about what might be their ultimate effects.

On the fifth day, as the young man was walking with Catharine Linmore, he came suddenly face to face with

Edith. There was a change in her that startled him. She looked at him, in passing, but gave no signs of re-cognition.

" Wasn't that Miss Walter ?" inquired the compan-ion of Edwin, in a tone of surprise.

" Yes," replied Florence.

" What's the matter with her ! Has she been sick ! How dreadful she looks !"

" I never saw her look so bad," remarked the young man. As they walked along, Miss Linmore kept al-luding to Edith, whose changed appearance had excited her sympathies.

" I've met her only a few times," said she, " but I have seen enough of her to give me a most exalted opinion of her character. Some one called her very plain ; but I have not thought so. There is something so good about her, that you cannot be with her long without perceiving a real beauty in the play of her countenance."

" No one can know her well, without loving her for ne goodness of which you have just spoken," said Edwin.

" You are intimate with her ?"

" Yes. She has been long to me as a sister." There was a roughness in the voice of Florence as he said this.

" She passed without recognizing you," said Miss Linmore.

" So I observed."

" And yet I noticed that she looked you in the face, though with a cold, stony, absent look   It is strange! What can have happened to her ?"

" I have observed a change in her for some time past," Florence ventured to say ; " but nothing like this. There is somethihg wrong." ·

When the time to part with his companion came, Edwin Florence felt a sense of relief. Weeks now passed without his seeing or hearing any thing from Edith. During the time he met Miss Linmore frequently ; and encouraged to approach, he at length ventured to speak to her of what was in his heart. The young lady heard with pleasure, and, though she did not accept the offered hand, by no means repulsed the ardent suitor. She had not thought of marriage, she said, and asked a short time for reflection.

Edwin saw enough in her manner to satisfy him that the result would be in his favor. This would have made him supremely happy, could he have blotted out all recollection of Edith and his conduct towards her. But, that was impossible. Her form and face, as he had last seen them, were almost constantly before his eyes. As he walked the streets, he feared lest he should meet her; and never felt pleasant in any company until certain that she was not there.

A few days after Mr. Florence had made an offer of his hand to Miss Linmore, and at a time when she was about making a favorable decision, that young lady happened to hear some allusion made to Edith Walter, in a tone that attracted her attention. She immediately asked some questions in regard to her, when one of the persons conversing said—

"Why, don't you know about Edith?"

"I know that there is a great change in her. But the reason of it I have not heard."

"Indeed! I thought it was pretty well known that her affections had been trifled with."

"Who could trifle with the affections of so sweet, so good a girl," said Miss Linmore, indignantly. "The man who could turn from her, has no true appreciation of what is really excellent and exalted in woman's character. I have seen her only a few times; but, often enough to make me estimate her as one among the loveliest of our sex."

"Edwin Florence is the man," was replied. "He won her heart, and then turned from her; leaving the waters of affection that had flowed at his touch to lose themselves in the sands at his feet. There must be something base in the heart of a man who could trifle thus with such a woman."

"It required a strong effort on the part of Miss Linnore to conceal the instant turbulence of feeling that succeeded so unexpected a declaration. But she had, naturally, great self-control, and this came to her aid.

"Edwin Florence!" said she, after a brief silence, speaking in a tone of surprise.

"Yes, he is the man. Ah, me! What a ruin has been wrought!" I never saw such a change in any one as Edith exhibits. The very inspiration of her life is gone. The love she bore towards Florence seems to have been almost the mainspring of her existence; for in touching that the whole circle of motion has grown feeble, and will, I fear, soon cease for ever."

"Dreadful! The falsehood of her lover has broken her heart."

"I fear that it is even so."

"Is she ill? I have not seen her for a long time," said Miss Linmore.

"Not ill, as one sick of a bodily disease; but drooping about as one whose spirits are broken, and who finds no sustaining arm to lean upon. When you meet her, she strives to be cheerful, and appear interested. But the effort deceives no one."

" Why did Mr. Florence. act towards her as he has done ?" asked Miss Linmore.

" A handsomer face and more brilliant exterior were the attractions, I am told."

The young lady asked no more questions. Those who observed her closely, saw the warm tints that made beautiful her cheeks grow fainter and fainter, until they had almost entirely faded. Soon after, she retired from the company.

In the ardor of his pursuit of a new object of affection, Edwin Florence scarcely thought of the old one. The image of Edith was hidden by the interposing form of Miss Linmore. The suspense occasioned by a wish for time to consider the offer he had made, grew more and more painful the longer it was continued. On the possession of the lovely girl as his wife, depended, so he felt, his future happiness. Were she to decline his offer he would be wretched. In this state of mind, he called one day upon Miss Linmore, hoping and fearing, yet resolved to know his fate. The moment he entered her presence he observed a change. She did not smile ; and there was something chilling in the steady glance of her large dark eyes.

" Have I offended you ?" he asked, as she declined taking his offered hand.

" Yes," was the firm·reply, while the young lady as
sumed a dignified air.

" In what ?" asked Florence.

" In proving false to her in whose ears you first
breathed words of affection."

The young man started as if stung by a serpent.

" The man," resumed Miss Linmore, " who has been
false to Edith Walter, never can be true to me.   I
wouldn't have the affection that could turn from one
like her.   I hold it to be light as the thistle-down.
Go ! heal the heart you have almost broken, if, per-
chance, it be not yet too late.   As for me, think of me
as if we had all our lives been strangers—such, henceforth, we must ever remain."

And saying this, Catharine Linmore turned from the
rebuked and astonished young man, and left the room.
He immediately retired.

CHAPTER II.

EVENING, with its passionless influences, was stealing softly down, and leaving on all things its hues of quiet and repose. The heart of nature was beating with calm and even pulses. Not so the heart of Edwin Florence. It had a wilder throb; and the face of nature was not reflected in the mirror of his feelings. He was alone in his room, where he had been during the few hours that had elapsed since his interview with Miss Linmore. In those few hours, Memory had turned over many leaves of the Book of his Life. He would fain have averted his eyes from the pages, but he could not. The record was before him, and he had read it. And, as he read, the eyes of Edith looked into his own; at first they were loving and tender, as of old; and then they were full of tears. Her hand lay, now, confidingly in his; and now it was slowly withdrawn. She sat by his side, and leaned upon him

—his lips were upon her lips ; his cheek touching her cheek ; their breaths were mingling. Another moment and he had turned from her coldly, and she was drooping towards the earth like a tender vine bereft of th support to which it had held by its clinging tendrils. Ah ! If he could only have shut out these images ! If he could have erased the record so that Memory could not read it ! How eagerly would he have drunk of Lethe's waters, could he have found the fabled stream !

More than all this. The rebuke of Miss Linmore almost maddened him. In turning from Edith, he had let his heart go out towards the other with a passionate devotion. Pride in her beauty and brilliant accomplishments had filled his regard with a selfishness that could ill bear the shock of a sudden repulse. Sleepless was the night that followed ; and when the morning, long looked for, broke at last, it brought no light for his darkened spirit. Yet he had grown calmer, and a gentle feeling pervaded his bosom. Thrown off by Miss Linmore, his thoughts now turned by a natural impulse, as the needle, long held by opposing attraction, turns to its polar point, again towards Edith Walter. As he thought of her longer and longer, tenderer emotions began to tremble in his heart. The beauty of her character was again seen ; and his better nature bowed before it once more in a genuine worship.

"How have I been infatuated! What syren spell has been on me!" Such were the words that fell from his lips, marking the change in his feelings.

Days went by, and still the change went on, until the old affection had come back ; the old tender, true affection. But, he had turned from its object—basely turned away. A more glaring light had dazzled his eyes so that he could see, for a time, no beauty, no attraction, in his first love. Could he turn to her again? Would she receive him? Would she let him dip healing leaves in the waters he had dashed with bitterness? His heart trembled as he asked these questions, for there was no confident answer.

At last Edwin Florence resolved that he would see Edith once more, and seek to repair the wrong done both to her and to himself. It was three months after his rejection by Miss Linmore when he came to this resolution. And then, some weeks elapsed before he could force himself to act upon it. In all that time he had not met the young girl, nor had he once heard of her. To the house of her aunt, where she resided, Florence took his way one evening in early autumn, his heart disturbed by many conflicting emotions. His love for Edith had come back in full force ; and his spirit was longing for the old communion.

" Can I see Miss Walter ?" he asked, on arriving at her place of residence.

" Walk in," returned the servant who had answered his summons.

Florence entered the little parlor where he had spent so many, never-to-be-forgotten hours with Edith—hours unspeakably happy in passing, but, in remembrance, burdened with pain—and looking around on each familiar object with strange emotions. Soon a light step was heard descending the stairs, and moving along the passage. The door opened, and Edith—no, her aunt—entered. The young man had risen in the breathlessness of expectation.

" Mr. Florence," said the aunt, coldly. He extended his hand ; but she did not take it.

" How is Edith ?" was half stammered.

" She is sinking rapidly," replied the aunt.

Edwin staggered back into a chair.

" Is she ill ?" he inquired, with a quivering lip.

" Ill ! She is dying !" There was something of in- dignation in the way this was said.

" Dying !" The young man clasped his hands to- gether with a gesture of despair.

" How long has she been sick ?" he next ventured to ask.

" For months she has been dying daily," said the

aunt. There was a meaning in her tones that the young man fully comprehended. He had not dream ed of this.

"Can I see her?"

The aunt shook her head, as she answered,

"Let her spirit depart in peace."

"I will not disturb, but calm her spirit," said the young man, earnestly. "Oh, let me see her, that I may call her back to life!"

"It is too late," replied the aunt. "The oil is exhausted, and light is just departing."

Edwin started to his feet, exclaiming passionately—

"Let me see her! Let me see her!"

"To see her thus, would be to blow the breath that would extinguish the flickering light," said the aunt. "Go home, young man! It is too late! Do not seek to agitate the waters long troubled by your hand, but now subsiding into calmness. Let her spirit depart in peace."

Florence sunk again into his chair, and, hiding his ace with his hands, sat for some moments in a state of mental paralysis.

In the chamber above lay the pale, almost pulseless form of Edith. A young girl, who had been as her sister for many years, sat holding her thin white hand. The face of the invalid was turned to the wall. Her

2

eyes were closed ; and she breathed so quietly that the motions of respiration could hardly be seen. Nearly ten minutes had elapsed from the time a servant whispered to the aunt that there was some one in the parlor, when Edith turned, and said to her companion, in a low, calm voice—

"Mr. Florence has come."

The girl started, and a flush of surprise went over her face.

"He is in the parlor now. Won't you ask him to come up ?" added the dying maiden, still speaking with the utmost composure.

Her friend stood surprised and hesitating for some moments, and then turning away, glided from the chamber. She found the aunt and Mr. Florence in the passage below, the latter pleading with the former for the privilege of seeing Edith, which was resolutely denied.

"Edith wants to see Mr. Florence," said the girl, as she joined them.

"Who told her that he was here ?" quickly asked the aunt.

"No one. I did not know it myself."

"Her heart told her that I was here," exclaimed Mr. Florence—and, as he spoke, he glided past the aunt, and, with hurried steps, ascended to the chamber where the dying one lay. The eyes of Edith were turned towards the door as he entered; but no sign of emotion passed over her countenance. Overcome by his feelings, at the sight of the shadowy remnant of one so loved and so wronged, the young man sunk into a chair by her side, as nerveless as a child; and, as his lips were pressed upon her lips and cheeks, her face was wet with his tears.

Coming in quickly after, the aunt took firmly hold of his arm and sought to draw him away, but, in a steady voice, the invalid said—

"No—no. I was waiting for him. I have expected him for days. I knew he would come; and he is here now."

All was silence for many minutes; and during this time Edwin Florence sat with his face covered, struggling to command his feelings. At a motion from the dying girl, the aunt and friend retired, and she was alone with the lover who had been false to his vows. As the door closed behind them, Edwin looked up. He had grown calm. With a voice of inexpressible tenderness, he said—

"Live for me, Edith."

"Not here," was answered. "The silver chord will soon be loosened and the golden bowl broken."

"Oh, say not that! Let me call you back to life

Turn to me again as I have turned to you with my whole heart. The world is still beautiful; and in it we will be happy together."

"No, Edwin," replied the dying maiden. "The story of my days here is written, and the angel is about sealing the record. I am going where the heart will never feel the touch of sorrow. I wished to see you once more before I died; and you are here. I have, once more, felt your breath upon my cheek; once more held your hand in mine. For this my heart is grateful. You had become the sun of my life, and when your face was turned away, the flower that spread itself joyfully in the light, drooped and faded. And now, the light has come back again; but it cannot warm into freshness and beauty the withered blossom."

"Oh, my Edith! Say not so! Live for me! I have no thoughts, no affection that is not for you. The drooping flower will lift itself again in the sunshine when the clouds have passed away."

As the young man said this, Edith raised herself up suddenly, and, with a fond gesture, flung herself forward upon his bosom. For a few moments her form quivered in his arms. Then all became still, and he felt her lying heavier and heavier against him. In a little while he was conscious that he clasped to his heart only the earthly semblance of one who had passed away forever.

Replacing the light and faded form of her who, a little while before, had been in the vigor of health, upon the bed, Edwin gazed upon the sunken features for a few moments, and then, leaving a last kiss upon her cold lips, hurried away.

Another page in his Book of Life was written. There was another record there from which memory, in after life, could read. And such a record! What would he not have given to erase that page!

When the body of Edith Walter was borne to its last resting-place, Florence was among the mourners. After looking his last look upon the coffin that contained the body, he went away, sadder in heart than he had ever been in his life. He was not only a prey to sadness, but to painful self-accusation. In his perfidy lay the cause of her death. He had broken the heart that confided in him, and only repented of his error when it was too late to repair the ruin.

As to what was thought or said of him by others, Edwin Florence cared but little. There was enough of pain in his own self-consciousness. He withdrew himself from the social circle, and, for several years, lived a kind of hermit-life in the midst of society But, he was far from being happy in his solitude:

for Memory was with him, and almost daily, from the
Book of his Life, read to him some darkly written
page.

One day,—it was three years from the time he
arted with Edith in the chamber of death, and when
he was beginning to rise in a measure above the
depressing influences attendant upon that event,—he
received an invitation to make one of a social party on
the next evening. The desire to go back again in
society had been gaining strength with him for some
time ; and, as it had gained strength, reason had
pointed out the error of his voluntary seclusion as
unavailing to alter the past.

"The past is past," he said to himself, as he mused
with the invitation in his hand. "I cannot recall it—
I cannot change it. If repentance can in any way
atone for error, surely I have made atonement ; for my
repentance has been long and sincere. If Edith can
see my heart, her spirit must be satisfied. Even she
could not wish for this living burial. It is better for
me to mingle in society as of old."

Acting on this view, Florence made one on the next
evening, in a social party. He felt strangely, for his
mind was invaded by old influences, and touched by
old impressions. He saw, in many a light and airy
form, as it glanced before him, the image of one long

since passed away; and heard, in the voices that filled
the rooms, many a tone that it seemed must have
come from the lips of Edith.   How busy was Memory
again with the past.   In vain he sought to shut out the
images that arose in his mind.   The page was open
before him, and what was impressed thereon he could
not but see and read.

This passed, in some degree, away as the evening
progressed, and he came nearer, so to speak, to some
of those who made up the happy company.   Among
those present was a young lady from a neighboring
city, who attracted much attention both from her
manners and person.   She fixed the eyes of Mr.
Florence soon after he entered the room, and, half
unconsciously to himself, his observation was frequently
directed towards her.

"Who is that lady?" he asked of a friend, an hour
after his arrival.

"Her name is Miss Welden.   She is from Albany."

"She has a very interesting face," said Florence.

"And quite as interesting a mind.   Miss Weldon is
a charming girl."

Not long after, the two were thrown near together,
when an introduction took place.   The conversation of
the young lady interested Florence, and in her society
he passed half an hour most pleasantly.   While talk-

ing with more than usual animation, in lifting his eyes
he saw that some one on the opposite side of the room
was observing him attentively. For the moment this
did not produce any effect. But, in looking up again,
he saw the same eyes upon him, and felt their expression as unpleasant. He now, for the first time, became aware that the aunt of Edith Walter was present. She it was who had been regarding him so attentively. From that instant his heart sunk in his bosom. Memory's magic mirror was before him, and in
it he saw pictured the whole scene of that last meeting
with Edith.

A little while afterward, and Edwin Florence was
missed from the pleasant company. Where was he !
Alone in the solitude of his own chamber, with his
thoughts upon the past. Again he had been reading
over those pages of his Book of Life in which was
written the history of his intimacy with and desertion
of Edith ; and the record seemed as fresh as if made
but the day before. It was in vain that he sought to
close or avert his eyes. There seemed a spell upon
him ; and he could only look and read.

"Fatal error !" he murmured to himself, as he
struggled to free himself from his thraldom to the past.
"Fatal error ! How a single act will curse a man
through life. Oh ! if I could but extinguish the whole

of this memory! If I could wipe out the hand-writing. Sorrow, repentance, is of no avail. The past is gone for ever. Why then should I thus continue to be unhappy over what I cannot alter? It avails nothing to Edith. She is happy—far happier than if she had remained on this troublesome earth."

But, even while he uttered these words, there came into his mind such a realizing sense of what the poor girl must have suffered, when she found her love thrown back upon her, crushing her heart by its weight, that he bowed his head upon his bosom and in bitter self-upbraidings passed the hours until midnight, when sleep locked up his senses, and calmed the turbulence of his feelings.

2*

CHAPTER III.

MONTHS elapsed before Edwin Florence ventured again into company.

"Why will you shut yourself up after this fashion?" said an acquaintance to him one day. "It isn't just to your friends. I've heard half a dozen persons asking for you lately. This hermit life you are leading is, let me tell you, a very foolish life."

The friend who thus spoke knew nothing of the young man's heart history.

"No one really misses me," said Florence, in reply.

"In that you are mistaken," returned the friend. You are missed. I have heard one young lady, at least, ask for you of late, more than a dozen times."

"Indeed! A *young* lady!"

"Yes; and a very beautiful young lady at that."

"In whose eyes can I have found such favor?"

"You have met Miss Clara Weldon?"

"Only once."

"But once !"

"That is all."

"Then it must be a case of love at first sight—at least on the lady's part—for Miss Weldon has asked for you, to my knowledge, not less than a dozen times."

"I am certainly flattered at the interest she takes in me."

"Well you may be. I know more than one young man who would sacrifice a good deal to find equal favor in her eyes. Now see what you have lost by this hiding of your countenance. And you are not the only loser."

Florence, who was more pleased at what he heard than he would like to have acknowledged, promised to come forth from his hiding place and meet the world in a better spirit. And he did so; being really drawn back into the social circle by the attraction of Miss Weldon. At his second meeting with this young lady he was still more charmed with her than at first; and she was equally well pleased with him. A few more interviews, and both their hearts were deeply interested.

Now there came a new cause of disquietude to Edwin; or, it might be said, the old cause renewed. The going out of his affections towards Miss Weldon revived the whole memory of the past; and, for a time, he found it almost impossible to thrust it from his mind. While sitting by her side and listening to her voice, the tones of Edith would be in his ears; and, often, when he looked into her face, he would see only the fading countenance of her who had passed away. This was the first state, and it was exceedingly painful while it lasted. But, it gradually changed into one more pleasant, yet not entirely free from the unwelcome intrusion of the past.

The oftener Florence and Miss Weldon met, the more strongly were their hearts drawn toward each other; and, at length, the former was encouraged to make an offer of his hand. In coming to this resolution, it was not without passing through a painful conflict. As his mind dwelt upon the subject, there was a reproduction of old states. Most vividly did he recall the time when he breathed into the ears of Edith vows to which he had proved faithless. He had, it is true, returned to his first allegiance. He had laid his heart again at her feet; but, to how little purpose! While in this state of agitation, the young man resolved, more than once, to abandon his suit for the hand of Miss Weldon, and shrink back again into the seclusion from which he had come forth. But, his affection for the lovely girl was too genuine to admit of this. When he thought of giving her up, his mind was still more deeply disturbed.

"Oh, that I could forget!" he exclaimed, while this ruggle was in progress. "Of what avail is this urning over of the leaves of a long passed history? I erred—sadly erred! But repentance is now too late. Why, then, should my whole existence be cursed for a single error? Ah, me! Art thou not satisfied, departed one? Is it, indeed, from the presence of thy spirit that I am troubled? My heart sinks at the thought. But, no, no! Thou wert too good to visit pain upon any; much less upon one who, though false to thee, thou didst so tenderly love."

But, upon this state there came a natural re-action. A peaceful calm succeeded the storm. Memory deposited her records in the mind's dimly lighted chambers. To the present was restored its better influences.

"I am free again," was the almost audible utterance f the young man, so strong was his sense of relief.

An offer of marriage was then made to Miss Weldon. Her heart trembled with joy when she received it. But, confiding implicitly in her uncle, who had been for the space of ten years her friend and guardian, she could not give an affirmative reply until his approval was gained. She, therefore, asked time for reflection and consultation with her friend.

Far different from what Florence had expected, was the reception of his offer. To him, Miss Weldon seemed instantly to grow cold and reserved. Vividly was now recalled his rejection by Miss Linmore, as well as the ground of her rejection.

"Is this to be gone over again?" he sighed to himself, when alone once more. "Is that one false step never to be forgotten nor forgiven? Am I to be followed, through life, by this shadow of evil?"

To no other cause than this could the mind of Florence attribute the apparent change and hesitation in Clara Weldon.

Immediately on receiving an offer of marriage, Miss Weldon returned to Albany. Before leaving, she dropped Florence a note, to the effect, that he should hear from her in a few days. A week passed, but the promised word came not. It was now plain that the friends of the young lady had been making inquiries about him, and were in possession of certain facts in his life, which, if known, would almost certainly blast his hopes of favor in her eyes. While in this state of uncertainty, he met the aunt of Edith, and the way she looked at him, satisfied his mind that his conjectures were true. A little while after a friend remarked to him casually—

"I saw Colonel Richards in town to-day."

"Colonel Richards! Miss Weldon's uncle?"

"Yes. Have you seen him?"

"No. I have not the pleasure of an acquaintance."

"Indeed! I thought you knew him. I heard him mention your name this morning."

"My name!"

"Yes."

"What had he to say of me?"

"Let me think. Oh! He asked me if I knew you."

"Well?"

"I said that I did, of course; and that you were a pretty clever fellow; though you had been a sad boy in your time."

The face of Florence instantly reddened.

"Why, what's the matter? Oh, I understand now! That little niece of his is one of your flames. But come! Don't take it so to heart. Your chances are one in ten, I have no doubt. By the way, I haven't seen Clara for a week. What has become of her? Gone back to Albany, I suppose. I hope you haven't frightened her with an offer. By the way, let me whisper a word of comfort in your ear. I heard her

say that she didn't believe in any thing but first love ;
and, as you are known to have had half a dozen
sweethearts, more or less, and to have broken the
hearts of two or three young ladies, the probability is,
that you won't be able to add her to the number of
your lady loves."

All this was mere jesting ; but the words, though
uttered in jest, fell upon the ears of Edwin Florence
with all the force of truth.

"Guilty, on your own acknowledgment," said the
friend, seeing the effect of his words. "Better always
to act fairly in these matters of the heart, Florence.
If we sow the wind, we will be pretty sure to reap the
whirlwind. But come ; let me take you down to the
Tremont, and introduce you to Colonel Richards. I
know he will be glad to make your acquaintance, and
will, most probably, give you an invitation to go home
with him and spend a week. You can then make all
fair with his pretty niece."

"I have no wish to make his acquaintance just at
this time," returned Florence ; "nor do I suppose he
cares about making mine, particularly after the high
opinion you gave him of my character."

"Nonsense, Edwin ! You don't suppose I said that
to him. Can't you take a joke ?"

"Oh, yes ; I can take a joke."

"Take that as one, then. Colonel Richards did ask for you, however; and said that he would like to meet you. He was serious. So come along, and let me introduce you."

"No; I would prefer not meeting with him at this time."

"You are a strange individual."

The young men parted; Florence to feel more disquieted than ever. Colonel Richards had been inquiring about him, and, in prosecuting his inquiries, would, most likely, find some one inclined to relate the story of Edith Walter. What was more natural? That story once in the ears of Clara, and he felt that she must turn from him with a feeling of repulsion.

Three or four days longer he was in suspense. He heard of Col. Richards from several quarters, and, in each case when he was mentioned, he was alluded to as making inquiries about him.

"I hear that the beautiful Miss Weldon is to be married," was said to Florence at a time when he was almost mad with the excitement of suspense.

"Ah!" he replied, with forced calmness, "I hope she will be successful in securing a good husband."

"So do I; for she is indeed a sweet girl. I was more than half inclined to fall in love with her myself;

and would have done so, if I had believed there was
any chance for me."

"Who is the favored one?" asked Florence.

"I have not been able to find out. She received
three or four offers, and went back to Albany to
consider them and make her election. This she has
done, I hear; and already, the happy recipient of her
favor is rejoicing over his good fortune. May they live
a thousand years to be happy with each other!"

Here was another drop of bitterness in the cup that
was at the lips of Edwin Florence. He went to his
office immediately, and, sitting down, wrote thus to
Clara:

"I do not wrongly interpret, I presume, a silence
continued far beyond the time agreed upon when we
parted. You have rejected my suit. Well, be it so; and
may you be happy with him who has found favor in your
eyes. I do not think he can love you more sincerely than
I do, or be more devoted to your happiness than I should
have been. It would have relieved the pain I cannot but
feel, if you had deemed my offer worthy a frank refusal.
But, to feel that one I have so truly loved does not think
me even deserving of this attention, is humiliating in the
extreme. But, I will not upbraid you. Farewell! May
you be happy."

Sealing up this epistle, the young man, scarcely pausing even for hurried reflection, threw it into the post office. This done, he sunk into a gloomy state of mind, in which mortification and disappointment struggled alternately for the predominance.

Only a few hours elapsed after the adoption of this hasty course, before doubts of its propriety began to steal across his mind. It was possible, it occurred to him, that he might have acted too precipitately. There might be reasons for the silence of Miss Weldon entirely separate from those he had been too ready to assume ; and, if so, how strange would his letter appear. It was too late now to recall the act, for already the mail that bore his letter was half way from New York to Albany. A restless night succeeded to this day. Early on the next morning he received a letter. It was in these words—

" MY DEAR MR. FLORENCE :—I have been very ill, and to-day am able to sit up just long enough to write a line or two. My uncle was in New York some days ago, but did not meet with you. Will you not come up and see me ?

" Ever Yours,   CLARA WELDON."

Florence was on board the next boat that left New York for Albany. The letter of Clara was, of course, written before the receipt of his hasty epistle. What troubled him now was the effect of this epistle on her mind. He had not only wrongly interpreted her silence, but had assumed the acceptance of another lover as confidently as if he knew to a certainty that such was the case. This was a serious matter, and might result in the very thing he had been so ready to assume—the rejection of his suit.

Arriving, at length, in Albany, Mr. Florence sought out the residence of Miss Weldon.

" Is Colonel Richards at home ?" he inquired.

On being answered in the affirmative, he sent up his name with a request to see him. The colonel made his appearance in a short time. He was a tall, thoughtful looking man, and bowed with a dignified air as he came into the room.

" How is Miss Weldon ?" asked Florence, with an eagerness he could not restrain.

" Not so well this morning," replied the guardian. " She had a bad night."

" No wonder," thought the young man, " after receiving that letter."

" She has been sleeping, however, since daylight," added Colonel Richards, and that is much in her favor."

" She received my letter, I presume," said Florence, in a hesitating voice

"A letter came for her yesterday," was replied; "but as she was more indisposed than usual, we did not give it to her."

".It is as well," said the young man, experiencing a sense of relief.

An hour afterwards he was permitted to enter the chamber, where she lay supported by pillows. One glance at her face dispelled from his mind every lingering doubt. He had suffered from imaginary fears, awakened by the whispers of a troubled conscience.

CHAPTER IV.

In a few days Clara was well enough to leave her room, and was soon entirely recovered from her sudden illness. That little matter of the heart had been settled within three minutes of their meeting, and they were now as happy as lovers usually are under such favorable circumstances.

When Edwin Florence went back to New York, it was with a sense of interior pleasure more perfect than he had experienced for years; and this would have remained, could he have shut out the past; or, so much of it as came like an unwelcome intruder. But, alas! this was not to be. Even while he was bending, in spirit, over the beautiful image of his last beloved, there would come between his eyes and that image a pale sad face, in which reproof was stronger than affection. It was all in vain that he sought to turn from that face. For a time it would remain present, and then fade slowly away, leaving his heart oppressed.

"Is it to be ever thus!" he would exclaim, in these seasons of darkness. "Will nothing satisfy this accusing spirit? Edith! Dear Edith! Art thou not mong the blessed ones? Is not thy heart happy oeyond mortal conception? Then why come to me thus with those tearful eyes, that shadowy face, those looks of reproof? Have I not suffered enough for purification!˜-Am I never to be forgiven?"

And then, with an effort, he would turn his eyes from the page laid open by Memory, and seek to forget what was written there. But it seemed as if every thing conspired to freshen his remembrance of the past, the nearer the time approached, when by a marriage union with one truly beloved, he was to weaken the bonds it had thrown around him. The marriage of Miss Linmore took place a few weeks after his engagement with Clara, and as an intimate friend led her to the altar, he could not decline making one of the nimber that graced the nuptial festivities. In meeting the young bride, he endeavored to push from his mind ll thoughts of their former relations. But she had not done this, and her thought determined his. Her mind recurred to the former time, the moment he came into her presence, and, of necessity his went back also. They met, therefore, with a certain reserve, that was to him most unpleasant, particularly as it stirred a hundred sleeping memories.

By a strong effort, Florence was able to conceal from other eyes much of what he felt. In doing this, a certain over action was the consequence; and he was gayer than usual. Several times he endeavored to be lightly familiar with the bride; but, in every instance that he approached her, he perceived a kind of instinctive shrinking; and, if she was in a laughing mood, when he drew near she became serious and reserved. All this was too plain to be mistaken; and like the repeated strokes of a hammer upon glowing iron, gradually bent his feelings from the buoyant form they had been endeavoring to assume. The effect was not wholly to be resisted. More than an hour before the happy assemblage broke up, Florence was not to be found in the brilliantly lighted rooms. Unable longer to conceal what he felt, he had retired.

For many days after this, the young man felt sober.

"Why haven't you called to see me?" asked th friend who had married Miss Linmore, a week or tw after the celebration of the nuptials.

Florence excused himself as best he could, and promised to call in a few days. Two weeks went by without the fulfillment of his promise.

"No doubt, we shall see you next week," said the

friend, meeting him one day about this time; "though I am not so sure we will receive your visits then."

"Why not?"

"A certain young lady with whom, I believe, you have some acquaintance, is to spend a short time with us."

"Who?" asked Florence, quickly.

"A young lady from Albany."

"Miss Weldon?"

"The same."

"I was not aware that she was on terms of intimacy with your wife."

"She's an old friend of mine; and, in that sense a friend of Kate's."

"Then they have not met."

"Oh, yes; frequently. And are warmly attached. We look for a pleasant visit. But, of course, we shall not expect to see you. That is understood."

"I rather think you will; that is, if your wife will admit me on friendly terms."

"Why do you say that?" inquired the friend, appearing a little surprised.

"I thought, on the night of your wedding, that she felt my presence as unwelcome to her."

"And is this the reason why you have not called to see us"

3

"I frankly own that it is."

"Edwin! I am surprised at you. It is all a piece of imagination. What could have put such a thing into your head?"

"It may have been all imagination. But I couldn't help feeling as I did. However, you may expect to see me, and that, too, before Miss Weldon's arrival."

"If you don't present yourself before, I am not so sure that we will let you come afterwards," said the friend, smiling.

On the next evening the young man called. Mrs. Hartley, the bride of his friend, endeavored to forget the past, and to receive him with all the external signs of forgetfulness. But, in this she did not fully succeed, and, of course, the visit of Florence was painfully embarrassing, at least, to himself. From that time until the arrival of Miss Weldon, he felt concerned and unhappy. That Mrs. Hartley would fully communicate or covertly hint to Clara certain events of his former life, he had too much reason to fear; and, were this done, he felt that all his fond hopes would be scattered to the winds. In due time, Miss Weldon arrived. In meeting her, Florence was conscious of a feeling of embarrassment, never before experienced in her presence. He understood clearly why this was so. At each successive visit, his embarrassment increased; and, the more so, from the fact that he perceived a change in Clara ere she had been in the city a week. As to the cause of this change, he had no doubts. It was evident that Mrs. Hartley had communicated certain matters touching his previous history.

Thus it went on, day after day, for two or three weeks, by which time the lovers met under the influence of a most chilling constraint. Both were exceedingly unhappy.

One day, in calling as usual, Mr. Florence was surprised to learn that Clara had gone back to Albany.

"She said nothing of this last night," remarked the young man to Mrs. Hartley.

"Her resolution was taken after you went away," was replied.

"And you, no doubt, advised the step," said Mr. Florence, with ill-concealed bitterness

"Why do you say that?" was quickly asked.

"How can I draw any other inference?" said the young man, looking at her with knit brows.

"Explain yourself, Mr. Florence!"

"Do my words need explanation?"

"Undoubtedly! For, I cannot understand them."

"There are events in my past life—I will not say how bitterly repented—of which only you could have informed her."

" What events ?" calmly asked the lady.

" Why lacerate my feelings by such a question !" said Florence, while a shadow of pain flitted over his face, as Memory presented a record of the past.

"I ask it with no such intention. I only wish to understand you," replied Mrs. Hartley. " You have brought against me a vague accusation. I wish it distinct, that I may affirm or deny it."

" Edith Walter," said Edwin Florence, in a low, unsteady voice, after he had been silent for nearly a minute.

Mrs. Hartley looked earnestly into his face. Every muscle was quivering.

" What of her ?" she inquired, in tones quite as low as those in which the young man had spoken.

" You know the history."

" Well ?"

" And, regardless of my suffering and repentance, made known to Clara the blasting secret."

" No ! By my hopes of heaven, no !" quickly exclaimed Mrs. Hartley.

" No ?" A quiver ran through the young man's frame.

" No, Mr. Florence ! That rested as silently in my own bosom as in yours."

" Who, then, informed her ?"

"No one."

"Has she not heard of it ?"

"No."

"Why, then, did she change towards me ?"

"You changed, first, towards her."

"Me !"

"Yes. From the day of her arrival in New York, she perceived in you a certain coldness and reserve, that increased with each repeated interview."

"Oh, no !"

"It is true. I saw it myself."

Florence clasped his hands together, and bent his eyes in doubt and wonder upon the floor.

"Did she complain of coldness and change in me ?" he inquired.

"Yes, often. And returned, last night, to leave you free, doubting not that you had ceased to love her."

"Ceased to love her ! While this sad work has been going on, I have loved her with the agony of one who is about losing earth's most precious thing. Oh ! write to her for me, and explain all. How strange has been my infatuation. Will you write for me ?"

"Yes."

"Say that my heart has not turned from her ar instant. That her imagined coldness has made me of all men most wretched."

" I will do so.   But why not write yourself ?"

" It will be better to come from you.   Ask her to
return.   I would rather meet her here than in her
uncle's house.   Urge her to come back."

Mrs. Hartley promised to do so, according to th
wish of Mr. Florence. Two days passed, and there
was no answer.   On the morning of the third day, the
young man, in a state of agitation from suspense
called at the house of his friend.   After sending up his
name, he sat anxiously awaiting the appearance of Mrs.
Hartley.   The door at length opened, and, to his
surprise and joy, Clara entered.   She came forward
with a smile upon her face, extending her hand as she
did so.   Edwin sprang to meet her, and catching her
hand, pressed it eagerly to his lips

" Strange that we should have so erred in regard to
each other," said Clara, as they sat communing tenderly.
" I trust no such error will come in the future to which
I look forward with so many pleasing hopes."

" Heaven forbid !" replied the young man, seriously
" But we are in a world of error.   Ah ! if we coulc
only pass through life without a mistake.   If the
heavy weight of repentance did not lie so often and so
long upon our hearts—this would be a far pleasanter
world than it is."

" Do not look so serious," remarked Clara, as she

bent forward and gazed affectionately into the young man's face. "To err is human. No one here is perfect. How often, for hours, have I mourned over errors; yet grief was of no avail, except to make my future more guarded."

"And that was much gained," said Florence, breathing deeply with a sense of relief. "If we cannot recall and correct the past, we can at least be more guarded in the future. This is the effect of my own experience. Ah! if we properly considered the action of our present upon the future, how guarded would we be. All actions are in the present, and the moment they are done the present becomes the past, over which Memory presides. What is past is fixed. Nothing can change it. The record is in marble, to be seen in all future time."

The serious character of the interview soon changed, and the young lovers forgot every thing in the joy of their reconciliation. Nothing arose to mar their intercourse until the appointed time for the nuptial ceremonies arrived, when they were united in holy wedlock. But, Edwin Florence did not pass on to this time without another visit from the rebuking Angel of the Past. He was not permitted to take the hand of Clara in his, and utter the words that bound him to her forever, without a visit from the one whose heart

he had broken years before. She came to him in the
dark and silent midnight, as he tossed sleeplessly upon
his bed, and stood and looked at him with her pale face
and despairing eyes, until he was driven almost to
madness. She was with him when the light of
morning dawned; she moved by his side as he went
forth to meet and claim his betrothed; and was near
him, invisible to all eyes but his own, when he stood at
the altar ready to give utterance to the solemn words
that bound him to his bride. And not until these
words were said, did the vision fade away.

No wonder the face of the bridegroom wore a
solemn aspect as he presented himself to the minister,
and breathed the vows of eternal fidelity to the living,
while before him, as distinct as if in bodily form, was
the presence of one long since sleeping in her grave,
who had gone down to her shadowy resting place
through his infidelity.

From this time there was a thicker veil drawn over
the past. The memory of that one event grew less
and less distinct; though it was not obliterated, for
nothing that is written in the Book of Life is ever
blotted out. There were reasons, even in long years
after his marriage, when the record stood suddenly
before him, as if written in words of light; and he
would turn from it with a feeling of pain.

Thus it is that our present blesses or curses our future. Every act of our lives affects the coming time for good or evil. We make our own destiny, and make it always in the present. The past is gone, the future is yet to come. The present only is ours, and, according to what we do in the present, will be the records of the past and its influence on the future. They are only wise who wisely regard their actions in the present.

THE BRILLIANT AND THE COMMONPLACE

DAY after day I worked at my life-task, and worked in an earnest spirit. Not much did I seem tc accomplish ; yet the little that was done had on it the impress of good. Still, I was dissatisfied, because my gifts were less dazzling than those of which many around me could boast. When I thought of the brilliant ones sparkling in the firmament of literature, and filling the eyes of admiring thousands, something like the evil spirit of envy came into my heart and threw a shadow upon my feelings. I was troubled because I had not their gifts. I wished to shine with a stronger light. To dazzle, as well as to warm and vivify.

Not long ago, there came among us one whom nature had richly endowed. His mind possessed exceeding brilliancy. Flashes of thought, like lightning from a summer cloud, were ever filling the air around him. There was a stateliness in the movement of his intellect,. and an evidence of power, that oppressed you at times with wonder.

Around him gathered the lesser lights in the hemisphere of thought, and veiled their feeble rays beneath his excessive brightness. He seemed conscious of his superior gifts, and displayed them more like a giant beating the air to excite wonder, than putting forth his strength to accomplish a good and noble work. Still, I was oppressed and paralyzed by the sphere of his presence. I felt puny and weak beside him, and unhappy because I was not gifted with equal power.

It so happened that a work of mine, upon which the maker's name was not stamped—work done with a purpose of good—was spoken of and praised by one who did not know me as the handicraftsman.

" It is tame, dull, and commonplace," said the brilliant one, in a tone of contempt ; and there were many present to agree with him.

Like the strokes of a hammer upon my heart, came these words of condemnation. " Tame, dull, and commonplace !" And was it, indeed, so ? Yes ; I felt that what he uttered was true. That my powers were exceedingly limited, and my gifts few. Oh, what would I not have then given for brilliant endowments like those possessed by him from whom had fallen the words of condemnation?

"You will admit," said one—I thought it strange at the time that there should be even one to speak a word in favor of my poor performance—"that it will do good?"

"Good!" was answered, in a tone slightly touched by contempt. "Oh, yes; it will do good!" and the brilliant one tossed his head. "Anybody can do good!"

I went home with a perturbed spirit. I had work to do; but I could not do it. I sat down and tried to forget what I had heard. I tried to think about the tasks that were before me. "Tame, dull, and commonplace!" Into no other form would my thoughts come.

Exhausted, at last, by this inward struggle, I threw myself upon my bed, and soon passed into the land of dreams.

Dream-land! Thou art thought by many to be *only* a land of fantasy and of shadows. But it is not so. Dreams, for the most part, *are* fantastic; but all are not so. Nearer are we to the world of spirits, in sleep; and, at times, angels come to us with lessons of wisdom, darkly veiled under similitude, or written in characters of light.

I passed into dream-land; but my thoughts went on

in the same current. " Tame, dull, and commonplace!"
I felt the condemnation more strongly than before.

I was out in the open air, and around me were
mountains, trees, green fields, and running waters ; and
above all bent the sky in its azure beauty. The sun
was just unveiling his face in the east, and his rays
were lighting up the dew-gems on a thousand blades
of grass, and making the leaves glitter as if studded
with diamonds.

" How calm and beautiful !" said a voice near me.
I turned, and one whose days were in the " sear and
yellow leaf," stood by my side.

" But all is tame and commonplace," I answered.
" We have this over and over again, day after day,
month after month, and year after year. Give me
something brilliant and startling, if it be in the fiery
comet or the rushing storm. I am sick of the
commonplace !"

" And yet to the commonplace the world is indebted
for every great work and great blessing. For every
thing good, and true, and beautiful !"

I looked earnestly into the face of the old man. He
went on.

" The truly good and great is the useful ; for in that
is the Divine image. Softly and unobtrusively has the
dew fallen, as it falls night after right. Silently it

distilled, while the vagrant meteors threw their lines of
dazzling light across the sky, and men looked up at
them in wonder and admiration. And now the soft
rass, the green leaves, and the sweet flowers, that
.rooped beneath the fervent heat of yesterday, are fresh
again and full of beauty, ready to receive the light and
warmth of the risen sun, and expand with a new vigor.
All this may be tame and commonplace; but is it not
a great and a good work that has been going on?

"The tiller of the soil is going forth again to his
work. Do not turn your eyes from him, and let a
feeling of impatience stir in your heart because he is
not a soldier rushing to battle, or a brilliant orator
holding thousands enchained by the power of a fervid
eloquence that is born not so much of good desires for
his fellow-men as from the heat of his own self-love.
Day after day, as now, patient and hopeful, the
husbandman enters upon the work that lies before him,
and, hand in hand with God's blessed sunshine, dews,
and rain, a loving and earnest co-laborer, brings forth
from earth's treasure-house of blessings good gifts for
his fellow-men. Is all this commonplace? How great
and good is the commonplace!"

I turned to answer the old man, but he was gone. I
was standing on a high mountain, and beneath me, as
far as the eye could reach, were stretched broad and

richly cultivated fields; and from a hundred farm-houses went up the curling smoke from the fires of industry. Fields were waving with golden grain, and trees bending with their treasures of fruit. Suddenly, the bright sun was veiled in clouds, that came whirling up from the horizon in dark and broken masses, and throwing a deep shadow over the landscape just before bathed in light. -Calmly had I surveyed the peaceful scene spread out before me. I was charmed with its quiet beauty. But now, stronger emotions stirred within me.

"Oh, this is sublime!" I murmured, as I gazed upon the cloudy hosts moving across the heavens in battle array.

A gleam of lightning sprang forth from a dark cavern in the sky, and then, far off, rattled and jarred the echoing thunder. Next came the rushing and roaring wind, bending the giant-limbed oaks as if they were but wands of willow, and tearing up lesser trees as a child tears up from its roots a weed or flower.

In this war of elements I stood, with my head bared, and clinging to a rock, mad with a strange and wild delight.

"Brilliant! Sublime! Grand beyond the power of description!" I said, as the storm deepened in intensity.

"An hour like this is worth all the commonplace, dull events of a lifetime!"

There came a stunning crash in the midst of a dazzling glare. For some moments I was blinded. When sight was restored, I saw, below me, the flames curling upward from a dwelling upon which the fierce lightning had fallen.

"What majesty! what awful sublimity!" said I, aloud. I thought not of the pain, and terror, and death that reigned in the human habitation upon which the bolt of destruction had fallen, but of the sublime power displayed in the strife of the elements.

There was another change. I no longer stood on the mountain, with the lightning and tempest around me; but was in the valley below, down upon which the storm had swept with devastating fury. Fields of grain were level with the earth; houses destroyed; and the trophies of industry marred in a hundred ways.

"How sublime are the works of the tempest!" said a voice near me. I turned, and the old man was again at my side.

But I did not respond to his words.

"What majesty! What awful sublimity and power!" continued the old man. "But," he added, in a changed voice, "there is a higher power in the gentle rain than lies in the rushing tempest. The power to destroy is an evil power, and has bounds beyond which it cannot go. But the gentle rain that falls noiselessly to the earth, is the power of restoration and recreation. See!"

I looked, and a man lay upon the ground apparently lifeless. He had been struck down by the lightning. His pale face was upturned to the sky, and the rain shaken free from the cloudy skirts of the retiring storm, was falling upon it. I continued to gaze upon the face of the prostrate man, until there came into it a flush of life. Then his limbs quivered; he threw his arms about. A groan issued from his constricted chest. In a little while, he arose.

"Which is best? Which is most to be loved and admired?" said the old man. "The wild, fierce, brilliant tempest, or the quiet rain that restores the image of life and beauty which the tempest has destroyed? See! The gentle breezes are beginning to move over the fields, and, hand in hand with the uplifting sunlight, to raise the grain that has been trodden beneath the crushing heel of the tempest, whose false sublimity you so much admired. There is nothing startling and brilliant in this work; but it is a good and a great work, and it will go on silently and efficiently until not a trace of the desolating storm can be found. In the still atmosphere, unseen, but all-potent, lies a power ever busy in the work of creating and restoring ; or, in other words, in the commonplace work of doing good.   Which office would you like best o assume—which is the most noble—the office of the destroyer or the restorer ?"

I lifted my eyes again, and saw men busily engaged in blotting out the traces of the storm, and in restoring all to its former use and beauty.

Builders were at work upon the house which had been struck by lightning, and men engaged in repairing fences, barns, and other objects upon which had been spent the fury of the excited elements.   Soon every vestige of the destroyer was gone.

" Commonplace work, that of nailing on boards and shingles," said the old man ; " of repairing broken fences ; of filling up the deep foot-prints of the passing storm ; but is it not a noble work ?   Yes ; for it is ennobled by its end.   Far nobler than the work of the brilliant tempest, which moved but to destroy."

The scene changed once more.   I was back again from the land of dreams and similitudes.   It was midnight, and the moon was shining in a cloudless sky. I arose, and going to the window, sat and looked forth, musing upon my dream.   All was hushed as if I were out in the fields, instead of in the heart of a populous city.   Soon came the sound of footsteps, heavy and measured, and the watchman passed on his round of duty. An humble man was he, forced by necessity into his position, and rarely thought of and little regarded by the many. There was nothing brilliant about him to attract the eye and extort admiration. The man and his calling were commonplace. He passed on ; and, as his form left my eye, the thought of him passed from my mind. Not long after, unheralded by the sound of footsteps, came one with a stealthy, crouching air ; pausing now, and listening : and now looking warily from side to side. It was plain that he was on no errand of good to his fellow-men. He, too, passed on, and was lost to my vision.

Many minutes went by, and I still remained at the window, musing upon the subject of my dream, when I was startled by a cry of terror issuing from a house not far away. It was the cry of a woman. Obeying the instinct of my feelings, I ran into the street and made my way hurriedly towards the spot from which the cry came.

"Help! help! murder!" shrieked a woman from the open window.

I tried the street door of the house, but it was fastened. I threw myself against it with all my strength, and it yielded to the concussion. As I entered the dark passage, I found myself suddenly grappled by a strong man, who threw me down and held me by the throat. I struggled to free myself, but in vain. His grip tightened. In a few moments I would have been lifeless. But, just at the instant when consciousness was about leaving me, the guardian of the night appeared. With a single stroke of his heavy mace, he laid the midnight robber and assassin senseless upon the floor.

How instantly was that humble watchman ennobled in my eyes! How high and important was his use in society! I looked at him from a new standpoint, and saw him in a new relation.

" Commonplace !" said I, on regaining my own room in my own house, panting from the excitement and danger to which I had been subjected. " Commonplace ! Thank God for the commonplace and the useful !"

Again I passed into the land of dreams, where I found myself walking in a pleasant way, pondering the theme which had taken such entire possession of my thoughts. As I moved along, I met the gifted one who had called my work dull and commonplace ; that work was a simple picture of human life, drawn for the purpose of inspiring the reader with trust in God and love towards his fellow-man. He addressed me with the air of one who felt that he was superior, and led

off the conversation by a brilliant display of words that
half concealed, instead of making clear, his ideas.
Though I perceived this, I was yet affected with
admiration. My eyes were dazzled as by a glare of
light.

"Yes, yes," I sighed to myself; "I am dull, tame,
and commonplace beside these children of genius.
How poor and mean is the work that comes from my
hands !"

"Not so !" said my companion. I turned to look at
him ; but the gifted being stood not by my side. In
his place was the ancient one who had before spoken to
me in the voice of wisdom.

"Not so !" he continued. "Nothing that is useful
is poor and mean. Look up ! In the fruit of our
labor is the proof of its quality."

I was in the midst of a small company, and the
gifted being whose powers I had envied was there, the
centre of attraction and the observed of all observers.
He read to those assembled from a book ; and what he
read flashed with a brightness that was dazzling. All
listened in the most rapt attention, and, by the power
of what the gifted one read, soared now, in thought,
among the stars, spread their wings among the swift-
moving tempest, or descended into the unknown depths
of the earth. As for myself, my mind seemed endowed

with new faculties, and to rise almost into the power of the infinite.

"Glorious! Divine! Godlike!" Such were the admiring words that fell from the lips of all.

And then the company dispersed. As we went forth from the room in which we had assembled, we met numbers who were needy, and sick, and suffering; mourners, who sighed for kind words from the comforter: little children, who had none to love and care for them; the faint and weary, who needed kind hands to help them on their toilsome journey. But no human sympathies were stirring in our hearts. We had been raised, by the power of the genius we so much admired, far above the world and its commonplace sympathies. The wings of our spirits were still beating the air, far away in the upper regions of transcendant thought.

Another change came. I saw a woman reading from the same book from which the gifted one had read. Ever and anon she paused, and gave utterance to words of admiration.

"Beautiful! beautiful!" fell, ever and anon, from her lips; and she would lift her eyes, and muse upon what she was reading. As she sat thus, a little child entered the room. He was crying.

"Mother! mother!" said the child, "I want—"

But the mother's thoughts were far above the regions of the commonplace. Her mind was in a world of ideal beauty. Disturbed by the interruption, a slight frown contracted on her beautiful brows as she arose and took her child by the arm to thrust it from the room.

A slight shudder went through my frame as I marked the touching distress that overspread the countenance of the child as it looked up into its mother's face and saw nothing there but an angry frown.

"Every thought is born of affection," said the old man, as this scene faded away, "and has in it the quality of the life that gave it birth; and when that thought is reproduced in the mind of another, it awakens its appropriate affection. If there had been a true love of his neighbor in the mind of the gifted one when he wrote the book from which the mother read, and if his purpose had been to inspire with human emotions—and none but these are God-like—the souls of men, his work would have filled the heart of tha mother with a deeper lore of her child, instead of freezing in her bosom the surface of love's celestial fountain. To have hearkened to the grief of that dear child, and to have ministered to its comfort, would have been a commonplace act, but, how truly noble and divine! And now, look again, and let what passes before you give strength to your wavering spirits."

I lifted my eyes, and saw a man reading, and I knew that he read that work of mine which the gifted one nad condemned as dull, and tame, and commonplace. And, moreover, I knew that he was in trouble so deep as to be almost hopeless of the future, and just ready to give up his life-struggle, and let his hands fall listless and despairing by his side. Around him were gathered his wife and his little ones, and they were looking to him, but in vain, for the help they needed.

As the man read, I saw a light come suddenly into his face. He paused, and seemed musing for a time; and his eyes gleamed quickly upwards, and as his lips parted, these words came forth : " Yes, yes; it must be so. God is merciful as he is wise, and will not forsake his creatures. He tries us in the fires of adversity but to consume the evil of our hearts. I will trust him, and again go forth, with my eyes turned confidingly upwards." And the man went forth in the spirit of confidence in Heaven, inspired by what I had written.

" Look again," said the one by my side.

I looked, and saw the same man in the midst of a smiling family. His countenance was full of life and happiness, for his trust had not been in vain. As I had written, so he had found it God is good, and lets no one feel the fires of adversity longer than is necessary for his purification from evil.

"Look again!" came like tones of music to my ear.

I looked, and saw one lying upon a bed. By the lines upon his brow, and the compression of his lips, it was evident that he was in bodily suffering. A book lay near him; it was written by the gifted one, and was full of bright thoughts and beautiful images. He took it, and tried to forget his pain in these thoughts and images. But in this he did not succeed, and soon laid it aside with a groan of anguish. Then there was handed to him my poor and commonplace work; and he opened the pages and began to read. I soon perceived that an interest was awakened in his mind. Gradually the contraction of his brow grew less severe, and, in a little while, he had forgotten his pain.

"I will be more patient," said he, in a calm voice, after he had read for a long time with a deep interest. "There are many with pain worse than mine to bear, who have none of the comforts and blessings so freely scattered along my way through life."

And then he gave directions to have relief sent to one and another whom he now remembered to be in need.

"It is a good work that prompts to good in others," said the old man. "What if it be dull and tame—

4

commonplace to the few—it is a good gift to the world, and thousands will bless the giver.   Look again !"

An angry mother, impatient and fretted by the conduct of a froward child, had driven her boy from her presence, when, if she had controlled her own feelings, she might have drawn him to her side and subdued him by the power of affection. She was unhappy, and her boy had received an injury.

The mother was alone. Before her was a table covered with books, and she took up one to read. I knew the volume ; it was written by one whose genius had a deep power of fascination. Soon the mother became lost in its exciting pages, and remained buried in them for hours. At length, after turning the last page, she closed the book ; and then came the thought of her wayward boy. But, her feelings toward him had undergone no change ; she was still angry, because of his disobedience.

Another book lay upon the table ; a book of no pretensions, and written with the simple purpose of doing good. It was commonplace, because it dealt with things in the common life around us. The mother took this up, opened to the title-page, turned a few leaves, and then laid it down again ; sat thoughtful for some moments, and then sighed. Again she lifted the book, opened it, and commenced reading. In a little while she was all attention, and ere long I saw a tear stealing forth upon her cheeks. Suddenly she closed the book, evincing strong emotion as she did so, and, rising up, went from the room. Ascending to a chamber above, she entered, and there found the boy at play. He looked towards her, and, remembering her anger, a shadow flitted across his face. But his mother smiled and looked kindly towards him. Instantly the boy dropped his playthings, and sprung to her side. She stooped and kissed him.

"Oh, mother! I do love you, and I will try to be good!"

Blinding tears came to my eyes, and I saw this scene no longer. I was out among the works of nature, and my instructor was by my side.

"Despise not again the humble and the commonplace," said he, "for upon these rest the happiness and well-being of the world. Few can enter into and appreciate the startling and the brilliant, but thousands and tens of thousands can feel and love the commonplace that comes to their daily wants, and inspires them with a mutual sympathy. Go on in your work. Think it not low and mean to speak humble, yet true and fitting words for the humble; to lift up the bowed and grieving spirit; to pour the oil and wine of consolation for the poor and afflicted. It is a great and a good work—the very work in which God's angels delight. Yea, in doing this work, you are brought nearer in spirit to Him who is goodness and greatness itself, for all his acts are done with the end of blessing his creatures."

There was another change. I was awake. It was broad daylight, and the sun had come in and awakened me with a kiss. Again I resumed my work, content to meet the common want in my labors, and let the more gifted and brilliant ones around me enjoy the honors and fame that gathered in cloudy incense around them.

It is better to be loved by the many, than admired by the few.

CHAPTER I.

MARK CLIFFORD had come up from New York to spend a few weeks with his maternal grandfather, Mr. Lofton, who lived almost alone on his beautiful estate a few miles from the Hudson, amid the rich valleys of Orange county. Mr. Lofton belonged to one of the oldest families in the country, and retained a large portion of that aristocratic pride for which they were distinguished. The marriage of his daughter to Mr. Clifford, a merchant of New York, had been strongly opposed on the ground that the alliance was degrading, —Mr. Clifford not being able to boast of an ancestor who was anything more than an honest man and a useful citizen. A closer acquaintance with his son-in-law, after the marriage took place, reconciled Mr. Lofton in a good measure to the union; for he found

Mr. Clifford to be a man of fine intelligence, gentle-manly feeling, and withal, tenderly attached to his daughter. The marriage was a happy one—and this is rarely the case when the external and selfish desire o make a good family connection is regarded above the mental and moral qualities on which a true union only can be based.

A few years previous to the time at which our story opens, Mrs. Clifford died, leaving one son and two daughters. Mark, the oldest of the children, was in his seventeenth year at the time the sad bereavement occurred—the girls were quite young. He had always been an active boy—ever disposed to get beyond the judicious restraints which his parents wisely sought to throw around him. After his mother's death, he attained a wider liberty. He was still at college when this melancholy event occurred, and continued there for two years; but no longer in correspondence with, and therefore not under the influence of one whose love for him sought ever to hold him back from evil, his natural temperament led him into the indulgence of a liberty that too often went beyond the bounds of propriety.

On leaving college Mr. Clifford conferred with his son touching the profession he wished to adopt, and to his surprise found him bent on entering the navy. All efforts to discourage the idea were of no avail. The

young man was for the navy and nothing else. Yield-
ing at last to the desire of his son, Mr. Clifford entered
the usual form of application at the Navy Yard in
Washington, but, at the same time, in a private letter
to the Secretary, intimated his wish that the application
might not be favorably considered.

Time passed on, but Mark did not receive the
anxiously looked for appointment. Many reasons were
conjectured by the young man, who, at last, resolved
on pushing through his application, if personal efforts
could be of any avail. To this end, he repaired to the
seat of government, and waited on the Secretary. In
his interviews with this functionary, some expressions
were dropped that caused a suspicion of the truth to
pass through his mind. A series of rapidly recurring
questions addressed to the Secretary were answered in
a way that fully confirmed this suspicion. The effect
of this upon the excitable and impulsive young man
will appear as our story progresses.

It was while Mark's application was pending, and a
hort time before his visit to Washington, that he came
up to Fairview, the residence of his grandfather.
Mark had always been a favorite with the old gentleman, who rather encouraged his desire to enter the
navy.

"The boy will distinguish himself," Mr. Lofton

would say, as he thought over the matter. And the idea of distinction in the army or navy, was grateful to his aristocratic feelings. "There is some of the right blood in his veins for all."

One afternoon, some two or three days after the young man came up to Fairview, he was returning from a ramble in the woods with his gun, when he met a beautiful young girl, simply attired, and bearing on her head a light bundle of grain which she had gleaned in a neighboring field. She was tripping lightly along, singing as gaily as a bird, when she came suddenly upon the young man, over whose face there passed an instant glow of admiration. Mark bowed and smiled, the maiden dropped a bashful courtesy, and then each passed on.; but neither to forget the other. When Mark turned, after a few steps, to gaze after the sweet wild flower he had met so unexpectedly, he saw the face again, for she had turned also. He did not go home on that evening, until he had seen the lovely being who glanced before him in her native beaut enter a neat little cottage that stood half a mile from Fairview, nearly hidden by vines, and overshadowed by two tall sycamores.

On the next morning Mark took his way toward the cottage with his gun. As he drew near, the sweet voice he had heard on the day before was warbling

tenderly an old song his mother had sung when he
was but a child; and with the air and words so well.
remembered, came a gentleness of feeling, and a love
of what was pure and innocent, such as he had not experienced for many years. In this state of mind he
entered the little porch, and stood listening for several
minutes to the voice that still flung itself plaintively or
joyfully upon the air, according to the sentiment
breathed in the words that were clothed in music; then
as the voice became silent, he rapped gently at the
door, which, in a few moments, was opened by the one
whose attractions had drawn him thither.

A warm color mantled the young girl's face as her
eyes fell upon so unexpected a visitor. She remembered him as the young man she had met on the evening before; about whom she had dreamed all night,
and thought much since the early morning. Mark
bowed, and, as an excuse for calling, asked if her
mother were at home.

"My mother died when I was but a child," replied
the girl, shrinking back a step or two; for Mark was
gazing earnestly into her face.

"Ah! Then you are living with your—your—"

"Mrs. Lee has been a mother to me since then,"
said she, dropping her eyes to the floor.

"Then I will see the good woman who has taken
4*

your mother's place." Mark stepped in as he spoke, and took a chair in the neat little sitting room into which the door opened.

"She has gone over to Mr. Lofton's," said the girl, in eply, "and won't be back for an hour."

"Has she, indeed ? Then you know Mr. Lofton ?"

"Oh, yes. We know him very well. He owns our little cottage."

"Does he ! No doubt you find him a good land-land."

"He's a kind man," said the girl, earnestly.

"He is, as I have good reason to know," remarked the young man. "Mr. Lofton is my grandfather."

The girl seemed much surprised at this avowal, and appeared less at ease than before.

"And now, having told you who I am," said Mark, "I think I may be bold enough to ask your name."

"My name is Jenny Lawson," replied the girl.

"A pretty name, that—Jenny—I always liked the sound of it. My mother's name was Jenny. Did you ever see my mother ? But don't tremble so! Sit down, and tell your fluttering heart to be still."

Jenny sunk into a chair, her bosom heaving, and the crimson flush still glowing on her cheeks, while Mark gazed into her face with undisguised admiration.

"Who would have thought," said he to himself,

"that so sweet a wild flower grew in this out of the way place."

"Did you ever see my mother, Jenny?" asked the young man, after she was a little composed.

"Mrs. Clifford?"

"Yes."

"Often."

"Then we will be friends from this moment, Jenny. If you knew my mother then, you must have loved her. She has been dead now over three years."

There was a shade of sadness in the young man's voice as he said this.

"When did you see her last?" he resumed.

"The summer before she died she came up from New York and spent two or three weeks here. I saw her then, almost every day."

"And you loved my mother? Say you did!"

The young man spoke with a rising emotion that he could not restrain.

"Every body loved her," replied Jenny, simply and earnestly.

For a few moments Mark concealed his face with his hands, to hide the signs of feeling that were playing over it; then looking up again, he said—

"Jenny, because you knew my mother and loved her, we must be friends It was a great loss to me when she died. The greatest loss I ever had, or, it may be, ever will have. I have been worse since then. Ah me! If she had only lived!"

Again Mark covered his face with his hands, and, this time, he could not keep the dimness from his eyes.

It was a strange sight to Jenny to see the young man thus moved. Her innocent heart was drawn toward him with a pitying interest, and she yearned to speak words of comfort, but knew not what to say.

After Mark grew composed again, he asked Jenny a great many questions touching her knowledge of his mother; and listened with deep interest and emotion to many little incidents of Jenny's intercourse with her, which were related with all the artlessness and force of truth. In the midst of this singular interview, Mrs. Lee came in and surprised the young couple, who, forgetting all reserve, were conversing with an interest in their manner, the ground of which she might well misunderstand. Jenny started and looked confused, but, quickly recovering herself, introduced Mark as th grandson of Mr. Lofton.

The old lady did not respond to this with the cordiality that either of the young folks had expected. No, not by any means. A flush of angry suspicion came into her face, and she said to Jenny as she Landed her the bonnet she hurriedly removed—

"Here—take this into the other room and put it away."

The moment Jenny retired, Mrs. Lee turned to Mark, and after looking at him somewhat sternly for a moment, surprised him with this speech—

"If I ever find you here again, young man, I'll complain to your grandfather."

"Will you, indeed!" returned Mark, elevating his person, and looking at the old lady with flashing eyes. "And pray, what will you say to the old gentleman!"

"Fine doings, indeed, for the likes o' you to come creeping into a decent woman's house when she is away!" resumed Mrs. Lee. "Jenny's not the kind you're looking after, let me tell you. What would your poor dear mother, who is in heaven, God bless her! think, if she knew of this?"

The respectful and even affectionate reference to his mother, softened the feelings of Mark, who was growing very angry.

"Good morning, old lady," said he, as he turned way; "you don't know what you're talking about!" and springing from the door, he hurried off with rapid steps. On reaching a wood that lay at some distance off, Mark sought a retired spot, near where a quiet stream went stealing noiselessly along amid its alder and willow-fringed banks, and sitting down upon a

grassy spot, gave himself up to meditation. Little
inclined was he now for sport. The birds sung in the
trees above him, fluttered from branch to branch, and
even dipped their wings in the calm waters of th
stream, but he heeded them not. He had othe
thoughts. Greatly had old Mrs. Lee, in the blindness
of her suddenly aroused fears, wronged the young
man. If the sphere of innocence that was around
the beautiful girl had not been all powerful to subdue
evil thoughts and passions in his breast, the reference to
his mother would have been effectual to that end.

For half an hour had Mark remained seated alone,
busy with thoughts and feelings of a less wandering
and adventurous character than usually occupied his
mind, when, to his surprise, he saw Jenny Lawson
advancing along a path that led through a portion of
the woods, with a basket on her arm. She did not
observe him until she had approached within some
fifteen or twenty paces; when he arose to his feet, and
she, seeing him, stopped suddenly, and looked pale an
alarmed.

"I am glad to meet you again, Jenny," said Mark,
going quickly toward her, and taking her hand, which
she yielded without resistance. "Don't be frightened.
Mrs. Lee did me wrong. Heaven knows I would not
hurt a hair of your head! Come and sit down with

me in this quiet place, and let us talk about my
mother. You say you knew her and loved her. Let
her memory make us friends."

Mark's voice trembled with feeling. There was
something about the girl that made the thought of his
mother a holier and tenderer thing. He had loved his
mother intensely, and since her death, had felt her loss
as the saddest calamity that had, or possibly ever
could, befall him. Afloat on the stormy sea of
human life, he had seemed like a mariner without
helm or compass. Strangely enough, since meeting
with Jenny at the cottage a little while before, the
thought of her appeared to bring his mother nearer to
him ; and when, so unexpectedly, he saw her approaching him in the woods, he felt momentarily, that it was
his mother's spirit guiding her thither.

Urged by so strong an appeal, Jenny suffered herself
to be led to the retired spot where Mark had been
reclining, half wondering, half fearful—yet impelled by
a certain feeling that she could not well resist. In fact,
each exercised a power over the other, a power not
arising from any determination of will, but from a
certain spiritual affinity that neither comprehended.
Some have called this " destiny," but it has a better
name.

" Jenny," said Mark, after they were seated—he

still retained her hand in his, and felt it tremble—" tell
me something about my mother. It will do me good
to hear of her from your lips."

The girl tried to make some answer, but found no
utterance. Her lips trembled so that she could not
speak. But she grew more composed after a time, and
then in reply to many questions of Mark, related
incident after incident, in which his mother's goodness
of character stood prominent. The young man listened intently, sometimes with his eyes upon the
ground, and sometimes gazing admiringly into the
sweet face of the young speaker.

Time passed more rapidly than either Mark or Jenny
imagined. For full an hour had they been engaged in
earnest conversation, when both were painfully surprised
by the appearance of Mrs. Lee, who had sent Jenny on
an errand, and expected her early return. A suspicion
that she might encounter young Clifford having flashed
through the old woman's mind, she had come forth to
learn if possible the cause of Jenny's long absence.
To her grief and anger, she discovered them sitting
together engaged in earnest conversation.

" Now, Mark Clifford !" she exclaimed as she
advanced, " this is too bad ! And Jenny, you weak
and foolish girl ! are you madly bent on seeking the

fowler's snare? Child! child! is it thus you repay me
for my love and care over you!"

Both Mark and Jenny started to their feet, the face
of the former flushed with instant anger, and that of
the other pale from alarm.

"Come!" and Mrs. Lee caught hold of Jenny's
arm and drew her away. As they moved off, the
former, glancing back at Mark, and shaking her finger
towards him, said—

"I'll see your grandfather, young man!"

Fretted by this second disturbance of an interview
with Jenny, and angry at an unjust imputation of
motive, Mark dashed into the woods, with his gun in
his hand, and walked rapidly, but aimlessly, for nearly
an hour, when he found himself at the summit of a
high mountain, from which, far down and away towards
the east, he could see the silvery Hudson winding along
like a vein of silver. Here, wearied with his walk, and
faint in spirit from over excitement, he sat down to
rest and to compose his thoughts. Scarcely intelligible
to himself were his feelings. The meeting with Jenny,
and the effect upon him, were things that he did not
clearly understand. Her influence over him was a
mystery. In fact, what had passed so hurriedly, was
to him more like a dream than a reality.

No further idea of sport entered the mind of the

young man on that day. He remained until after the sun had passed the meridian in this retired place, and then went slowly back, passing the cottage of Mrs. Lee on his return. He did not see Jenny as he had hoped. On meeting Mr. Lofton, Mark became aware of a change in the old man's feelings towards him, and he guessed at once rightly as to the cause. If he had experienced any doubts, they would have been quickly removed.

" Mark !" said the old gentleman, sternly, almost the moment the grandson came into his presence, " I wish you to go back to New York to-morrow. I presume I need hardly explain my reason for this wish, when I tell you that I have just had a visit from old Mrs Lee."

The fiery spirit of Mark was stung into madness by this further reaction on him in a matter that involved nothing of criminal intent. Impulsive in his feelings, and quick to act from them, he replied with a calmness and even sadness in his voice that Mr. Lofton did not expect—the calmness was from a strong effort : the sadness expressed his real feelings :

" I will not trouble you with my presence an hour longer. If evil arise from this trampling of good impulse out of my heart, the sin rest on your own head. I never was and never can be patient under a false judgment. Farewell, grandfather! We may never meet again. If you hear of evil befalling me, think of it as having some connection with this hour."

With these words Mark turned away and left the house. The old man, in grief and alarm at the effec of his words, called after him, but he heeded him not.

"Run after him, and tell him to come back," he cried to a servant who stood near and had listened to what had passed between them. The order was obeyed, but it was of no avail. Mark returned a bitter answer to the message he brought him, and continued on his way. As he was hurrying along, suddenly he encountered Jenny. It was strange that he should meet her so often. There was something in it more than accident, and he felt that it was so.

"God bless you, Jenny!" he exclaimed with much feeling, catching hold of her hand and kissing it. "We may never meet again. They thought I meant you harm, and have driven me away. But, Heaven knows how little of evil purpose was in my heart! Farewell! Sometimes, when you are kneeling to say your nightly prayers, think of me, and breathe my name in your petitions. I will need the prayers of the innocent. Farewell!"

And under the impulse of the moment, Mark bent forward and pressed his lips fervently upon her pure

forehead ; then, springing away, left her bewildered and
in tears.

Mark hurried on towards the nearest landing place
on the river, some three miles distant, which he
reached just as a steamboat was passing. Waving his
handkerchief, as a signal, the boat rounded to, and
touching at the rude 'pier, took him on board. He
arrived in New York that evening, and on the next
morning started for Washington to see after his
application for a midshipman's appointment in the
navy. It was on this occasion that the young man
became aware of the secret influence of his father
against the application which had been made. His
mind, already feverishly excited, lost its balance under
this new disturbing cause.

"He will repent of this !" said he, bitterly, as he left
the room of the Secretary of the Navy, "and repent it
until the day of his death. Make a fixture of me in a
counting room ! Shut me up in a lawyer's office !
Lock me down in a medicine chest ! Mark Clifford
never will submit ! If I cannot enter the service in one
way I will in another."

Without pausing to weigh the consequences of his
act, Mark, in a spirit of revenge towards his father, went,
while the fever was on him, to the Navy Yard, and
there entered the United States service as a common

sailor, under the name of Edward James.   On the day following, the ship on board of which he had enlisted was gliding down the Potomac, and, in a week after, left Hampton Roads and went to sea.

From Norfolk, Mr. Clifford received a brief note written by his son, upbraiding him for having defeated the application to the department, and avowing the fact that he had gone to sea in the government service, as a common sailor.

CHAPTER II.

IT was impossible for such passionate interviews, brief though they were, to take place without leaving on the heart of a simple minded girl like Jenny Lawson, a deep impression. New impulses were given to her feelings, and a new direction to her thoughts. Nature told her that Mark Clifford loved her; and nothing but his cold disavowal of the fact could possibly have affected this belief. He had met her, it was true, only three or four times; but their interviews during these meetings had been of a character to leave no ordinary effect behind. So long as her eyes, dimmed by overflowing tears, could follow Mark's retiring form, she gazed eagerly after him; and when he was at length hidden from her view, she sat down to pour out her heart in passionate weeping.

Old Mrs. Lee, while she tenderly loved the sweet flower that had grown up under her care, was not, in all things, a wise and discreet woman; not deeply versed in the workings of the human heart.

Rumor of Mark's wildness had found its way to the neighborhood of Fairview, and made an unfavorable impression. Mrs. Lee firmly believed that he was moving with swift feet in the way to destruction, and rolling evil under his tongue as a sweet morsel. When she heard of his arrival at his grandfather's, a fear came upon her lest he should cast his eyes upon Jenny. No wonder that she met the young man with such a quick repulse, when, to her alarm, she found that he had invaded her home, and was already charming the ear of the innocent child she so tenderly loved and cared for. To find them sitting alone in the woods, only a little while afterwards, almost maddened her; and so soon as she took Jenny home, she hurried over to Mr. Lofton, and in a confused, exaggerated, and intemperate manner, complained of the conduct of Mark.

"Together alone in the woods!" exclaimed the old gentleman, greatly excited. "What does the girl mean?"

"What does he mean, thus to entice away my innocent child?" said Mrs. Lee, equally excited. "Oh, Mr. Lofton! for goodness' sake, send him back to New York! If he remain here a day longer, all may be lost! Jenny is bewitched with him. She cried as if her heart would break when I took her back home, and said that I had done wrong to Mark in what I had said to him."

"Weak and foolish child! How little does she know of the world—how little of the subtle human heart! Yes—yes, Mrs. Lee, Mark shall go back at once. He shall not remain here a day longer, to breathe his blighting breath on so sweet a flower. Jenny is too good a girl to be exposed to such an influence."

The mind of Mr. Lofton remained excited for hours after this interview; and when Mark appeared, he met him as has already been seen. The manner in which the young man received the angry words of his grandfather, was a little different from what had been anticipated. Mr. Lofton expected some explanation by which he could understand more clearly what was in the young man's thoughts. When, therefore, Mark abruptly turned from him with such strange language on his tongue, Mr. Lofton's anger cooled, and he felt that he had suffered himself to be misled by a hasty judgment. That no evil had been in the young man's mind he was sure. It was this change that had prompted him to make an effort to recall him. But, the effort was fruitless.

On Jenny's return home, after her last interview with Mark, she found a servant there with a summons from Mr. Lofton. With much reluctance she repaired to the mansion house. On meeting with the old gentleman he received her in a kind but subdued manner; but, as for Jenny herself, she stood in his presence weeping and trembling.

"Jenny," said Mr. Lofton, after the girl had grown more composed, "when did you first meet my grandson?"

Jenny mentioned the accidental meeting on the day before, and the call at the cottage in the morning.

"And you saw him first only yesterday?"

"Yes."

"What did he say when he called this morning?"

"He asked for my mother."

"Your mother?"

"Yes. I told him that my mother was dead, and that I lived with Mrs. Lee. He then wanted to see her; but I said that she had gone over to your house.'

"What did he say then?"

"He spoke of you, and said you were a good man, and that we no doubt found you a good landlord. I had mentioned that you owned our cottage."

Mr. Lofton appeared affected at this.

"What then?" he continued.

5

"He told me who he was, and then asked me my name. When I told him that it was Jenny, he said it was a good name, and that he always liked the sound of it, for his mother's name was Jenny. Then he asked me if I had known his mother, and when I said yes, he wanted to know if I loved her. I said yes— for you know we all loved her. Then he covered his face with his hands, and I saw the tears coming through his fingers. 'Because you knew my mother, and loved her, Jenny,' said he, 'we will be friends.' Afterwards he asked me a great many questions about her, and listened with the tears in his eyes, when I told him of many things she had said and done the last time she was up here. We were talking together about his mother, when Mrs. Lee came in. She spoke cross to him, and threatened to complain to you, if he came there any more. He went away angry. But I'm sure he meant nothing wrong, sir. How could he, and talk as he did about his mother in heaven?"

"But, how came you to meet him in the woods, Jenny?" said Mr. Lofton. "Did he tell you that he would wait there for you?"

"Oh, no, sir. The meeting was accidental. I was sent over to Mrs. Jasper's on an errand, and, in passing through the woods, saw him sitting alone and looking very unhappy. I was frightened ; but he told me that he wouldn't hurt a hair of my head. Then he made me sit down upon the grass beside him, and talk to him about his mother. He asked me a great many questions, and I told him all that I could remember about her. Sometimes the tears would steal over his cheeks; and sometimes he would say—'Ah! if my mother had not died. Her death was a great loss to me, Jenny—a great loss—and I have been worse for it.'"

"And was this all you talked about, Jenny," asked Mr. Lofton, who was much affected by the artless narrative of the girl.

"It was all about his mother," replied Jenny. "He said that I not only bore her name, but that I looked like her, and that it seemed to him, while with me, that she was present."

"He said that, did he!" Mr. Lofton spoke more earnestly, and looked intently upon Jenny's face. "Yes—yes—it is so. She does look like dear Jenny," he murmured to himself. "I never saw this before. Dear boy! We have done him wrong. These hasty conclusions—ah, me! To how much evil do they lead!"

"And you were talking thus, when Mrs. Lee found you?"

"Yes, sir."

" What did she say ?"

" I can hardly tell what she said, I was so frightened. But I know she spoke angrily to him and to me, and threatened to see you."

Mr. Lofton sighed deeply, then added, as if the remark were casual—

" And that is the last you have seen of him."

" No, sir ; I met him a little while ago, as he was hurrying away from your house."

" You did !"   Mr. Lofton started at Jenny's unexpected reply.

" Yes, sir."

" Did he speak to you ?"

" Yes ; he stopped and caught hold of my hand, saying, ' God bless you, Jenny !   We may never meet again.   They have driven me away, because they thought I meant to harm you.'   But he said nothing wrong was in his heart, and asked me to pray for him, as he would need my prayers."

At this part of her narrative, Jenny wept bitterly, and her auditor's eyes became dim also.

Satisfied that Jenny's story was true in every particular, Mr. Lofton spoke kindly to her and sent her home.

A week after Mark Clifford left Fairview, word came that he had enlisted in the United States' service and gone to sea as a common sailor; accompanying this intelligence was an indignant avowal of his father that he would have nothing more to do with him. To old Mr. Lofton this was a serious blow. In Mark he had hoped to see realized some of his ambitious desires. His daughter Jenny had been happy in her marriage, but the union never gave him much satisfaction. She was to have been the wife of one more distinguished than a mere plodding money-making merchant.

Painful was the shock that accompanied the prostration of old Mr. Lofton's ambitious hopes touching his grandson, of whom he had always been exceedingly fond. To him he had intended leaving the bulk of his property when he died. But now anger and resentment arose in his mind against him as unworthy such a preference, and in the warmth of a moment's impulse, he corrected his will and cut him off with a dollar. This was no sooner done than better emotions stirred in the old man's bosom, and he regretted the hasty act; but pride of consistency prevented his recalling it.

From that time old Mr. Lofton broke down rapidly. In six months he seemed to have added ten years to his life. During that period no news had come from Mark; who was not only angry with both his father and grandfather, but felt that in doing what he had done, he had offended them beyond the hope of

forgiveness. He, therefore, having taken a rash step,
moved on in the way he had chosen, in a spirit of
recklessness and defiance. The ties of blood which had
bound him to his home were broken; the world was all
before him, and he must make his way in it, alone.
The life of a common sailor in a government ship he
found to be something different from what he had
imagined, when, acting under a momentary excitement,
he was so mad as to enlist in the service. Unused to
work or ready obedience, he soon discovered that his
life was to be one not only of bodily toil, pushed sometimes to the extreme of fatigue, but one of the most
perfect subordination to the will of others, under pain
of corporeal punishment. The first insolent word of
authority passed to him by a new fledged midshipman,
his junior by at least three years, stung him so deeply
that it was only by a most violent effort that he could
master the impulse that prompted him to seize and
throw him overboard. He did not regret this successful effort at self-control, when, a few hours afterwards,
he was compelled to witness the punishment of the cat
inflicted on a sailor for the offence of insolence to an
officer. The sight of the poor man, writhing under the
brutality of the lash, made an impression on him that
nothing could efface. It absorbed his mind and

brought it into a healthier state of reflection than it had yet been.

"I have placed myself in this position by a rash act," he said to himself, as he turned, sick at heart away from the painful and disgusting sight. "And all rebellion against the authority around me will but make plainer my own weakness. I have degraded myself; but there is a lower degradation still, and that I must avoid. Drag me to the gangway, and I am lost!"

Strict obedience and submission was from that time self-compelled on the part of Mark Clifford. It was not without a strong effort, however, that he kept down the fiery spirit within him. A word of insolent command—and certain of the young midshipmen on board could not speak to a sailor even if he were old as their father, except in a tone of insult—would send the blood boiling through his veins.

It was only by the narrowest chances that Mark escaped punishment during the first six months of the cruise, which was in the Pacific. If he succeeded in bridling his tongue, and restraining his hands from violence, he could not hide the indignant flash of his eyes, nor school the muscles of his face into submission. They revealed the wild spirit of rebellion that was in his heart. Intelligent promptness in duty saved him.

This was seen by his superior officers, and it was so much in his favor when complaints came from the petty tyrants of the ship who sometimes shrunk from the fierce glance that in a moment of struggling passion would be cast upon them. After a trying ordeal of six months, he was favored by one of the officers who saw deeper than the rest, and gathered from him a few hints as to his true character. In pitying him, he made use of his influence to save him from some of the worst consequences of his position.

Jenny Lawson was a changed girl after her brief meeting with Mark Clifford. Before, she had been as light hearted and gay as a bird. But, her voice was no longer heard pouring forth the sweet melodies born of a happy heart. Much of her time she sought to be alone; and when alone, she usually sat in a state of dreamy absent-mindedness. As for her thoughts, they were most of the time on Clifford. His hand had stirred the waters of affection in her gentle bosom; and they knew no rest. Mr. Lofton frequently sent for her to come over to the mansion house. He never spoke to her of Mark; nor did she mention his name—though both thought of him whenever they were together. The oftener Mr. Lofton saw Jenny, and the more he was with her, the more did she remind him of his own lost child—his Jenny, the mother of Mark—now in heaven. The incident of meeting with young Clifford had helped to develop Jenny's character, and give it a stronger type than otherwise would have been the case. Thus, she became to Mr. Lofton companionable; and, ere a year had elapsed from the time Mark went away, Mrs. Lee, having passed to her account, she was taken into his house, and he had her constantly with him. As he continued to fail, he leaned upon the affectionate girl more and more heavily; and was never contented when she was away from him.

It would be difficult to represent clearly Jenny's state of feeling during this period. A simple minded, innocent, true-hearted girl, in whose bosom scarce beat a single selfish impulse, she found herself suddenly approached by one in station far above her, in a way that left her heart unguarded. He had stooped to her, and leaned upon her, and she, obeying an impulse of her nature, had stood firmer to support him as he leaned. Their tender, confiding, and delightful intercourse, continued only for a brief season, and was then rudely broken in upon; forced separation was followed by painful consequences to the young man. When Jenny thought of how Mark had been driven away on her account, she felt that in order to save him from the evils that must be impending over him, she would devote even her life in his service. But, what could

5*

she do ? This desire to serve him had also another origin. A deep feeling of love had been awakened; and, though she felt it to be hopeless, she kept the flame brightly burning.

Intenser feelings produced more active thoughts, and the mind of Jenny took a higher development. A constant association with Mr. Lofton, who required her to read to him sometimes for hours each day, filled her thoughts with higher ideas than any she had known, and gradually widened the sphere of her intelligence. Thus she grew more and more companionable to the old man, who, in turn, perceiving that her mind was expanding, took pains to give it a right direction, so far as external knowledges were concerned.

Soon after Mark went to sea, Jenny took pains to inform herself accurately as to the position and duties of a common sailor on board of a United States' vessel. She was more troubled about Mark after this, for she understood how unfitted he was for the hard service he entered upon so blindly.

One day, it was over a year from the time that Mark left Fairview, Mr. Lofton sent for Jenny, and, on her coming into his room, handed her a sealed letter, but without making any remark. On it was superscribed her name ; and it bore, besides, the word "Ship" in red printed letters, " Valparaiso," also, was written upon it.

Jenny looked at the letter wonderingly, for a moment or two, and then, with her heart throbbing wildly, left the room. On breaking the seal, she found the letter to be from Mark. It was as follows :

"U. S. Ship ——,

Valparaiso, September 4, 18—,

"My Gentle Friend.—A year has passed since our brief meeting and unhappy parting. I do not think you have forgotten me in that time; you may be sure I have not forgotten you. The memory of one about whom we conversed, alone would keep your image green in my thoughts. Of the rash step I took you have no doubt heard. In anger at unjust treatment both from my father and grandfather, I was weak enough to enter the United States' service as a sailor. Having committed this folly, and being unwilling to humble myself, and appeal to friends who had wronged me for their interest to get me released, I have looked the hardship and degradation before me in the face, and sought to encounter it manfully. The ordeal has been thus far most severe, and I have yet two years of trial before me. As I am where I am by my own act, I will not complain, and yet, I have felt it hard to be cut off from all the sympathy and kind interest of my friends—to have no word from home—to feel that none cares for me. I know that I have offended both my father and grandfather past forgiveness, and my mind is made up to seek for no reconciliation with them. I cannot stoop to that. I have too much of the blood of the Loftons in my veins.

"But why write this to you, Jenny? You will hardly understand how such feelings can govern any heart—your own is so gentle and innocent in all of its impulses. I have other things to say to you! Since our meeting I have never ceased to think of you! I need no picture of your face, for I see it ever before me as distinctly as if sketched by the painter's art. I sometimes ask myself wonderingly, how it is that you, a simple country maiden, could, in one or two brief meetings, have made so strong an impression upon me? But, you bore my mother's name, and your face was like her dear face. Moreover, the beauty of goodness was in your countenance, and a sphere of innocence around you; and I had not strayed so far from virtue's paths as to be insensible to these. Since we parted, Jenny, you have seemed ever present with me, as an angel of peace and protection. In the moment when passion was about overmastering me, you stood by my side, and I seemed to hear your voice speaking to the rising storm, and hushing all into calmness. When my feet have been ready to step aside, you instantly approached and pointed to the better way. Last night I had a dream, and it is because of that dream that I now write to you. I have often felt like writing before; now I write because I cannot help it. I am moved to do so by something that I cannot resist.

"Yesterday I had a difficulty with an officer who has shewn a disposition to domineer over me ever since the cruise commenced. He complained to the commander, who has, in more than one instance shown me kindness. The commander said that I must make certain concessions to the officer, which I felt as humiliating; that good discipline required this, and that unless I did so, he would be reluctantly compelled to order me to the gangway. Thus far I had avoided punishment by a strict obedience to duty. No lash had ever touched me. That degradation I felt would be my ruin; and in fear of the result I bore much, rather than give any petty officer the power to have me punished. 'Let me sleep over it, Captain,' said I, so earnestly, that my request was granted.

"Troubled dreams haunted me as I lay in my hammock that night. At last I seemed to be afloat on the wide ocean, on a single plank, tossing about with the hot sun shining fiercely upon me, and monsters of the great deep gathering around, eager for their prey. I was weak, faint, and despairing. In vain did my eyes sweep the horizon, there was neither vessel nor land in sight. At length the sun went down, and the darkness drew nearer and nearer. Then I could see nothing but the stars shining above me. In this moment, when hope seemed about leaving my heart orever, a light came suddenly around me. On looking up I saw a boat approaching. In the bow stood my mother, and you sat guiding the helm! She took my hand, and I stepped into the boat with a thrill of joy at my deliverance. As I did so, she kissed me, looked tenderly towards you, and faded from my sight. Then I awoke.

"The effect of all this was to subdue my haughty spirit. As soon as an opportunity offered, I made every desired concession for my fault, and was forgiven. And now I am writing to you, I feel as if there was something in that dream, Jenny. Ah! Shall I ever see your face again? Heaven only knows!

"I send this letter to you in care of my grandfather. I know that he will not retain it or seek to know its contents. Unless he should ask after me, do not speak to him or any one of what I have written to you. Farewell! Do not forget me in your prayers.

MARK CLIFFORD."

The effect of this letter upon Jenny, was to interest her intensely. The swell of emotion went deeper, and the activity of her mind took a still higher character. It was plain to her, when she next came into Mr. Lofton's presence, that his thoughts had been busy about the letter she had received. · But he asked her no questions, and, faithful to the expressed wish of Mark, she made no reference to the subject whatever.

One part of Jenny's service to the failing old man, had been to read to him daily from the newspapers. This made her familiar with what was passing in the world, gave her food for thought, and helped her to develop and strengthen her mind. Often had she pored over the papers for some news of Mark, but never having heard the name of the vessel in which he had gone to sea, she had possessed no clue to find what she sought for. But now, whenever a paper was opened, her first search was for naval intelligence. With what a throb of interest did she one day, about a week after Mark's letter came to hand, read an announcement that the ship —— had been ordered home, and might be expected to arrive daily at Norfolk.

A woman thinks quickly to a conclusion ; or, rather, arrives there by a process quicker than thought ; especially where her conclusions are to affect a beloved object. In an hour after Jenny had read the fact just stated, she said to Mr. Lofton, who had now come to be much attached to her—

" Will you grant me a favor ?"

" Ask what you will, my child," replied Mr. Loftin, with more than usual affection in his tones.

" Let me have fifty dollars."

" Certainly. I know you will use it for a good purpose."

Two days after this Jenny was in Washington. She made the journey alone, but without timidity or fear. Her purpose made her self-possessed and courageous. On arriving at the seat of government, Jenny inquired for the Secretary of the Navy. When she arrived at the Department over which he presided, and obtained an interview, she said to him, as soon as she could compose herself—

" The ship —— has been ordered home from the Pacific ?"

" She arrived at Norfolk last night, and is now hourly expected at the Navy Yard," replied the Secretary.

At this intelligence, Jenny was so much affected that it was some time before she could trust herself to speak.

" You have a brother on board ?" said the Secretary.

" There is a young man on board," replied Jenny, in a tremulous voice, " for whose discharge I have come to ask."

The Secretary looked grave.

" At whose instance do you come ?" he inquired

" Solely at my own."

" Who is the young man ?"

" Do you know Marshal Lofton ?"

" I do, by reputation, well. He belongs to a distinguished family in New York, to which the country owes much for service rendered in trying times."

" The discharge I ask, is for his grandson."

" Young Clifford, do you mean ?" The Secretary looked surprised as he spoke. " He is not in the service."

" He is on board the ship —— as a common sailor."

" Impossible !"

" It is too true. In a moment of angry disappointment he took the rash step. And, since then, no communication has passed between him and his friends."

The Secretary turned to the table near which he was sitting, and, after writing a few lines on a piece of paper, rung a small hand-bell for the messenger, who came in immediately.

" Take this to Mr J——, and bring me an answer immediately."

The messenger left the room, and the Secretary said to Jenny—

" Wait a moment or two, if you please."

In a little while the messenger came back and handed the Secretary a memorandum from the clerk to whom he had sent for information.

"There is no such person as Clifford on board the hip ——, nor, in fact, in the service as a common sailor," said the Secretary, addressing Jenny, after glancing at the memorandum he had received.

"Oh, yes, there is; there must be," exclaimed the now agitated girl. "I received a letter from him at Valparaiso, dated on board of this ship. And, besides, he wrote home to his father, at the time he sailed, declaring what he had done."

"Strange. His name doesn't appear in the Department as attached to the service. Hark! There's a gun. It announces, in all probability, the arrival of the ship —— at the Navy Yard."

Jenny instantly became pale.

"Perhaps," suggested the Secretary, "your best way will be to take a carriage and drive down, at once, to the Navy Yard. Shall I direct the messenger to call a carriage for you?"

"I will thank you to do so," replied Jenny, faintly.

The carriage was soon at the door. Jenny was much agitated when she arrived at the Navy Yard. To her question as to whether the ship —— had arrived, she was pointed to a large vessel which lav moored at the dock. How she mounted its side she hardly knew ; but, in what seemed scarcely an instant of time, she was standing on the deck. To an officer who met her, as she stepped on board, she asked for Mark Clifford.

" What is he ?   A sailor or marine ?"

" A sailor."

" There is no such person on board, I believe," said the officer.

Poor Jenny staggered back a few paces, while a deadly paleness overspread her face. As she leaned against the side of the vessel for support, a young man, dressed as a sailor, ascended from the lower deck. Their eyes met, and both sprung towards each other.

" Jenny ! Jenny ! is it you !" fell passionately from his lips, as he caught her in his arms, and kissed her fervently. " Bless you ! Bless you, Jenny ! This is more than I had hoped for," he added, as he gazed fondly into her beautiful young face.

" They said you were not here," murmured Jenny, " and my heart was in despair."

" You asked for Mark Clifford ?"

" Yes."

" I am not known in the service by that name. I entered it as Edward James."

This meeting, occurring as it did, with many

spectators around, and they of the ruder class, was se earnest and tender, yet with all, so mutually respectfu. and decorous, that even the rough sailors were touched by the manner and sentiment of the interview; and more than one eye grew dim.

Not long did Jenny linger on the deck of the ——. Now that she had found Mark, her next thought was to secure his discharge.

CHAPTER III.

It was little more than half an hour after the Secretary of the Navy parted with Jenny, ere she entered his office again; but now with her beautiful face flushed and eager.

"I have found him!" she exclaimed; "I knew he was on board this ship!"

The Secretary's interest had been awakened by the former brief interview with Jenny, and when she came in with the announcement, he was not only affected with pleasure, but his feelings were touched by her manner. "How is it, then," he inquired, "that his name is not to be found in the list of her crew?"

"He entered the service under the name of Edward James."

"Ah! that explains it."

"And now, sir," said Jenny, in a voice so earnest and appealing, that her auditor felt like granting her desire without a moment's reflection : " I have come to entreat you to give me his release."

" On what ground do you make this request ?" inquired the Secretary, gazing into the sweet youn face of Jenny, with a feeling of respect blended witl admiration.

" On the ground of humanity," was the simple yet earnestly spoken reply.

" How can you put it on that ground ?"

" A young man of his education and abilities can serve society better in another position."

" But he has chosen the place he is in."

" Not deliberately.   In a moment of disappointment and blind passion he took a false step.   Severely has he suffered for this act.   Let it not be prolonged, lest it destroy him.   One of his spirit can scarcely pass through so severe an ordeal without fainting."

" Does Mr. Lofton, his grandfather, desire what you ask ?"

" Mr. Lofton is a proud man.   He entertained high hopes for Mark, who has, in this act, so bitterly disap pointed them, that he has not been known to utter his name since the news of his enlistment was received."

" And his father ?"

Jenny shook her head, sighing—

"I don't know anything about him. He was angry, and, I believe, cast him off."

"And you, then, are his only advocate?"

Jenny's eyes dropped to the floor, and a deeper tinge overspread her countenance.

"What is your relation to him, and to his friends?" asked the Secretary, his manner becoming more serious.

It was some moments before Jenny replied. Then she said, in a more subdued voice:

"I am living with Mr. Lofton. But—"

She hesitated, and then became silent and embarrassed.

"Does Mr. Lofton know of your journey to Washington?"

Jenny shook her head.

"Where did you tell him you were going?"

"I said nothing to him, but came away the moment I heard the ship was expected to arrive at Norfolk."

"Suppose I release him from the service?"

"I will persuade him to go back with me to Fairview, and then I know that all will be forgiven between him and his grandfather. You don't know how Mr Lofton has failed since Mark went away," added Jenny in a tone meant to reach the feelings of her auditor

"He looks many years older. Ah, sir, if you would only grant my request!"

"Will the young man return to his family! Have you spoken to him about it?"

"No; I wished not to create hopes that might fail. But give me his release, and I will have a claim on him."

"And you will require him to go home in acknowledgment of that claim."

"I will not leave him till he goes back," said Jenny.

"Is he not satisfied in the service?"

"How could he be satisfied with it?" Jenny spoke with a quick impulse, and with something like rebuke in her voice. "No! It is crushing out his very life. Think of your own son in such a position!"

There was something in this appeal, and in the way it was uttered, that decided the Secretary's mind. A man of acute observation, and humane feelings, he not only understood pretty clearly the relation that Jenny bore to Mark and his family, but sympathised with the young man and resolved to grant the maiden's request. Leaving her for a few minutes, he went into an adjoining room. When he returned, he had a sealed letter in his hand directed to the commander of the ship ——— .

" This will procure his dismissal from the service," said he, as he reached it towards Jenny.

" May heaven reward you!" fell from the lips of the young girl, as she received the letter. Then, with the tears glistening in her eyes, she hurriedly left the apartment.

While old Mr. Lofton was yet wondering what Jenny could want with fifty dollars, a servant came and told him that she had just heard from a neighbor who came up a little while before from the landing, that he had seen Jenny go on board of a steamboat that was on its way to New York.

" It can't be so," quickly answered Mr. Lofton.

" Mr. Jones said, positively, that it was her."

" Tell Henry to go to Mr. Jones and ask him, as a favor, to step over and see me."

In due time Mr. Jones came.

" Are you certain that you saw Jenny Lawson go on board the steamboat for New York to-day ?" asked Mr. Lofton, when the neighbor appeared.

" Oh, yes, sir ; it was her," replied the man.

" Did you speak to her ?"

" I was going to, but she hurried past me without looking in my face."

" Had she anything with her ?"

" There was a small bundle in her hand."

6

"Strange—strange—very strange,' murmured the old man to himself. "What does it mean? Where can she have gone?"

"Did she say nothing about going away?"

"Nothing—nothing!"

Mr. Lofton's eyes fell to the floor, and he sat thinking for some moments.

"Mr. Jones," said he, at length, "can you go to New York for me?"

"I suppose so," replied Mr. Jones.

"When will the morning boat from Albany pass here?"

"In about two hours."

"Then get yourself ready, if you please, and come over to me. I do not like this of Jenny, and must find out where she has gone."

Mr. Jones promised to do as was desired, and went to make all necessary preparations. Before he returned, a domestic brought Mr. Lofton a sealed note bearing his address, which she had found in Jenny's chamber. It was as follows:

"Do not be alarmed at my telling you that, when you receive this, I will be on a journey of two or three hundred miles in extent, and may not return for weeks. Believe me, that my purpose is a good one. I hope to be back much sooner than I have said. When I do get home, I know you will approve of what I have done. My errand is one of Mercy.

"Humbly and faithfully yours,   JENNY."

It was some time before Mr. Lofton's mind grew calm and clear, after reading this note. That Jenny's absence was, in some way, connected with Mark, was a thought that soon presented itself. But, in what way, he could not make out; for he had never heard the name of the ship in which his grandson sailed, and knew nothing of her expected arrival home.

By the time Mr. Jones appeared, ready to start on the proposed mission to New York, Mr. Lofton had made up his mind not to attempt to follow Jenny, but to wait for some word from her. Not until this sudden separation took place did Mr. Lofton understand how necessary to his happiness the affectionate girl had become. So troubled was he at her absence, and so anxious for her safety, that when night came he found himself unable to sleep. In thinking about the dangers that would gather around one so ignorant of the world, his imagination magnified the trials and temptations to which, alone as she was, she would be exposed. Such thoughts kept him tossing anxiously upon his pillow, or restlessly pacing the chamber floor until day dawn. Then, from over-excitement and loss of rest, he was seriously indisposed—so much so, that his physician had to be called in during the day. He found him with a good deal of fever, and deemed it necessary to resort to depletion, as well as to the application of ther remedies to allay the over-action of his vital system. These prostrated him at once—so much so, that he was unable to sit up. Before night he was so seriously ill that the physician had to be sent for again. The fever had returned with great violence, and the pressure on his brain was so great that he had become slightly delirious.

During the second night, this active stage of the disease continued ; but all the worst symptoms subsided towards morning. Daylight found him sleeping quietly, with a cool moist skin, and a low, regular pulse. Towards mid-day he awoke ; but the anxiety that came with thought brought back many of the unfavorable symptoms, and he was worse again towards evening. On the third day he was again better, but so weak as to be unable to sit up.

How greatly did old Mr. Lofton miss the gentle girl, who had become almost as dear to him as a child, during this brief illness, brought on by her strange absence. No hand could smooth his pillow like hers. No presence could supply her place by his side. He was companionless, now that she was away ; and his heart reached vainly around for something to lean upon for support.

On the fourth day he was better, and sat up a little. But his anxiety for Jenny was increasing. Where could she be? He read her brief letter over and over again.

"May not return for weeks," he said, as he held the letter in his hand. "Where can she have gone? Foolish child! Why did she not consult with me? I would have advised her for the best."

Late on the afternoon of that day, Jenny, in company with Mark, the latter in the dress of a seaman in the United States service, passed from a steamboat at the landing near Fairview, and took their way towards the mansion of Mr. Lofton. They had not proceeded far, before the young man began to linger, while Jenny showed every disposition to press on rapidly. At length Mark stopped.

"Jenny," said he, while a cloud settled on his face, "you've had your own way up to this moment. I'v been passive in your hands. But I can't go on with you any further."

"Don't say that," returned Jenny, her voice almost imploring in its tones. And in the earnestness of her desire to bring Mark back to his grandfather, she seized one of his hands, and, by a gentle force, drew

him a few paces in the direction they had been going.
But he resisted that force, and they stood still again.

"I don't think I can go back, Jenny," said Mark, in
a subdued voice: "I have some pride left, much as
has been crushed out of me during the period of my
absence, and this rises higher and higher in my heart
the nearer I approach my grandfather. How can I
meet him!"

"Only come into his presence, Mark," urged Jenny,
speaking tenderly and familiarly. She had addressed
him as Mr. Clifford, but he had forbidden that,
saying—

"To you my name is Mark—let none other pass
your lips!"

"Only come into his presence. You need not speak
to him, nor look towards him. This is all I ask."

"But, the humiliation of going back after my
resentment of his former treatment," said Mark. "I
can bear anything but this bending of my pride—this
humbling of myself to others."

"Don't think of yourself, Mark," replied Jenny.
"Think of your grandfather, on whom your absence
has wrought so sad a change. Think of what he must
have suffered to break down so in less than two years.
In pity to him, then, come back. Be guided by me,

Mark, and I will lead you right. Think of that strange dream!"

At this appeal, Mark moved quickly forward by the side of the beautiful girl, who had so improved in every way—mind and body having developed wonderfully since he parted with her—that he was filled all the while by wonder, respect and admiration. He moved by her side as if influenced by a spell that subdued his own will.

In silence they walked along, side by side, the pressure of thought and feeling on each mind being so strong as to take away the desire to speak, until the old mansion house of Mr. Lofton appeared in view. Here Mark stopped again; but the tenderly uttered " Come," and the tearful glance of Jenny, effectually controlled the promptings of an unbroken will. Together, in a few minutes afterwards, they approached the house and entered.

" Where is Mr. Lofton?" asked Jenny of a servant who met them in the great hall.

" He's been very ill," replied the servant.

" Ill!" Jenny became pale.

" Yes, very ill. But he is better now."

" Where is he?"

" In his own chamber."

For a moment Jenny hesitated whether to go up

alone, or in company with Mark. She would have
preferred going alone; but fearing that, if she parted
even thus briefly from Mark, her strong influence over
him, by means of which she had brought him, almost
as a struggling prisoner, thus far, would be weakened,
and he tempted to turn from the house, she resolved
to venture upon the experiment of entering Mr. Lofton's
sick chamber, in company with his grandson.

"Is he sitting up?" she asked of the servant.

"He's been sitting up a good deal to-day, but is
lying down now."

"He's much better?"

"Oh, yes!"

"Come," said Jenny, turning to Mark, and moving
towards the stairway. Mark followed passively. On
entering the chamber of Mr. Lofton, they found him
sleeping.

Both silently approached, and looked upon his
venerable face, composed in deep slumber. Tears came
to the eyes of Mark as he gazed at the countenance of
his grandfather, and his heart became soft as the heart
of a child. While they yet stood looking at him, his
lips moved, and he uttered both their names. Then he
seemed disturbed, and moaned, as if in pain.

"Grandfather!" said Mark, taking the old man'
hand, and bending over him.

Quickly his eyes opened. For a few moments he gazed earnestly upon Mark, and then tightened his hand upon that of the young man, closed his eyes again, and murmured in a voice that deeply touched the returning wanderer—

"My poor boy! My poor boy! Why did you do so? Why did you break my heart? But, God be thanked, you are back again! God be thanked!"

"Jenny!" said the old man, quickly, as he felt her take his other hand and press it to her lips. "And it was for this you left me! Dear child, I forgive you!"

As he spoke, he drew her hand over towards the one that grasped that of Mark, and uniting them together, murmured—

"If you love each other, it is all right. My blessing shall go with you."

How mild and delicious was the thrill that ran through each of the hearts of his auditors. This was more than they expected. Mark tightly grasped the hand that was placed within his own, and that hand gave back an answering pressure. Thus was the past reconciled with the present; while a vista was opened toward a bright future.

Little more than a year has passed since this joyful event took place. Mark Clifford, with the entire approval of his grandfather, who furnished a handsome

6*

capital for the purpose, entered, during the time, into
the mercantile house of his father as a partner, and is
now actively engaged in business, well sobered by his
evere experience.   He has taken a lovely bride, who is
the charm of all circles into which she is introduced ;
and her name is Jenny.   But few who meet her dream
that she once grew, a beautiful wild flower, near the
banks of the Hudson.

Old Mr. Lofton could not be separated from Jenny ;
and, as he could not separate her from her husband, he
has removed to the city, where he has an elegant
residence, in which her voice is the music and her
smiles the ever present sunshine.

SHADOWS.

A HAPPY-HEARTED child was Madeline Henry, for the glad sunshine ever lay upon the threshold of her early home. Her father, a cheerful, unselfish man, left the world and its business cares behind him when he placed his hand upon the door of entrance to his household treasures. Like other men, he had his anxieties, his hopes and losses, his disappointments and troubles; but he wisely and humanely strove to banish these from his thoughts, when he entered the home-sanctuary, lest his presence should bring a shadow instead of sunshine.

Madeline was just twenty years of age, when, as the wife of Edward Leslie, she left this warm down-covered nest, and was borne to a new and more elegant home. Mr. Leslie was her senior by eight or nine years. He began his business life at the age of twenty-two, as partner in a well established mercantile house, and, as he was able to place ten thousand dollars in the concern, his position, in the matter of profits, was good from the beginning.   Yet, for all this, notwithstanding* more than one loving-hearted girl, in whose eyes he might have found favor, crossed his path, he resolutely turned his thoughts away, lest the fascination should be too strong for him.   He resolved not to marry until he felt able to maintain a certain style of living.

Thus were the heart's impulses checked ; thus were the first tender leaves of affection frozen in the cold breath of mere calculation.   He wronged himself in this ; yet, in his worldliness and ignorance, did he feel proud of being above, what he called, the weaknesses of other men.

It was but natural that Mr. Leslie should become, in a measure, reserved towards others.   Should assume a statelier step, and more set forms of speech.   Should repress, more and more, his heart's impulses.

In Leslie, the love of money was strong ; yet there was in his character a firmly laid basis of integrity. Though shrewd in his dealings, he never stooped to a system of overreaching.   He was not long, therefore, in establishing a good reputation among business men. In social circles, where he occasionally appeared, almost as a matter of course he became an object of interest.

Observation, as it regards character, is, by far, too

superficial. With most persons, merely what strikes the eye is sufficient ground for an opinion ; and this opinion is freely and positively expressed. Thus, a good reputation comes, as a natural consequence, to a man who lives in the practice of most of the apparent social virtues, while he may possess no real kindness of heart, may be selfish to an extreme degree.

Thus it was with Mr. Leslie. He was generally regarded as a model of a man ; and when he, at length, approached Madeline Henry as a lover, the friends of the young lady regarded her as particularly fortunate.

As for Madeline, she rather shrunk, at first, from his advances. There was a coldness in his sphere that chilled her ; a rigid propriety of speech and action that inspired too much respect and deference. Gradually, however, love for the maiden, (if by such a term it might be called) fused his hard exterior, and his manner became so softened, gentle and affectionate, bat she yielded up to him a most precious treasure— the love of her young and trusting heart.

Just twenty years old, as we have said, was Madeline when she passed, as the bride of Mr. Leslie, from the warm home-nest in which she had reposed so happily, to become the mistress of an elegant mansion. Though in age a woman, she was, in many things, but a child in feelings. Tenderly cared for and petted by her father, her spirit had been, in a measure, sustained by love as an aliment.

One like Madeline is not fit to be the wife of such a man as Edward Leslie. For him, a cold, calculating woman of the world were a better companion. One who has her own selfish ends to gain ; and who can find, in fashion, gaiety, or personal indulgence, full compensation for a husband's love.

Madeline was scarcely the bride of a week, ere shadows began to fall upon her heart ; and the form that interposed itself between her and the sunlight, was the form of her husband. As a daughter, love had ever gone forth in lavish expression. This had been encouraged by all the associations of home. But, from the beginning of her wedded life, she felt the manner of her husband like the weight of a hand on her bosom, repressing her heart's outgushing impulses.

It was on the fifth evening of their marriage, about the early twilight hour, and Madeline, alone, almost for the first time since morning, sat awaiting the return of her husband. Full of pleasant thoughts was her mind, and warm with love her heart. A few hours of separation from Edward had made her impatient to meet him again. When, at length, she heard him enter, she sprang to meet him, and, with an exclamation of delight, threw her arms about his neck.

There was a cold dignity in the way this act was received by Edward Leslie, that chilled the feelings of his wife. Quickly disengaging her arms, she assumed a more guarded exterior; yet, trying all the while, to be cheerful in manner. We say "trying;" for a shadow had fallen on her young heart—and, to seem cheerful was from an effort. They sat down, side by side, in the pensive twilight close to the windows, through which came fragrant airs; and Madeline laid her hand upon that of her husband. Checked in the first gush of feelings, she now remained silent, yet with her yearning spirit intently listening for words of tenderness and endearment.

" I have been greatly vexed to-day."

These were the very words he uttered. How chilly they fell upon the ears of his expectant wife.

" What has happened ?" she asked, in a voice of concern.

" Oh, nothing in reality more than usual. Men in business are exposed to a thousand annoyances. If all the world were honest, trade would be pleasant enough. But you have to watch every one you deal with as closely as if he were a rogue. A man, whom I had confided in and befriended, tried to overreach me to-day, and it has hurt me a good deal. I couldn't have believed it of him."

Nothing more was said on either side for several minutes. Leslie, absorbed in thoughts of business, so far forgot the presence of his wife, as to withdraw the hand upon which her's was laid. How palpable to her was the coldness of his heart! She felt it as an atmosphere around him.

After tea, Leslie remarked, as he arose from the table, that he wished to see a friend on some matter of business; but would be home early. Not even a kiss did he leave with Madeline to cheer her during his absence. His selfish dignity could not stoop to such childishness.

The young bride passed the evening with no companionship but her tears. When Leslie came home, and looked upon her sober face, he was not struck with its aspect as being unusual. It did not enter his imagination that she could be otherwise than happy. Was she not *his* wife? And had she not, around her, every thing to make the heart satisfied? He verily believed that she had. He spoke to her kindly, yet, as she felt, indifferently, while her heart was pining for words of warm affection.

This was the first shadow that fell, darkly, across the young wife's path. For hours after her husband's senses were locked in slumber, she lay wakeful and weeping. He understood not, if he remarked the fact, why her cheeks had less color and her eyes less brightness on the morning that succeeded to this, on Madeline's part, never forgotten evening.

We need not present a scene from the sixth, the seventh, or even the twentieth day of Madeline's married life. All moved on with a kind of even tenor. Order—we might almost say, mercantile order—reigned throughout the household. And yet, shadows were falling more and more heavily over the young wife's feelings. To be loved, was an element of her existence —to be loved with expression. But, expressive fondness was not one of the cold, dignified Mr. Leslie's weaknesses. He loved Madeline—as much as he was capable of loving anything out of himself. And he had given her the highest possible evidence of this love, by making her his wife.—What more could she ask? It never occurred to his unsentimental thought, that words and acts of endearment were absolutely essential to her happiness. That her world of interest was a world of affections, and that without his companionship in this world, her heart would feel an aching void.

Who will wonder that, as weeks and months went by, shadows were more apparent on the sunny face of Madeline? Yet, such shadows, when they became visible to casual eyes, did excite wonder. What was there to break the play of sunshine on her countenance?

"The more some people have, the more dissatisfied they are," remarked one superficial observer to another, in reply to some communication touching Mrs. Leslie's want of spirits.

"Yes," was answered. "Nothing but *real* trouble ever brings such persons to their senses."

Ah! Is not heart-trouble the most real of all with which we are visited? There comes to it, so rarely, a balm of healing. To those external evils which merely affect the personal comfort, the mind quickly accommodates itself. We may find happiness in either prosperity or adversity. But, what true happiness is there for a loving heart, if, from the only source of reciprocation, there is but an imperfect response? A strong mind may accommodate itself, in the exercise of a firm religious philosophy, to even these circumstances, and like the wisely discriminating bee, extract honey from even the most unpromising flower. But, it is hard—nay, almost impossible—for one like Madeline, reared as she was in so warm an atmosphere of love, to fall back upon and find a sustaining power, in such a philosophy. Her spirit first must droop. There must be a passing through the fire, with painful purification.

Alas! How many perish in the ordeal!—How many gentle, loving ones, unequally mated, die, daily, around us; moving on to the grave, so far as the world knows, by the way of some fatal bodily ailment; yet, in truth, failing by a heart-sickness that has dried up the fountains of life.

And so it was with the wife of Edward Leslie. Greatly her husband wondered at the shadows which fell, more and more heavily, on Madeline—wondered as time wore on, at the paleness of her cheeks—the sadness which, often, she could not repress when he was by; the variableness of her spirits—all tending to destroy the balance of her nervous system, and, finally, ending in confirmed ill-health, that demanded, imperiously, the diversion of his thoughts from business and worldly schemes to the means of prolonging her life.

Alas! What a sad picture to look upon, would it be, were we to sketch, even in outline, the passing events of the ten years that preceded this conviction on the part of Mr. Leslie. To Madeline, his cold, hard, impatient, and, too frequently, cruel re-actions upon what he thought her unreasonable, captious, dissatisfied states of mind, having no ground but in her imagination, were heavy heart-strokes—or, as a discordant hand dashed among her life-chords, putting them forever out of tune. Oh! The wretchedness, struggling with patience and concealment, of those weary years. The days and days, during which her husband maintained towards her a moody silence, that it seemed would kill her.   And yet, so far as the world went, Mr. Leslie was among the best of husbands.   How little does the world, so called, look beneath the surface of things !

With the weakness of failing health, came, to Madeline, the loss of mental energy.   She had less and less self-control.   A brooding melancholy settled upon her feelings ; and she often spent days in her chamber, refusing to see any one except members of her own family, and weeping if she were spoken to.

"You will die, Madeline.   You will kill yourself!" said her husband, repeating, one day, the form of speech so often used when he found his wife in these states of abandonment.   He spoke with more than his usual tenderness, for, to his unimaginative mind had come a quickly passing, but vivid realization, of what he would lose if she were taken from him.

"The loss will scarcely be felt," was her murmured answer.

"Your children will, at least, feel it," said Mr. Leslie, in a more captious and meaning tone than, upon reflection, he would have used.   He felt her words as expressing indifference for himself, and his quick retort involved, palpably, the same impression in regard to his wife.

Madeline answered not farther, but her husband's words were not forgotten—"My children will feel my loss." This thought became so present to her mind, that none other could, for a space, come into manifest perception. The mother's heart began quickening into life a sense of the mother's duty. Thus it was, when her oldest child—named for herself, and with as loving and dependent a nature—opened the chamber door, and coming up to her father, made some request that he did not approve. To the mother's mind, her desire was one that ought to have been granted; and, she felt, in an instant, that the manner, as well as the fact of the father's denial, were both unkind, and that Madeline's heart would be almost broken. She did not err in this. The child went sobbing from the room.

How distinctly came before the mind of Mrs. Leslie a picture of the past. She was, for a time, back in he father's house; and she felt, for a time, the ever present, considerate, loving kindness of one who had made all sunshine in that early home. Slowly came back the mind of Mrs. Leslie to the present, and she said to herself, not passively, like one borne on the current of a down-rushing stream, but resolutely, as one with a purpose to struggle—to suffer, and yet be strong—

"Yes; my children will feel my loss. I could pass away and be at rest. I could lie me down and sleep weetly in the grave. But, is all my work done? Can I leave these little ones to his tender mer—"

She checked herself in the mental utterance of this sentiment, which referred to her husband. But, the feeling was in her heart; and it inspired her with a new purpose. Her thought, turned from herself, and fixed, with a yearning love upon her children, gave to the blood a quicker motion through the veins, and to her mind a new activity. She could no longer remain passive, as she had been for hours, brooding over her own unhappy state, but arose and left her chamber. In another room she found her unhappy child, who had gone off to brood alone over her disappointment, and to weep where none could see her.

"Madeline, dear!" said the mother, in a loving, sympathetic voice.

Instantly the child flung herself into her arms, and laid her face, sobbing, upon her bosom.

Gently, yet wisely—for there came, in that moment, to Mrs. Leslie, a clear perception of all her duty—did the mother seek to soften Madeline's disappointment, and to inspire her with fortitude to bear. Beyond her

own expectation came success in this effort. The
reason she invented or imagined, for the father's
refusal, satisfied the child; and soon the clouded brow
was lit up by the heart's sunshine.

From that hour, Mrs. Leslie was changed. From
that hour, a new purpose filled her heart. She could
not leave her children, nor could she take them with
her if she passed away; and so, she resolved to live for
them,—to forget her own suffering, in the tenderness
of maternal care. The mother had risen superior to
the unhappy, unappreciated wife.

All marked the change; yet in none did it awaken
more surprise than in Mr. Leslie. He never fully
understood its meaning; and, no wonder, for he had
never understood her from the beginning. He was too
cold and selfish to be able fully to appreciate her
character or relation to him as a wife.

Yet, for all this change—though the long drooping
form of Mrs. Leslie regained something of its erect-
ness, and her exhausted system a degree of tension—
the shadow passed not from her heart or brow; nor
did her cheeks grow warm again with the glow of
health. The delight of her life had failed; and now,
she lived only for the children whom God had given
her.

A man of Mr. Leslie's stamp of character too rarely

grows wiser in the true sense. Himself the centre of
his world, it is but seldom that he is able to think
enough out of himself to scan the effect of his daily
actions upon others. If collisions take place, he thinks
only of the pain he feels, not of the pain he gives.
He is ever censuring; but rarely takes blame. During
the earlier portions of his married life, Mr. Leslie's
mind had chafed a good deal at what seemed to him
Madeline's unreasonable and unwomanly conduct; the
soreness of this was felt even after the change in her
exterior that we have noticed, and he often indulged in
the habit of mentally writing bitter things against her.
He had well nigh broken her heart; and was yet
impatient because she gave signs indicative of pain.

And so, as years wore on, the distance grew wider
instead of becoming less and less. The husband had
many things to draw him forth into the busy world,
where he established various interests, and sought
pleasure in their pursuits, while the wife, seldom seen
abroad, buried herself at home, and gave her very life
for her children.

But, even maternal love could not feed for very
many years the flame of her life. The oil· was too
nearly exhausted when that new supply came. For a
time, the light burned clearly; then it began to fail,

and ere the mother's tasks were half done, it went out in darkness.

How heavy the shadows which then fell upon the household and upon the heart of Edward Leslie! As he stood, alone, in the chamber of death, with his eyes fixed upon the pale, wasted countenance, no more to quicken with life, and felt on his neck the clinging arms that were thrown around it a few moments before the last sigh of mortality was breathed; and still heard the eager, " Kiss me, Edward, once, before I die !"—a new light broke upon him,—and he was suddenly stung by sharp and self-reproaching thoughts. Had he not killed her, and, by the slowest and most agonizing process by which murder can be committed ? There was in his mind a startling perception that such was the awful crime of which he had been guilty.

Yes, there were shadows on the heart of Edward Leslie ; shadows that never entirely passed away.

7

THE THANKLESS OFFICE.

"An object of real charity," said Andrew Lyon to his wife, as a poor woman withdrew from the room in which they were seated.

"If ever there was a worthy object, she is one," returned Mrs. Lyon. "A widow, with health so feeble that even ordinary exertion is too much for her; yet obliged to support, with the labor of her own hands, not only herself, but three young children. I do not wonder that she is behind with her rent."

"Nor I," said Mr. Lyon in a voice of sympathy. "How much did she say was due to her landlord?"

"Ten dollars."

"She will not be able to pay it."

"I fear not. How can she! I give her all my extra sewing, and have obtained work for her from several ladies; but, with her best efforts she can barely obtain food and decent clothing for herself and babes."

"Does it not seem hard," remarked Mr. Lyon, "that

one like Mrs. Arnold, who is so earnest in her efforts to take care of herself and family, should not receive a helping hand from some one of the many who could help her without feeling the effort? If I didn't find it so hard to make both ends meet, I would pay off her arrears of rent for her, and feel happy in so doing."

"Ah!" exclaimed the kind-hearted wife, "how much I wish that we were able to do this. But we are not."

"I'll tell you what we can do," said Mr. Lyon, in a cheerful voice—"or, rather what *I* can do. It will be a very light matter for, say ten persons, to give a dollar a-piece, in order to relieve Mrs. Arnold from her present trouble. There are plenty who would cheerfully contribute for this good purpose; all that is wanted is some one to take upon himself the business of making the collections. That task shall be mine."

"How glad, James, to hear you say so," smilingly replied Mrs. Lyon. "Oh! what a relief it will be to poor Mrs. Arnold. It will make her heart as light as a feather. That rent has troubled her sadly. Old Links, her landlord, has been worrying her about it a good deal, and, only a week ago, threatened to put her things in the street if she didn't pay up."

"I should have thought of this before," remarked Andrew Lyon. "There are hundreds of people who are willing enough to give if they were only certain in

regard to the object.   Here is one worthy enough in
every way.   Be it my business to present her claims to
benevolent consideration.   Let me see.   To whom shall
I go ?   There are Jones, and Green, and Tompkins.   I
can get a dollar from each of them.   That will be
three dollars—and one from myself, will make four.
Who else is there ?   Oh ! Malcolm ! I'm sure of a
dollar from him ; and, also, from Smith, Todd, and
Perry."

Confident in the success of his benevolent scheme,
Mr. Lyon started forth, early on the very next day, for
the purpose of obtaining, by subscription, the poor
widow's rent.   The first person he called on was Malcolm.

"Ah, friend Lyon," said Malcolm, smiling blandly.
"Good morning !   What can I do for you to-day ?"

"Nothing for me, but something for a poor widow,
who is behind with her rent," replied Andrew Lyon.
"I want just one dollar from you, and as much more
from some eight or nine as benevolent as yourself."

At the words "poor widow," the countenance of
Malcolm fell, and when his visiter ceased, he replied in
a changed and husky voice, clearing his throat two or
three times as he spoke,

"Are you sure she is deserving, Mr. Lyon ?"   The
man's manner had become exceedingly grave.

" None more so," was the prompt answer. " She is
in poor health, and has three children to support with
the product of her needle. If any one needs assist·
ance it is Mrs. Arnold."

"Oh! ah! The widow of Jacob Arnold?"

" The same," replied Andrew Lyon.

Malcolm's face did not brighten with a feeling of
heart-warm benevolence. But, he turned slowly away,
and opening his money-drawer, *very slowly*, toyed with
his fingers amid its contents. At length he took therefrom a dollar bill, and said, as he presented it to Lyon,
—sighing involuntarily as he did so—

" I suppose I must do my part. But, we are called
upon so often."

The ardor of Andrew Lyon's benevolent feelings
suddenly cooled at this unexpected reception. He had
entered upon his work under the glow of a pure enthusiasm ; anticipating a hearty response the moment his
errand was made known.

" I thank you in the widow's name," said he, as he
ook the dollar. When he turned from Mr. Malcolm's
store, it was with a pressure on his feelings, as if he
had asked the coldly-given favor for himself.

It was not without an effort that Lyon compelled
himself to call upon Mr. Green, considered the " next
best man" on his list. But he entered his place of

business with far less confidence than he had felt when calling upon Malcolm. His story told, Green without a word or smile, drew two half dollars from his pocket, and presented them.

" Thank you," said Lyon.

" Welcome," returned Green.

Oppressed with a feeling of embarrassment, Lyon stood for a few moments. Then bowing, he said—

" Good morning."

" Good morning," was coldly and formally responded.

And thus the alms-seeker and alms-giver parted.

" Better be at his shop, attending to his work," muttered Green to himself, as his visitor retired. " Men ain't very apt to get along too well in the world who spend their time in begging for every object of charity that happens to turn up. And there are plenty of such, dear knows. He's got a dollar out of me ; may it do him, or the poor widow he talked so glibly about, much good."

Cold water had been poured upon the feelings of Andrew Lyon. He had raised two dollars for the poor widow, but, at what a sacrifice for one so sensitive as himself. Instead of keeping on in his work of benevolence, he went to his shop, and entered upon the day's employment. How disappointed he felt ;—and this disappointment was mingled with a certain sense

of humiliation, as if he had been asking alms for him
self.

"Catch me at this work again!" he said, half aloud,
as his thoughts dwelt upon what had so recently
occurred. "But this is not right," he added, quickly.
"It is a weakness in me to feel so. Poor Mrs. Arnold
must be relieved; and it is my duty to see that she
gets relief. I had no thought of a reception like this.
People can talk of benevolence; but putting the hand
in the pocket is another affair altogether. I never
dreamed that such men as Malcolm and Green could be
insensible to an appeal like the one I made."

"I've got two dollars towards paying Mrs. Arnold's
rent," he said to himself, in a more cheerful tone, sometime afterwards; "and it will go hard if I don't raise
the whole amount for her. All are not like Green and
Malcolm. Jones is a kind-hearted man, and will
instantly respond to the call of humanity. I'll go and
see him."

So, off Andrew Lyon started to see this individual.

"I've come begging, Mr. Jones," said he, on meeting
him. And he spoke in a frank, pleasant manner.

"Then you've come to the wrong shop; that's all I
have to say," was the blunt answer.

"Don't say that, Mr. Jones. Hear my story, first."

"I do say it, and I'm in earnest," returned Jones. "I feel as poor as Job's turkey, to-day."

"I only want a dollar to help a poor widow pay her rent," said Lyon.

"Oh, hang all the poor widows! If that's your game, you'll get nothing here. I've got my hands full to pay my own rent. A nice time I'd have in handing out a dollar to every poor widow in town to help pay her rent! No, no, my friend, you can't get anything here."

"Just as you feel about it," said Andrew Lyon. "There's no compulsion in the matter."

"No, I presume not," was rather coldly replied.

Lyon returned to his shop, still more disheartened than before. He had undertaken a thankless office.

Nearly two hours elapsed before his resolution to persevere in the good work he had begun came back with sufficient force to prompt to another effort. Then he dropped in upon his neighbor Tompkins, to whom he made known his errand.

"Why, yes, I suppose I must do something in a case like this," said Tompkins, with the tone and air of a man who was cornered. "But, there are so many calls for charity, that we are naturally enough led.to hold on pretty tightly to our purse strings. Poor woman! I feel sorry for her. How much do you want?"

"I am trying to get ten persons, including myself, to give a dollar each."

"Well, here's my dollar." And Tompkins forced a smile to his face as he handed over his contribution— but the smile did not conceal an expression which said very plainly—

"I hope you will not trouble me again in this way."

"You may be sure I will not," muttered Lyon, as he went away. He fully understood the meaning of the expression.

Only one more application did the kind-hearted man make. It was successful ; but, there was something in the manner of the individual who gave his dollar, that Lyon felt as a rebuke.

"And so poor Mrs. Arnold did not get the whole of her arrears of rent paid off," says some one who has felt an interest in her favor.

Oh, yes she did. Mr. Lyon begged five dollars, and added five more from his own slender purse. But, he cannot be induced again to undertake the thankless office of seeking relief from the benevolent for a fellow creature in need. He has learned that a great many who refuse alms on the plea that the object presented is not worthy, are but little more inclined to charitable deeds, when on this point there is no question.

How many who read this can sympathise with
7*

Andrew Lyon. Few men who have hearts to feel for others but have been impelled, at some time in their lives, to seek aid for a fellow-creature in need. That their office was a thankless one, they have too soon become aware. Even those who responded to their call most liberally, in too many instances gave in a way that left an unpleasant impression behind. How quickly has the first glow of generous feeling, that sought to extend itself to others, that they might share the pleasure of humanity, been chilled; and, instead of finding the task an easy one, it has proved to be hard, and, too often, humiliating! Alas, that this should be! That men should shut their hearts so instinctively at the voice of charity.

We have not written this to discourage active efforts in the benevolent; but to hold up a mirror in which another class may see themselves. At best, the office of him who seeks of his fellow-men aid for the suffering and indigent, is an unpleasant one. It is all sacrifice on his part, and the least that can be done is to honor his disinterested regard for others in distress, and treat him with delicacy and consideration.

GOING TO THE SPRINGS;

OR, VULGAR PEOPLE.

"I suppose you will all be off to Saratoga, in a week or two," said Uncle Joseph Garland to his three nieces, as he sat chatting with them and their mother, one hot day, about the first of July.

"We're not going to Saratoga this year," replied Emily, the eldest, with a toss of her head.

"Indeed! And why not, Emily?"

"Everybody goes to Saratoga, now."

"Who do you mean by everybody, Emily?"

"Why, I mean merchants, shop-keepers, and trades men, with their wives and daughters, all mixed up together, into a kind of hodge-podge. It used to be a fashionable place of resort—but people that think any thing of themselves, don't go there now."

"Bless me, child!" ejaculated old Uncle Joseph, in

surprise. "This is all new to me. But you were there last year."

"I know. And that cured us all. There was not a day in which we were not crowded down to the table among the most vulgar kind of people."

". How, vulgar, Emily ?"

" Why, there was Mr. Jones, the watchmaker, with his wife and two daughters. I need not explain what I mean by vulgar, when I give you that information."

" I cannot say that I have any clearer idéa of what you mean, Emily."

" You talk strangely, uncle ! You do not suppose that we are going to associate with the Joneses ?"

" I did not say that I did. Still, I am in the dark as to what you mean by the most vulgar kind of people."

" Why, common people, brother," said Mrs. Ludlow, coming up to the aid of her daughter. " Mr. Jones is only a watchmaker, and therefore has no business to push himself and family into the company of genteel people."

" Saratoga is a place of public resort," was the quiet reply.

" Well, genteel people will have to stay away, then, that's all. I, at least, for one, am not going to be annoyed as I have been for the last two or three seasons at Saratoga, by being thrown amongst all sorts of people."

"They never troubled me any," spoke up Florence Ludlow, the youngest of the three sisters. "For my part, I liked Mary Jones very much. She was——"

"You are too much of a child to be able to judge in matters of this kind," said the mother, interrupting Florence.

Florence was fifteen; light-hearted and innocent. She had never been able, thus far in life, to appreciate the exclusive principles upon which her mother and sisters acted, and had, in consequence, frequently fallen under their censure. Purity of heart, and the genuine graces flowing from a truly feminine spirit, always attracted her, no matter what the station of the individual in whose society she happened to be thrown. The remark of her mother silenced her, for the time, for experience had taught her that no good ever resulted from a repetition of her opinions on a subject of this kind.

"And I trust she will ever remain the child she is, in these matters," said Uncle Joseph, with emphasis. "It is the duty of every one, sister, to do all that he can to set aside the false ideas of distinction prevailing in the social world, and to build up on a broader and truer foundation, a right estimate of men and things.

Florence, I have observed, discriminates according to the quality of the person's mind into whose society she is thrown, and estimates accordingly. But you, and Emily, and Adeline, judge of people according to their ank in society—that is according to the position to which wealth alone has raised them. In this way, and in no other, can you be thrown so into association with ' all kinds of people,' as to be really affected by them. For, the result of my observation is, that in any circle where a mere external sign is the passport to association, ' all sorts of people,' the good, the bad, and the indifferent, are mingled. It is not a very hard thing for a bad man to get rich, sister ; but for a man of evil principles to rise above them, is very hard, indeed ; and is an occurrence that too rarely happens. The consequence is, that they who are rich, are not always the ones whom we should most desire to mingle with."

"I don't see that there is any use in our talking about these things, brother," replied Mrs. Ludlow. " You know that you and I never did agree in matters of this kind. As I have often told you, I think you incline to be rather low in your social views."

" How can that be a low view which regards the quality of another, and estimates him accordingly ?" was the reply.

" I don't pretend to argue with you, on these subjects,

brother; so you will oblige me by dropping them," said Mrs. Ludlow, coloring, and speaking in an offended tone.

"Well, well, never mind," Uncle Joseph replied soothingly. "We will drop them."

Then turning to Emily, he continued—

"And so your minds are made up not to go to Saratoga?"

"Yes, indeed."

"Well, where do you intend spending the summer months?"

"I hardly know yet. But, if I have my say, we will take a trip in one of the steamers. A flying visit to London would be delightful."

"What does your father say to that?"

"Why, he won't listen to it. But I'll do my best to bring him round—and so will Adeline. As for Florence, I believe I will ask father to let her go to Saratoga with the Joneses."

"I shall have no very decided objections," was the quiet reply of Florence. A half angry and reproving glance from her mother, warned her to be more discreet in the declaration of her sentiments.

A young lady should never attempt to influence her father," said Uncle Joseph. "She should trust to his judgment in all matters, and be willing to deny

herself any pleasure to which he objected. If your
father will not listen to your proposition to go to
London, be sure that he has some good reason for
it."

"Well, I don't know that he has such very good
reasons, beyond his reluctance to go away from business," Emily replied, tossing her head.

"And should not you, as his daughter, consider this
a most conclusive reason ? Ought not your father's
wishes and feelings be considered first ?"

"You may see it so, Uncle ; but I cannot say that I
do."

"Emily," and Uncle Joseph spoke in an excited tone
of voice, "If you hold these sentiments, you are
unworthy of such a man as your father !"

"Brother, you must not speak to the girls in that
way," said Mrs. Ludlow.

"I shall always speak my thoughts in your house
Margaret," was the reply ; "at least to you and the
girls. As far as Mr. Ludlow is concerned, I have rarely
occasion to differ with him."

A long silence followed, broken at last by an allusion
to some other subject ; when a better understanding
among all parties ensued.

On that evening, Mr. Ludlow seemed graver than
usual when he came in. After tea, Emily said, break

ing in upon a conversation that had become somewhat interesting to Mr. Ludlow—

"I'm not going to let you have a moment's peace, Pa, until you consent to go to England with us this season."

"I'm afraid it will be a long time before I shall have any peace, then, Emily," replied the father, with an effort to smile, but evidently worried by the remark. This, Florence, who was sitting close by him, perceived instantly, and said—

"Well, I can tell you, for one, Pa, that I don't wish to go. I'd rather stay at home a hundred times."

"It's no particular difference, I presume, what you like," remarked Emily, ill-naturedly. "If you don't wish to go, I suppose no one will quarrel with you for staying at home."

"You are wrong to talk so, Emily," said Mr. Ludlow, calmly but firmly, "and I cannot permit such remarks in my presence."

Emily looked rebuked, and Mr. Ludlow proceeded.

"As to going to London, that is altogether out of the question. The reasons why it is so, are various, and I cannot now make you acquainted with all of them. One is, that I cannot leave my business so long as such a journey would require. Another is, that I do not think it altogether right for me to indulge you in

such views and feelings as you and Adeline are beginning to entertain.   You wish to go to London, because
you don't want to go to Saratoga, or to any other of
ur watering places ; and you don't want to go there,
because certain others, whom you esteem below you in
rank, can afford to enjoy themselves, and recruit their
health at the same places of public resort.   All this I
do not approve, and cannot encourage."

"You certainly cannot wish us to associate with
every one," said Emily, in a tone less arrogant.

"Of course not, Emily," replied Mr. Ludlow ; " but I
do most decidedly condemn the spirit from which you
are now acting.   It would exclude others, many of
whom, in moral character, are far superior to yourself,
from enjoying the pleasant, health-imparting recreation
of a visit to the Springs, because it hurts your self-
importance to be brought into brief contact with
them."

"I can't understand what you mean by speaking of
these kind of people as superior in moral character to
us," Mrs. Ludlow remarked.

"I said some of them.   And, in this, I mean what I
say.   Wealth and station in society do not give moral
tone.   They are altogether extraneous, and too frequently exercise a deteriorating influence upon the
character.   There is Thomas, the porter in my store—

a plain, poor man, of limited education ; yet possessing
high moral qualities, that I would give much to
call my own.   This man's character I esteem far above
that of many in society .to whom no one thinks of
objecting.   There are hundreds and thousands of
humble and unassuming persons like him, far superior
in the high moral qualities of mind to the mass of self-
esteeming exclusives, who think the very air around
them tainted by their breath.   Do you suppose that I
would enjoy less the pleasures of a few weeks at
Saratoga, because Thomas was there ?   I would, rather,
be gratified to see him enjoying a brief relaxation, if
his duties at the store could be remitted in my absence."

There was so much of the appearance of truth in
what Mr. Ludlow said, combined with a decided tone
and manner, that neither his wife or daughters ventured
a reply.   But they had no affection for the truth he
utttered, and of course it made no salutary impression
on their minds.

"What shall we do, Ma ?" asked Adeline, as they
sat with their mother, on the next afternoon.   "We
must go somewhere this summer, and Pa seems in
earnest about not letting us visit London."

"I don't know, I am sure, child," was the reply.

" I can't think of going to Saratoga," said Emily, in a positive tone.

" The Emmersons are going," Adeline remarked.

" How do you know?" asked Emily in a tone of surprise.

" Victorine told me so this morning."

" She did!"

" Yes. I met her at Mrs. Lemmington's and she said that they were all going next week."

" I don't understand that," said Emily, musingly.

" It was only last week that Victorine told me that they were done going to Saratoga; that the place had become too common. It had been settled, she said, that they were to go out in the next steamer."

" Mr. Emmerson, I believe, would not consent, and so, rather than not go anywhere, they concluded to visit Saratoga, especially as the Lesters, and Milfords, and Luptons are going."

" Are they all going?" asked Emily, in renewed surprise.

" So Victorine said."

" Well, I declare! there is no kind of dependence to be placed in people now-a-days. They all told me that they could not think of going to such a vulgar place as Saratoga again."

Then, after a pause, Emily resumed,

" As it will never do to stay at home, we will have to go somewhere. What do you think of the Virginia Springs, Ma ?"

" I think that I am not going there, to be jolted hal. .o death in a stage coach by the way."

" Where, then, shall we go ?"

"I don't know, unless to Saratoga."

" Victorine said," remarked Adeline, " that a large number of distinguished visiters were to be there, and that it was thought the season would be the gayest spent for some time."

" I suppose we will have to go, then," said Emily.

" I am ready," responded Adeline."

" And so am I," said Florence.

That evening Mr. Ludlow was graver and more silent than usual. After tea, as he felt no inclination to join in the general conversation about the sayings and doings of distinguished and fashionable individuals, he took a newspaper, and endeavored to become interested n its contents. But he tried in vain. There was something upon his mind that absorbed his attention at the same time that it oppressed his feelings. From a deep reverie he was at length roused by Emily, who said —

" So, Pa, you are determined not to let us go out in the next steamer ?"

"Don't talk to me on that subject any more, if you please," replied Mr. Ludlow, much worried at the remark.

"Well, that's all given up now," continued Emily, "and we've made up our minds to go to Saratoga. How soon will you be able to go with us?"

"Not just now," was the brief, evasive reply.

"We don't want to go until next week."

"I am not sure that I can go even then."

"O, but we must go then, Pa."

"You cannot go without me," said Mr. Ludlow, in a grave tone.

"Of course not," replied Emily and Adeline at the same moment.

"Suppose, then, I cannot leave the city next week?"

"But you can surely."

"I am afraid not.   Business matters press upon me, and will, I fear, engage my exclusive attention for several weeks to come."

"O, but indeed you must lay aside business," said Mrs. Ludlow.   "It will never do for us to stay at home, you know, during the season when everybody is away."

"I shall be very sorry if circumstances arise to prevent you having your regular summer recreation," was replied, in a serious, even sad tone.   "But, I trust my wife and daughters will acquiesce with cheerfulness."

"Indeed, indeed, Pa! We never can stay at home," said Emily, with a distressed look. "How would it appear? What would people say if we were to remain in the city during all the summer?"

"I don't know, Emily, that you should consider that as having any relation to the matter. What have other people to do with matters which concerns us alone?"

"You talk very strangely of late, Mr. Ludlow," said his wife.

"Perhaps I have reason for so doing," he responded, a shadow flitting across his face:

An embarrassing silence ensued, which was broken, at last, by Mr. Ludlow.

"Perhaps," he began, "there may occur no better time than the present, to apprise you all of a matter that must, sooner or later, become known to you. We will have to make an effort to reduce our expenses—and it seems to me that this matter of going to the Springs, which will cost some three or four hundred dollars, might as well be dispensed with. Business is in a worse condition than I have ever known it; and I am sustaining, almost daily, losses that are becoming alarming. Within the last six weeks I have lost, beyond hope, at least twenty thousand dollars. How much more will go I am unable to say. But there are large sums due me that may follow the course of that lready gone. Under these circumstances, I am driven to the necessity of prudence in all my expenditures."

"But three or four hundred are not much, Pa," Emily urged, in a husky voice, and with dimmed eyes. For the fear of not being able to go somewhere, was terrible to her. None but vulgar people staid at home during the summer season.

"It is too large a sum to throw away now. So I think you had all better conclude at once not to go from home this summer," said Mr. Ludlow.

A gush of tears from Emily and Adeline followed this annunciation, accompanied by a look of decided disapprobation from the mother. Mr. Ludlow felt deeply tried, and for some moments his resolution wavered; but reason came to his aid, and he remained firm. He was accounted a very rich merchant. In good times, he had entered into business, and prosecuted it with great energy. The consequence was, that he had accumulated money rapidly. The social elevation consequent upon this, was too much for his wife. Her good sense could not survive it. She not only became impressed with the idea, that, because she was richer, she was better than others, but that only such customs were to be tolerated in "good society," as were different from prevalent usages in the mass. Into this idea her two eldest daughters were thoroughly inducted. Mr. Ludlow, immersed in business, thought little about such matters, and suffered himself to be led into almost anything that his wife and daughters proposed. But Mrs. Ludlow's brother—Uncle Joseph, as he was called—a bachelor, and a man of strong common sense, steadily opposed his sister in her false notions, but with little good effect. Necessity at last called into proper activity the good sense of Mr. Ludlow, and he commenced the opposition that has just been noticed. After reflecting some time upon the matter, he resolved not to assent to his family leaving home at all during the summer.

All except Florence were exceedingly distressed at this. She acquiesced with gentleness and patience, although she had much desired to spend a few weeks at Saratoga. But Mrs. Ludlow, Emily, and Adeline, closed up the front part of the house, and gave directions to the servants not to answer the door bell, nor to do anything that would give the least suspicion that the family were in town. Then ensconcing themselves in the back buildings of their dwelling, they waited in gloomy indolence for the "out of the city" season to pass away; consoling themselves with the idea, that if they were not permitted to join the fashionables at the Springs, it would at least be supposed that they had gone some where into the country, and thus they hoped to escape the terrible penalty of losing *caste* for not conforming to an indispensable rule of high life.

Mr. Ludlow was compelled to submit to all this, and he did so without much opposition; but it all determined him to commence a steady opposition to the false principles which prompted such absurd observances. As to Uncle Joseph, he was indignant, and failing to gain admittance by way of the front door after one or two trials, determined not to go near his sister and nieces, a promise which he kept for a few weeks, at least.

Meantime, every thing was passing off pleasantly at Saratoga. Among the distinguished and undistinguished visitors there, was Mary Jones, and her father, a man of both wealth and worth, notwithstanding he was only a watchmaker and jeweller. Mary was a girl of no ordinary character. With beauty of person far exceeding that of the Misses Ludlow, she had a well cultivated mind, and was far more really and truly accomplished than they were. Necessarily, therefore, she attracted attention at the Springs; and this had been one cause of Emily's objection to her.

A day or two after her arrival at Saratoga, she was sitting near a window of the public parlor of one of the hotels, when a young man, named Armand, whom she had seen there several times before, during the watering season, in company with Emily Ludlow, with whose family he appeared to be on intimate terms came up to her and introduced himself.

"Pardon me, Miss Jones," said he, "but not seeing any of the Miss Ludlows here, I presumed that you might be able to inform me whether they intend visiting Saratoga or not, this season, and, therefore, I have broken through all formalities in addressing you. You are well acquainted with Florence, I believe?"

"Very well, sir," Mary replied.

"Then perhaps you can answer my question?"

"I believe I can, sir. I saw Florence several times within the last week or two; and she says that they shall not visit any of the Springs this season."

"Indeed! And how comes that?"

"I believe the reason is no secret," Mary replied, utterly unconscious that any one could be ashamed of a right motive, and that an economical one. "Florence tells me that her father has met with many heavy losses in business; and that they think it best not to incur any unnecessary expenses. I admire such a course in them."

"And s do I, most sincerely," replied Mr. Armand.
Then, after thinking for a moment, he added—

"I will return to the city in the next boat. All of
their friends being away, they must feel exceedingly
lonesome."

"It will certainly be a kind act, Mr. Armand, and
one, the motive for which they cannot but highly
appreciate," said Mary, with an inward glow of
admiration.

It was about eleven o'clock on the next day that Mr.
Armand pulled the bell at the door of Mr. Ludlow's
beautiful dwelling, and then waited with a feeling of
impatience for the servant to answer the summons.
But he waited in vain. No servant came. He rang
again, and again waited long enough for a servant to
come half a dozen times. Then he looked up at the
house and saw that all the shutters were closed; and
down upon the marble steps, and perceived that they
were covered with dust and dirt; and on the bell-
handle, and noted its loss of brightness.

"Miss Jones must have been mistaken," he said to
himself, as he gave the bell a third pull, and then
waited, but in vain, for the hall-door to be swung open.

"Who can it be?" asked Emily, a good deal
disturbed, as the bell rang violently for the third time,

and, in company with Adeline, went softly into the parlor to take a peep through one of the shutters.

"Mr. Armand, as I live !" she ejaculated, in a low husky whisper, turning pale. "I would not have *him* know that we are in town for the world !"

And then she stole away quietly, with her heart leaping and fluttering in her bosom, lest he should instinctively perceive her presence.

Finding that admission was not to be obtained, Mr. Armand concluded that the family had gone to some other watering place, and turned away irresolute as to his future course. As he was passing down Broadway, he met Uncle Joseph.

"So the Ludlows are all out of town," he said.

"So they are not !" replied Uncle Joseph, rather crustily, for he had just been thinking over their strange conduct, and it irritated him.

"Why, I have been ringing there for a quarter of an hour, and no one came to the door ; and the house is all shut up."

"Yes ; and if you had rung for a quarter of a century, it would all have been the same."

"I can't understand you," said Mr. Armand.

"Why, the truth is, Mr. Ludlow cannot go to the Springs with them this season, and they are so afraid that it will become known that they are burying them-

selves in the back part of the house, and denying all
visiters."

" Why so!   I cannot comprehend it."

" All fashionable people, you know, are expected to
o to the sea-shore or the Springs ; and my sister and
her two eldest daughters are so silly, as to fear that
they will lose *caste*, if it is known that they could not
go this season.   Do you understand now ?"

" Perfectly."

" Well, that's the plain A B C of the case.   But it
provokes me out of all patience with them."

" It's a strange idea, certainly," said Mr. Armand, in
momentary abstraction of thought ; and then bidding
Uncle Joseph good morning, he walked hastily along,
his mind in a state of fermentation.

The truth was, Mr. Armand had become much
attached to Emily Ludlow, for she was a girl of
imposing appearance and winning manners.   But this
staggered him.   If she were such a slave to fashion
and observance, she was not the woman for his wife.
As he reflected upon the matter, and reviewed his
intercourse with her, he could remember many things
in her conversation and conduct that he did not like.
He could distinctly detect a degree of self-estimation
consequent upon her station in society, that did not
meet his approbation—because it indicated a weakness

of mind that he had no wish to have in a wife. The wealth of her father he had not regarded, nor did now regard, for he was himself possessor of an independence.

Two days after, he was again at Saratoga. The brief interview that had passed between him and Mary Jones was a sufficient introduction for him ; and, taking advantage of it, he threw himself in her way frequently, and the more he saw of her, the more did he admire her winning gentleness, sweet temper, and good sense. When he returned to New York, he was more than half in love with her.

"Mr. Armand has not been to see us once this fall," said Adeline, one evening in October. They were sitting in a handsomely furnished parlor in a neat dwelling, comfortable and commodious, but not so splendid as the one they had occupied a few months previous. Mr. Ludlow's affairs had become so embarrassed, that he determined, in spite of the opposition of his family, to reduce his expenses. This resolution he carried out amid tears and remonstrances—for he could not do it n any other way.

"Who could expect him to come *here ?*" Emily replied, to the remark of her sister. "Not I, certainly."

"I don't believe that would make any difference with him," Florence ventured to say, for it was little that she could say, that did not meet with opposition.

" Why don't you ?" asked Adeline.

" Because Mary Jones——"

" Mary Jones again !" ejaculated Emily.   " I believe you don't think of anybody but Mary Jones.   I'm surprised that Ma lets you visit that girl !"

" As good people as I am visit her," replied Florence. " I've seen those there who would be welcome here."

" What do you mean ?"

" If you had waited until I had finished my sentence, you would have known before now.   Mary Jones lives in a house no better than this, and Mr. Armand goes to see her."

" I don't believe it !" said Emily, with emphasis.

" Just as you like about that.   Seeing is believing, they say, and as I have seen him there, I can do no less than believe he was there."

" When did you see him there ?" Emily now asked with eager interest, while her face grew pale.

" I saw him there last evening—and he sat conversing with Mary in a way that showed them to be no strangers to each other."

A long, embarrassed, and painful silence followed this announcement.   At last, Emily got up and went off to her chamber, where she threw herself upon her bed and burst into tears.   After these ceased to flow, and her mind had become, in some degree, tranquillized, her

thoughts became busy. She remembered that Mr.
Armand had called, while they were hiding away in
fear lest it should be known that they were not on a
fashionable visit to some watering place—how he had
rung and rung repeatedly, as if under the idea that
they were there, and how his countenance expressed
disappointment as she caught a glimpse of it through
the closed shutters. With all this came, also, the idea
that he might have discovered that they were at home,
and have despised the principle from which they acted,
in thus shutting themselves up, and denying all visiters.
This thought was exceedingly painful. It was evident
to her, that it was not their changed circumstances that
kept him away—for had he not visited Mary Jones?

Uncle Joseph came in a few evenings afterwards,
and during his visit the following conversation took
place.

"Mr. Armand visits Mary Jones, I am told," Adeline
remarked, as an opportunity for saying so occurred.

"He does? Well, she is a good girl—one in a thousand," replied Uncle Joseph.

"She is only a watchmaker's daughter," said Emily,
with an ill-concealed sneer.

"And you are only a merchant's daughter. Pray,
what is the difference?"

"Why, a good deal of difference!"

8*

" Well state it."

" Mr. Jones is nothing but a mechanic."

" Well ?"

" Who thinks of associating with mechanics ?"

" There may be some who refuse to do so ; but upon what grounds do they assume a superiority ?"

" Because they are really above them."

" But in what respect ?"

" They are better and more esteemed in society."

" As to their being better, that is only an assumption. But I see I must bring the matter right home.   Would you be really any worse, were your father a mechanic ?"

" The question is not a fair one. You suppose an impossible case."

" Not so impossible as you might imagine.   You are the daughter of a mechanic."

" Brother, why will you talk so ?   I am out of all patience with you !" said Mrs. Ludlow, angrily.

" And yet, no one knows better than you, that I speak only the truth.   No one knows better than you, that Mr. Ludlow served many years at the trade of a shoemaker.   And   that,   consequently,   these   high-minded   young   ladies,   who   sneer   at   mechanics,   are themselves a shoemaker's daughters—a fact that is just as well known   abroad   as   anything   else   relating   to   the family.   And now, Misses Emily and Adeline, I hope

you will hereafter find it in your hearts to be a little
more tolerant of mechanics' daughters."

And thus saying, Uncle Joseph rose, and bidding
them good night, left them to their own reflections,
which were not of the most pleasant character, especially
as the mother could not deny the allegation he had
made.

During the next summer, Mr. Ludlow, whose business was no longer embarrassed, and who had become
satisfied that, although he should sink a large propor-
tion of a handsome fortune, he would still have a com-
petence left, and that well secured—proposed to visit
Saratoga, as usual. There was not a dissenting voice
—no objecting on the score of meeting vulgar people
there. The painful fact disclosed by Uncle Joseph, of
their plebeian origin, and the marriage of Mr. Armand—
whose station in society was not to be questioned—
with Mary Jones, the watchmaker's daughter, had softened and subdued their tone of feeling, and caused
them to set up a new standard of estimation. The old
one would not do, for, judged by that, they would have
to hide their diminished heads. Their conduct at the
Springs was far less objectionable than it had been
heretofore, partaking of the modest and retiring in
deportment, rather than the assuming, the arrogant,

and the self-sufficient.   Mrs. Armand was there, with her sister, moving in the first circles ; and Emily Ludlow and her sister Adeline felt honored rather than humiliated by an association with them.   It is to be hoped they will yet make sensible women.

THE WIFE.

"I AM hopeless!" said the young man, in a voice that was painfully desponding. "Utterly hopeless! Heaven knows I have tried hard to get employment! But no one has need of my service. The pittance doled out by your father, and which comes with a sense of humiliation that is absolutely heart-crushing, is scarcely sufficient to provide this miserable abode, and keep hunger from our door. But for your sake, I would not touch a shilling of his money if I starved."

"Hush, dear Edward!" returned the gentle girl, who had left father, mother, and a pleasant home, to share the lot of him she loved ; and she laid a finger on his lips, while she drew her arm around him.

"Agnes," said the young man, "I cannot endure this life much longer. The native independence of my character revolts at our present condition. Months have elapsed, and yet the ability I possess finds no employment. In this country every avenue is crowded."

The room in which they were overlooked the sea.

"But there is another land, where, if what we her be true, ability finds employment and talent a sure reward." And, as Agnes said this, in a voice of encouragement, she pointed from the window towards the expansive waters that stretched far away towards the south and west.

"America!" The word was uttered in a quick, earnest voice.

"Yes."

"Agnes, I thank you for this suggestion! Return to the pleasant home you left for one who cannot procure for you even the plainest comforts of life, and I will cross the ocean to seek a better fortune in that land of promise. The separation, painful to both, will not, I trust, be long."

"Edward," replied the young wife with enthusiasm, as she drew her arm more tightly about his neck, " will never leave thee nor forsake thee! Where thou goest I will go, and where thou liest I will lie. Thy people shall be my people, and thy God my God."

"Would you forsake all," said Edward, in surprise, " and go far away with me into a strange land!"

"It will be no stranger to me than it will be to you, Edward."

"No, no, Agnes! I will not think of that," said Edward Marvel, in a positive voice. "If I go to that land of promise, it must first be alone."

"Alone!" A shadow fell over the face of Agnes. "Alone! It cannot—it must not be!"

"But think, Agnes. If I go alone, it will cost me but a small sum to live until I find some business, which may not be for weeks, or even months after I arrive in the New World."

"What if you were to be sick?" The frame of Agnes slightly quivered as she made this suggestion.

"We will not think of that."

"I cannot help thinking of it, Edward. Therefore entreat me not to leave thee, nor to return from following after thee. Where thou goest, I will go."

Marvel's countenance became more serious.

"Agnes," said the young man, after he had reflected for some time, "let us think no more about this. I cannot take you far away to this strange country. We will go back to London. Perhaps another trial there may be more successful."

After a feeble opposition on the part of Agnes, it was finally agreed that Edward should go once more to

London, while she made a brief visit to her parents.
If he found employment, she was to join him immediately ; if not successful, they were then to talk further
of the journey to America.

With painful reluctance, Agnes went back to her
father's house, the door of which ever stood open to
receive her ; and she went back alone.   The pride of
her husband would not permit him to cross the threshold
of a dwelling where his presence was not a welcome
one.   In eager suspense, she waited for a whole week
ere a letter came from Edward.   The tone of this letter
was as cheerful and as hopeful as it was possible for
the young man to write.   But, as yet, he had found no
employment.   A week elapsed before another came.
It opened in these words :—

"MY DEAR, DEAR AGNES ! Hopeless of doing anything here, I have turned my thoughts once more to
the land of promise ; and, when you receive this, I will
be on my journey thitherward.   Brief, very brief, I
trust, will be our separation.   The moment I obtain
employment, I will send for you, and then our re-union
will take place with a fulness of delight such as we
have not yet experienced."

Long, tender, and hopeful was the letter; but it
brought a burden of grief and heart-sickness to the

tender young creature, who felt almost as if she had been deserted by the one who was dear to her as her own life.

Only a few days had Edward Marvel been at sea, when he became seriously indisposed, and, for the remaining part of the voyage, was so ill as to be unable to rise from his berth. He had embarked in a packet ship from Liverpool bound for New York, where he arrived, at the expiration of five weeks. Then he was removed to the sick wards of the hospital on Staten Island, and it was the opinion of the physicians there that he would die.

"Have you friends in this country?" inquired a nurse who was attending the young man. This question was asked on the day after he had become an inmate of the hospital.

"None," was the feebly uttered reply.

"You are very ill," said the nurse.

The sick man looked anxiously into the face of his attendant.

"You have friends in England?"

"Yes."

"Have you any communication to make to them?"

Marvel closed his eyes, and remained for some time silent.

"If you will get me a pen and some paper, I will write a few lines," said he at length.

"I'm afraid you are too weak for the effort," replied the nurse.

"Let me try," was briefly answered.

The attendant left the room.

"Is there any one in your part of the house named Marvel?" asked a physician, meeting the nurse soon after she had left the sick man's room. "There's a young woman down in the office inquiring for a person of that name."

"Marvel—Marvel?" the nurse shook her head.

"Are you certain?" remarked the physician.

"I'm certain there is no one by that name for whom any here would make inquiries. There's a young Englishman who came over in the last packet, whose name is something like that you mention. But he has no friends in this country."

The physician passed on without further remark.

Soon after, the nurse returned to Marvel with the writing materials for which he had asked. She drew a table to the side of his bed, and supported him as he leaned over and tried, with an unsteady hand, to write.

"Have you a wife at home?" asked the nurse; her eyes had rested on the first words he wrote.

"Yes," sighed the young man, as the pen dropped from his fingers, and he leaned back heavily, exhausted by even the slight effort he had made.

"Your name is Marvel?"

"Yes."

"A young woman was here just now inquiring if we had a patient by that name."

"By my name?" There was a slight indication of surprise.

"Yes."

Marvel closed his eyes, and did not speak for some moments.

"Did you see her?" he asked at length, evincing some interest.

"Yes."

"Did she find the one for whom she was seeking?"

"There is no person here, except yourself, whose name came near to the one she mentioned. As you said you had no friends in this country, we did not suppose that you were meant."

"No, no." And the sick man shook his head slowly. "There is none to ask for me. Did you say it was a young woman?" he inquired, soon after. His mind dwelt on the occurrence.

"Yes. A young woman with a fair complexion and deep blue eyes."

Marvel looked up quickly into the face of the attendant, while a flush came into his cheeks.

"She was a slender young girl, with light hair, and her face was pale, as from trouble."

"Agnes! Agnes!" exclaimed Marvel, rising up. "But, no, no," he added, mournfully, sinking back again upon the bed; "that cannot be. I left her far away over the wide ocean."

"Will you write?" said the nurse after some moments.

The invalid, without unclosing his eyes, slowly shook his head. A little while the attendant lingered in his room, and then retired.

"Dear, dear Agnes!" murmured Edward Marvel, closing his eyes, and letting his thoughts go, swift-winged, across the billowy sea. "Shall I never look on your sweet face again? Never feel your light arms about my neck, or your breath warm on my cheek! Oh, that I had never left you! Heaven give thee strength to bear the trouble in store!"

For many minutes he lay thus, alone, with his eyes closed, in sad self-communion. Then he heard the door open and close softly; but he did not look up. His thoughts were far, far away. Light feet approached quickly; but he scarcely heeded them. A form bent over him; but his eyes remained shut, nor did he op

them until warm lips were pressed against his own,
and a low voice, thrilling through his whole being,
said—

" Edward !"

" Agnes !" was his quick response, while his arms
were thrown eagerly around the neck of his wife,
Agnes ! Agnes !   Have I awakened from a fearful
dream ?"

Yes, it was indeed her of whom he had been thinking. The moment she received his letter, informing
her that he had left for the United States, she resolved
to follow him in the next steamer that sailed. This
purpose she immediately avowed to her parents. At
first, they would not listen to her ; but, finding that she
would, most probably, elude their vigilance, and get
away in spite of all efforts to prevent her, they deemed
it more wise and prudent to provide her with everything
necessary for the voyage, and to place her in the care
of the captain of the steamship in which she was to go.
In New York they had friends, to whom they gave her
letters fully explanatory of her mission, and earnestly
commending her to their care and protection.

Two weeks before the ship in which Edward Marvel
sailed reached her destination, Agnes was in New
York. Before her departure, she had sought, but in
vain, to discover the name of the vessel in which her

husband had embarked.   On arriving in the New
World, she was therefore uncertain whether he had
preceded her in a steamer, or was still lingering on the
way.

The friends to whom Agnes brought letters received
her with great kindness, and gave her all the advice and
assistance needed under the circumstances.   But two
weeks went by without a word of intelligence on the
one subject that absorbed all her thoughts.   Sadly was
her health beginning to suffer.   Sunken eyes and
pale cheeks attested the weight of suffering that was on
her.

One day it was announced that a Liverpool packet
had arrived with the ship fever on board, and that
several of the passengers had been removed to the
hospital.

A thrill of fear went through the heart of the
anxious wife.   It was soon ascertained that Marvel had
been a passenger on board of this vessel; but, from
some cause, nothing in regard to him beyond this fact
could she learn.   Against all persuasion, she started
for the hospital, her heart oppressed with a fearful
presentiment that he was either dead or struggling in
the grasp of a fatal malady.   On making inquiry at
the hospital, she was told the one she sought was not

there, and she was about returning to the city, when the truth reached her ears.

"Is he very ill?" she asked, struggling to compose herself.

"Yes, he is extremely ill," was the reply. "And it might not be well for you, under the circumstances, to see him at present."

"Not well for his wife to see him?" returned Agnes. Tears sprung to her eyes at the thought of not being permitted to come near in his extremity. "Do not say that. Oh, take me to him! I will save his life."

"You must be very calm," said the nurse; for it was with her she was talking. "The least excitement may be fatal."

"Oh, I will be calm and prudent." Yet, even while she spoke, her frame quivered with excitement.

But she controlled herself when the moment of meeting came, and, though her unexpected appearance produced a shock, it was salutary rather than injurious.

"My dear, dear Agnes!" said Edward Marvel, a month from this time, as they sat alone in the chamber of a pleasant house in New York, "I owe you my life. But for your prompt resolution to follow me across the sea, I would, in all probability, now be sleeping the sleep of death. Oh, what would I not suffer for your sake !"

As Marvel uttered the last sentence, a troubled expression flitted over his countenance. Agnes gazed tenderly into his face, and asked—

"Why this look of doubt and anxiety ?"

"Need I answer the question ?" returned the young man. "It is, thus far, no better with me than when we left our old home. Though health is coming back through every fibre, and my heart is filled with an eager desire to relieve these kind friends of the burden of our support, yet no prospect opens."

No cloud came stealing darkly over the face of the young wife. The sunshine, so far from being dimmed, was brighter.

"Let not your heart be troubled," said she, with a beautiful smile. "All will come out right."

"Right, Agnes? It is not right for me thus to depend on strangers."

"You need depend but a little while longer. I have already made warm friends here, and, through them, secured for you employment. A good place awaits you so soon as strength to fill it comes back to your weakened frame."

"Angel !" exclaimed the young man, overcome with emotion at so unexpected a declaration.

"No, not an angel," calmly replied Agnes, "only a wife. And now, dear Edward," she added, "never again, in any extremity, think for a moment of meeting trials or enduring privations alone. Having taken a wife, you cannot move safely on your journey unless she moves by your side."

"Angel! Yes, you are my good angel," repeated Edward.

"Call me what you will," said Agnes, with a sweet smile, as she brushed, with her delicate hand, the hair from his temples; "but let me be your wife. I ask no better name, no higher station."

NOT GREAT, BUT HAPPY.

How pure and sweet is the love of young hearts! How little does it contain of earth—how much of heaven! No selfish passions mar its beauty. Its tenderness, its pathos, its devotion, who does not remember, even when the sere leaves of autumn are rustling beneath his feet? How little does it regard the cold and calculating objections of worldly-mindedness. They are heard but as a passing murmur. The deep, unswerving confidence of young love, what a blessed thing it is! Heart answers to heart without an unequal throb. The world around is bright and beautiful: the atmosphere is filled with spring's most delicious perfumes.

From this dream—why should we call it a dream?—Is it not a blessed reality?—Is not young, fervent love, true love? Alas! this is an evil world, and man's heart is evil. From this dream there is too often a tearful awaking. Often, too often, hearts are suddenly torn asunder, and wounds are made that never heal, or, healing, leave hard, disfiguring scars. But this is not always so. Pure love sometimes finds its own sweet reward. I will relate one precious instance.

The Baron Holbein, after having passed ten years of active life in a large metropolitan city of Europe, retired to his estate in a beautiful and fertile valley, far away from the gay circle of fashion—far away from the sounds of political rancor with which he had been too long familiar—far away from the strife of selfish men and contending interests. He had an only child, Nina, just fifteen years of age. For her sake, as well as to indulge his love of quiet and nature, he had retired from the world. Her mother had been with the angels for some years. Without her wise counsels and watchful care, the father feared to leave his innocent-minded child exposed to the temptations that must gather around her in a large city.

For a time Nina missed her young companions, and pined to be with them. The old castle was lonely, and the villagers did not interest her. Her father urged her to go among the peasantry, and, as an inducement, placed a considerable sum of money at her command, to be used as she might see best in works of benevolence. Nina's heart was warm, and her impulse, generous. The idea pleased her, and she acted upon it. She soon found employment enough both for her time and the money placed at her disposal. Among the villagers was a woman named Blanche Delebarre, a widow, whose only son had been from home since his tenth year, under the care of an uncle, who had offered to educate him, and fit him for a life of higher useful ness than that of a mere peasant. There was a gentleness about this woman, and something that marked her as superior to her class. Yet she was an humble villager, dependent upon the labor of her own hands, and claimed no higher station.

Nina became acquainted with Blanche soon after the commencement of her residence at the castle. When she communicated to her the wishes of her father, and mentioned the money that had been placed at her disposal, the woman took her hand and said, while a beautiful light beamed from her countenance—

"It is more blessed to give than to receive, my child. Happy are they who have the power to confer benefits, and who do so with willing hearts. I fear, however, that you will find your task a difficult one. Every-where are the idle and undeserving, and these are more apt to force themselves forward as objects of benevo-lence than the truly needy and meritorious. As I know every one in the village, perhaps I may be able to guide you to such objects as deserve attention."

"My good mother," replied Nina, "I will confide in 'ur judgment. I will make you my almoner."

"No, my dear young lady, it will be better for you to dispense with your own hands. I will merely aid you to make a wise dispensation."

"I am ready tõ begin. Show me but the way."

"Do you see that company of children on the green ?" said Blanche.

"Yes. And a wild company they are."

"For hours each day they assemble as you see them, and spend their time in idle sports. Sometimes they disagree and quarrel. That is worse than idleness. Now, come here. Do you see that little cottage yonder on the hill-side, with vines clustering around the door ?"

"Yes."

"An aged mother and her daughter reside there. The labor of the daughter's hands provides food and raiment for both. These children need instruction, and Jennet Fleury is fully qualified to impart it. Their parents cannot, or will not, pay to send them to school, and Jennet must receive some return for her labors, whatever they be."

"I see it all," cried Nina with animation. "There

must be a school in the village. Jenne. shall be the teacher."

"If this can be done, it will be a great blessing," said Blanche.

"It shall be done. Let us go over to that sweet little cottage at once and see Jennet."

The good Blanche Delebarre made no objection. In a little while they entered the cottage. Every thing was homely, but neat and clean. Jennet was busy at her reel when they entered. She knew the lady of Castle Holbein, and arose up quickly and in some confusion. But she soon recovered herself, and welcomed, with a low courtesy, the visiters who had come to grace her humble abode. When the object of this visit was made known, Jennet replied that the condition of the village children had often pained her, and that she had more than once prayed that some way would open by which they could receive instruction. She readily accepted the proposal of Nina to become their teacher, and wished to receive no more for the service than what she could now earn by reeling silk.

It did not take long to get the proposed school in operation. The parents were willing to send their children, the teacher was willing to receive them, and the young lady patroness was willing to meet the expenses.

Nina said nothing to her father of what she was doing. She wished to surprise him some day, after every thing was going on prosperously. But a matter of so much interest to the neighborhood could not remain a secret. The school had not been in operation two days before the baron heard all about it. But he said nothing to his daughter. He wished to leave her the pleasure which he knew she desired, that of telling him herself.

At the end of a month Nina presented her father with an account of what she had done with the money he had placed in her hands. The expenditure had been moderate enough, but the good done was far beyond the baron's anticipations. Thirty children were receiving daily instructions; nurses had been employed, and medicines bought for the sick; needy persons, who had no employment, were set to work in making up clothing for children, who, for want of such as was suitable, could not attend the school. Besides, many other things had been done. The account was looked over by the Baron Holbein, and each item noted with sincere pleasure. He warmly commended Nina for what she had done; he praised the prudence with which she had managed what she had undertaken, and begged her to persevere in the good work.

For the space of more than a year did Nina submit

to her father, for approval, every month an accurate statement of what she had done, with a minute account of all the moneys expended. But after that time she failed to render this account, although she received the usual supply, and was as actively engaged as before in works of benevolence among the poor peasantry. The father often wondered at this, but did not inquire the cause. He had never asked an account : to render it had been a voluntary act, and he could not, therefore, ask why it was withheld. He noticed, however, a change in Nina. She was more thoughtful, and conversed less openly than before. If he looked at her intently, her eyes would sink to the floor, and the color deepen on her cheek. She remained longer in her own room, alone, than she had done since their removal to the castle. Every day she went out, and almost always took the direction of Blanche Delebarre's cottage, where she spent several hours.

Intelligence of his daughter's good deeds did not, so often as before, reach the old baron's ears ; and yet Nina drew as much money as before, and had twice asked to have the sum doubled. The father could not understand the meaning of all this. He did not believe that any thing was wrong—he had too much confidence in Nina—but he was puzzled. We will briefly apprise the reader of the cause of this change.

One day—it was nearly a year from the time Nina had become a constant visitor at Blanche Delebarre's—the young lady sat reading a book in the matron's cottage. She was alone—Blanche having gone out to visit a sick neighbor at Nina's request. A form suddenly darkened the door, and some one entered hurriedly. Nina raised her eyes, and met the gaze of a youthful stranger, who had paused and stood looking at her with surprise and admiration. With more confusion, but with not less of wonder and admiration, did Nina return the stranger's gaze.

"Is not this the cottage of Blanche Delebarre?" asked he, after a moment's pause. His voice was low and musical.

"It is," replied Nina. "She has gone to visit a sick neighbor, but will return shortly."

"Is my mother well?" asked the youth.

Nina rose to her feet. This, then, was Pierre Delebarre, of whom his mother had so often spoke. The heart of the maiden fluttered.

"The good Blanche is well," was her simple reply. "I will go and say to her that her son has come home. It will make her heart glad."

"My dear young lady, no!" said Pierre. "Do not disturb my mother in her good work. Let her come home and meet me here—the surprise will add to the

9*

pleasure. Sit down again. Pardon my rudeness—but
are not you the young lady from the castle, of whom
my mother so often writes to me as the good angel of
the village ? I am sure you must be, or you would
not be alone in my mother's cottage."

Nina's blushes deepened, but she answered without
disguise that she was from the castle.

A full half hour passed before Blanche returned.
The young and artless couple did not talk of love with
their lips during that time, but their eyes beamed with
a mutual passion. When the mother entered, so much
were they interested in each other, that they did not
hear her approaching footstep. She surprised them
leaning toward each other in earnest conversation.

The joy of the mother's heart was great on meeting
her son. He was wonderfully improved since she last
saw him—had grown several inches, and had about
him the air of one born of gentle blood, rather than
the air of a peasant. Nina staid only a very short
time after Blanche returned, and then hurried away
from the cottage.

The brief interview held with young Pierre sealed
the maiden's fate. She knew nothing of love before
the beautiful youth stood before her—her heart was
as pure as an infant's—she was artlessness itself. She
had heard him so often spoken of by his mother, that

she had learned to think of Pierre as the kindest and best of youths. She saw him, for the first time, as one to love. His face, his tones, the air of refinement and intelligence that was about him, all conspired to win her young affections. But of the true nature of her feelings, Nina was as yet ignorant. She did not think of love. She did not, therefore, hesitate as to the propriety of continuing her visits at the cottage of Blanche Delebarre, nor did she feel any reserve in the presence of Pierre. Not until the enamored youth presumed to whisper the passion her presence had awakened in his bosom, did she fully understand the cause of the delight she always felt while by his side.

After Pierre had been home a few weeks, he ventured to explain to his mother the cause of his unexpected and unannounced return. He had disagreed with his uncle, who, in a passion, had reminded him of his dependence. This the high-spirited youth could not bear, and he left his uncle's house within twenty-four hours, with a fixed resolution never to return. He had come back to the village, resolved, he said, to lead a peasant's life of toil, rather than live with a relative who could so far forget himself as to remind him of his dependence. Poor Blanche was deeply grieved. All her fond hopes for her son were at an end. She looked at his small, delicate hands and slender proportions, and wept when she thought of a peasant's life of hard labor.

A very long time did not pass before Nina made a proposition to Blanche, that relieved, in some measure, the painful depression under which she labored. It was this. Pierre had, from a child, exhibited a decided talent for painting. This talent had been cultivated by the uncle, and Pierre was, already, quite a respectable artist. But he needed at least a year's study of the old masters, and more accurate instruction than he had yet received, before he would be able to adopt the painter's calling as one by which he could take an independent position in society as a man. Understanding this fully, Nina said that Pierre must go to Florence, and remain there a year, in order to perfect himself in the art, and that she would claim the privilege of bearing all the expense. For a time, the young man's proud spirit shrunk from an acceptance of this generous offer; but Nina and the mother overruled all his objections, and almost forced him to go.

It may readily be understood, now, why Nina ceased to render accurate accounts of her charitable expenditures to her father. The baron entertained not the slightest suspicion of the real state of affairs, until about a year afterward, when a fine looking youth presented himself one day, and boldly preferred a claim to his daughter's hand. The old man was astounded.

"Who, pray, are you," he said, "that presume to make such a demand?"

"I am the son of a peasant," replied Pierre, bowing, and casting his eyes to the ground, "and you may think it presumption, indeed, for me to aspire to the hand of your noble daughter. But a peasant's love is as pure as the love of a prince; and a peasant's heart may beat with as high emotions."

"Young man," returned the baron, angrily, "your assurance deserves punishment. But go—never dare cross my threshold again! You ask an impossibility. When my daughter weds, she will not think of stooping to a presumptuous peasant. Go, sir!"

Pierre retired, overwhelmed with confusion. He had been weak enough to hope that the Baron Holbein would at least consider his suit, and give him some chance of showing himself worthy of his daughter's hand. But this repulse dashed every hope to th earth.

As soon as he parted with the young man, the father sent a servant for Nina. She was not in her chamber—nor in the house. It was nearly two hours before she came home. When she entered the pres ence of her father, he saw, by her countenance, that all was not right with her.

"Who was the youth that came here some hours ago ?" he asked, abruptly.

Nina looked up with a frightened air, but did not answer.

"Did you know that he was coming ?" said the father.

The maiden's eyes drooped to the ground, and her lips remained sealed.

"A base-born peasant ! to dare—"

"Oh, father ! he is not base ! His heart is noble," replied Nina, speaking from a sudden impulse.

"He confessed himself the son of a peasant ! Who is he ?"

"He is the son of Blanche Delebarre," returned Nina, timidly. "He has just returned from Florence, an artist of high merit. There is nothing base about him, father !"

"The son of a peasant, and an artist, to dare approach ne and claim the hand of my child ! And worse, that child to so far forget her birth and position as to favor the suit ! Madness ! And this is your good Blanche ! —your guide in all works of benevolence ! She shall be punished for this base betrayal of the confidence I have reposed in her."

Nina fell upon her knees before her father, and with tears and earnest entreaties pleaded for the mother of Pierre; but the old man was wild and mad with anger. He uttered passionate maledictions on the head of Blanche and her presumptuous son, and positively forbade Nina again leaving the castle on any pretext whatever, under the penalty of never being permitted to return.

Had so broad an interdiction not been made, there would have been some glimmer of light in Nina's dark horizon; she would have hoped for some change—would have, at least, been blessed with short, even if stolen, interviews with Pierre. But not to leave the castle on any pretext—not to see Pierre again! This was robbing life of every charm. For more than a year she had loved the young man with an affection to which every day added tenderness and fervor. Could this be blotted out in an instant by a word of command? No! That love must burn on the same.

The Baron Holbein loved his daughter; she was the bright spot in life. To make her happy, he would sacrifice almost anything. A residence of many years in the world had shown him its pretensions, its heartlessness, the worth of all its titles and distinctions. He did not value them too highly. But, when a peasant approached and asked the hand of his daughter, the

old man's pride, that was smouldering in the ashes,
burned up with a sudden blaze. He could hardly find
words to express his indignation. It took but a few
days for this indignation to burn low. Not that he felt
more favorable to the peasant—but less angry with his
daughter. It is not certain that time would not have
done something favorable for the lovers in the baron's
mind. But they could not wait for time. Nina, from
the violence and decision displayed by her father, felt
hopeless of any change, and sought an early opportunity to steal away from the castle and meet Pierre, notwithstanding the positive commands that had been
issued on the subject. The young man, in the thoughtless enthusiasm of youth, urged their flight.

"I am master of my art," he said, with a proud air.
"We can live in Florence, where I have many friends."

The youth did not find it hard to bring the confiding,
artless girl into his wishes. In less than a month the
baron missed his child. A letter explained all. She
had been wedded to the young peasant, and they ha
left for Florence. The letter contained this clause,
signed by both Pierre and Nina :—

"When our father will forgive us, and permit our
return, we shall be truly happy—but not till then."

The indignant old man saw nothing but impertinent
assurance in this. He tore up the letter, and trampled

it under his feet in a rage. He swore to renounce his child forever !

For the Baron Holbein, the next twelve months were the saddest of his life. Too deeply was the image of his child impressed upon his heart, for passion to efface it. As the first ebullitions subsided, and the atmosphere of his mind grew clear again, the sweet face of his child was before him, and her tender eyes looking into his own. As the months passed away, he grew more and more restless and unhappy. There was an aching void in his bosom. Night after night he would dream of his child, and awake in the morning and sigh that the dream was not reality. But pride was strong —he would not countenance her disobedience.

More than a year had passed away, and not one word had come from his absent one, who grew dearer to his heart every day. Once or twice he had seen the name of Pierre Delebarre in the journals, as a young artist residing in Florence, who was destined to become eminent. The pleasure these announcements gave him was greater than he would confess even to himself.

One day he was sitting in his library, endeavoring to banish the images that haunted him too continually when two of his servants entered, bearing a large square box in their arms, marked for the Baron Holbein. When the box was opened, it was found to contain a large picture, enveloped in a cloth. This was removed and placed against the wall, and the servants retired with the box. The baron, with unsteady hands, and a heart beating rapidly, commenced removing the cloth that still held the picture from view. In a few moments a family group was before him. There sat Nina, his lovely, loving and beloved child, as perfect, almost, as if the blood were glowing in her veins. Her eyes were bent fondly upon a sleeping cherub that lay in her arms. By her side sat Pierre, gazing upon her face in silent joy. For only a single instant did the old man gaze upon this scene, before the tears were gushing over his cheeks and falling to the floor like rain. This wild storm of feeling soon subsided, and, in the sweet calm that followed, the father gazed with unspeakable tenderness for a long time upon the face of his lovely child, and with a new and sweeter feeling upon the babe that lay, the impersonation of innocence, in her arms. While in this state of mind, he saw, for the first time, written on the bottom of the picture— "Not Great, but Happy."

A week from the day on which the picture was received, the Baron Holbein entered Florence. On inquiring for Pierre Delebarre, he found that every one knew the young artist.

" Come," said one, " let me go with you to the exhibition, and show you his picture that has taken the prize. It is a noble production. All Florence is alive with its praise."

The baron went to the exhibition. The first picture that met his eyes on entering the door was a counterpart of the one he had received, but larger, and, in the admirable lights in which it was arranged, looked even more like life.

"Isn't it a grand production?" said the baron's conductor.

"My sweet, sweet child!" murmured the old man, in a low thrilling voice. Then turning, he said, abruptly—

"Show me where I can find this Pierre Delebarre."

"With pleasure. His house is near at hand," said his companion.

A few minutes' walk brought them to the artist's dwelling.

"That is an humble roof," said the man, pointing to where Pierre lived, "but it contains a noble man." He turned away, and the baron entered alone. He did not pause to summon any one, but walked in through the open door. All was silent. Through a neat vestibule, in which were rare flowers, and pictures upon the wall, he passed into a small apartment, and through that to the door of an inner chamber. It was half open. He looked in. Was it another picture? No, it was in very truth his child; and her babe lay in her arms, as he had just seen it, and Pierre sat before her looking tenderly in her face. He could restrain himself no longer. Opening the door, he stepped hurriedly forward, and, throwing his arms around the group, said, in a broken voice—" God bless you, my children !"

The tears that were shed; the smiles that beamed from glad faces; the tender words that were spoken, and repeated again and again ; why need we tell of all these? Or why relate how happy the old man was when the dove that had flown from her nest came back with her mate by her side ? The dark year had passed, and there was sunshine again in his dwelling, brighter sunshine than before. Pierre never painted so good a picture again as the one that took the prize— that was his masterpiece.

*   *   *   *   *

The young Baron Holbein has an immense picture gallery, and is a munificent patron of the arts. There is one composition on his walls he prizes above all the rest. The wealth of India could not purchase it. It is the same that took the prize when he was but a babe and lay in his mother's arms. The mother who held

him so tenderly, and the father who gazed so lovingly
upon her pure young brow, have passed away, but they
live before him daily, and he feels their gentle presence
ever about him for good.

THE MARRIED SISTERS.

" Come, William, a single day, out of three hundred
and sixty-five, is not much."

" True, Henry Thorne. Nor is the single drop of
water, that first finds its way through the dyke, much;
and yet, the first drop but makes room for a small
stream to follow, and then comes a flood. No, no,
Henry, I cannot go with you, to-day; and if you will
be governed by a friend's advice, you will not neglect
your work for the fancied pleasures of a sporting
party."

" All work and no play, makes Jack a dull boy. W
were not made to be delving forever with tools in close
rooms. The fresh air is good for us. Come, William,
you will feel better for a little recreation. You look
pale from confinement. Come; I cannot go without
you."

" Henry Thorne," said his friend, William Moreland,

with an air more serious than that at first assumed,. " let me in turn, urge you to stay."

" It is in vain, William," his friend said, interrupting him.

" I trust not, Henry. Surely, my early friend and companion is not deaf to reason."

" No, not to right reason."

" Well, listen to me. As I said at first, it is not the loss of a single day, though even this is a serious waste of time, that I now take into consideration. It is the danger of forming a habit of idleness. It is a mistake, that a day of idle pleasure recreates the mind and body, and makes us return to our regular and necessary employments with renewed delight. My own experience is, that a day thus spent, causes us to resume our labors with reluctance, and makes irksome what before was pleasant. Is it not your own ?"

" Well, I don't know; I can't altogether say that it is; indeed, I never thought about it."

" Henry, the worst of all kinds of deception is self-deception. Don't, let me beg of you, attempt to deceive yourself in a matter so important. I am sure you have experienced this reluctance to resuming work after a day of pleasure. It is a universal experience. And now that we are on this subject, I will add, that I have observed in you an increasing desire to get away

from work. You make many excuses and they seem
to you to be good ones. Can you tell me how many
days you have been out of the shop in the last three
months ?"

"No, I cannot," was the reply, made in a tone indicating a slight degree of irritation.

"Well, I can, Henry."

"How many is it, then ?"

"Ten days."

"Never !"

"It is true, for I kept the count."

"Indeed, then, you are mistaken. I was only out a
gunning three times, and a fishing twice."

"And that makes five times. But don't you remember the day you were made sick by fatigue ?"

"Yes, true, but that is only six."

"And the day you went up the mountain with the
party ?"

"Yes."

"And the twice you staid away because it stormed ?"

"But, William, that has nothing to do with the
matter. If it stormed so violently that I couldn't come
to the shop, that surely is not to be set down to the
account of pleasure-taking."

"And yet, Henry, I was here, and so were all the
workmen but yourself. If there had not been in your

mind a reluctance to coming to the shop, I am sure the storm would not have kept you away. I am plain with you, because I am your friend, and you know it. Now, it is this increasing reluctance on your part, that alarms me. Do not, then, add fuel to a flame, that, if thus nourished, will consume you."

"But, William——"

"Don't make excuses, Henry. Think of the aggregate of ten lost days. You can earn a dollar and a half a day, easily, and do earn it whenever you work steadily. Ten days in three months is fifteen dollars. All last winter, Ellen went without a cloak, because you could not afford to buy one for her; now the money that you could have earned in the time wasted in the last three months, would have bought her a very comfortable one—and you know that it is already October, and winter will soon be again upon us. Sixty dollars a year buys a great many comforts for a poor man."

Henry Thorne remained silent for some moments. He felt the force of William Moreland's reasoning; but his own inclinations were stronger than his friend's arguments. He wanted to go with two or three companions a gunning, and even the vision of his young wife shrinking in the keen winter wind, was not sufficient to conquer this desire.

10

"I will go this once, William," said he, at length, with a long inspiration; "and then I will quit it. I see and acknowledge the force of what you say, I never viewed the matter so seriously before."

"This once may confirm a habit now too strongly fixed," urged his companion. "Stop now, while your mind is rationally convinced that it is wrong to waste your time, when it is so much needed for the sake of making comfortable and happy one who loves you, and has cast her lot in life with yours. Think of Ellen, and be a man."

"Come, Harry!" said a loud, cheerful voice at the shop door; "we are waiting for you!"

"Ay, ay," responded Henry Thorne. "Good morning, William! I am pledged for to-day. But after this, I will swear off!" And so saying, he hurried away.

Henry Thorne and William Moreland were workmen in a large manufacturing establishment in one of our thriving inland towns. They had married sisters and thus a friendship that had long existed, was confirmed by closer ties of interest.

They had been married about two years, at the time of their introduction to the reader, and, already, Moreland could perceive that his earnings brought many more comforts for his little family than did Henry's.

The difference was not to be accounted for in the days the other spent in pleasure taking, although their aggregate loss was no mean item to be taken from a poor man's purse. It was to be found, mainly, in disposition to spend, rather than to save; to pay away for trifles that were not really needed, very small sums, whose united amounts in a few weeks would rise to dollars. But, when there was added to this constant check upon his prosperity the frequent recurrence of a lost day, no wonder that Ellen had less of good and comfortable clothing than her sister Jane, and that her house was far less neatly furnished.

All this had been observed, with pain, by William Moreland and his wife, but, until the conversation recorded in the opening of this story, no word or remonstrance or warning had been ventured upon by the former. The spirit in which Moreland's words were received, encouraged him to hope that he might exer-cise a salutary control over Henry, if he persevered, and he resolved that he would extend thus far towards him the offices of a true friend.

After dinner on the day during which her husband was absent, Ellen called in to see Jane, and sit the afternoon with her. They were only sisters, and had always loved each other much. During their conversation, Jane said, in allusion to the season:

" It begins to feel a little chilly to-day, as if winter were coming.   And, by the way, you are going to get a cloak this fall, Ellen, are you not ?"

" Indeed, I can hardly tell, Jane," Ellen replied, in a erious tone ; " Henry's earnings, somehow or other, don't seem to go far with us ; and yet I try to be as prudent as I can.   We have but a few dollars laid by, and both of us want warm underclothing.   Henry must have a coat and pair of pantaloons to look decent this winter ; so I must try and do without the cloak, I suppose."

" I am sorry for that.   But keep a good heart about it, sister.   Next fall, you will surely be able to get a comfortable one ; and you shall have mine as often as you want it, this winter.   I can't go out much, you know ; our dear little Ellen, your namesake, is too young to leave often."

" You are very kind, Jane," said Ellen, and her voice slightly trembled.

A silence of some moments ensued, and then the subject of conversation was changed to one more cheer-ful.

That evening, just about nightfall, Henry Thorne came home, much fatigued, bringing with him half a dozen squirrels and a single wild pigeon.

" There, Ellen, is something to make a nice pie for

us to-morrow," said he, tossing his game bag upon the table.

"You look tired, Henry," said his wife, tenderly; I wouldn't go out any more this fall, if I were you."

"I don't intend going out any more, Ellen," was replied, "I'm sick of it."

"You don't know how glad I am to hear you say so! Somehow, I always feel troubled and uneasy when you are out gunning or fishing, as if you were not doing right."

"You shall not feel so any more, Ellen," said Thorne: "I've been thinking all the afternoon about your cloak. Cold weather is coming, and we haven't a dollar laid by for anything. How I am to get the cloak, I do not see, and yet I cannot bear the thought of your going all this winter again without one."

"O, never mind that, dear," said Ellen, in a cheerful tone, her face brightening up. "We can't afford it this fall, and so that's settled. But I can have Jane's whenever I want it, she says; and you know she is so kind and willing to lend me anything that she has. I don't like to wear her things; but then I shall not want the cloak often."

Henry Thorne sighed at the thoughts his wife's words stirred in his mind.

"I don't know how it is," he at length said, despondingly ; " William can't work any faster than I can, nor earn more a week, and yet he and Jane have every thing comfortable, and are saving money into the bargain, while we want many things that they have, nd are not a dollar ahead."

One of the reasons for this, to her husband so unaccountable, trembled on Ellen's tongue, but she could not make up her mind to reprove him ; and so bore in silence, and with some pain, what she felt as a reflection upon her want of frugality in managing household affairs.

Let us advance the characters we have introduced, a year in their life's pilgrimage, and see if there are any fruits of these good resolutions.

" Where is Thorne, this morning?" asked the owner of the shop, speaking to Moreland, one morning, an hour after all the workmen had come in.

" I do not know, really," replied Moreland. "I saw him yesterday, when he was well "

" He's off gunning, I suppose, again. If so, it is the tenth day he has lost in idleness during the last two months. I am afraid I shall have to get a hand in his place, upon whom I can place more dependence. I shall be sorry to do this for your sake, and for the sake of his wife. But I do not like such an example to the workmen and apprentices; and besides being away from the shop often disappoints a job."

"I could not blame you, sir," Moreland said; "and yet, I do hope you will bear with him for the sake of Ellen. I think if you would talk with him it would do him good."

"But, why don't you talk to him, William?"

"I have talked to him frequently, but he has got so that he won't bear it any longer from me."

"Nor would he bear it from me, either, I fear, William."

Just at that moment the subject of the conversation came in.

"You are late this morning, Henry," said the owner of the shop to him, in the presence of the other workmen.

"It's only a few minutes past the time," was replied, moodily.

"It's more than an hour past."

"Well, if it is, I can make it up."

"That is not the right way, Henry. Lost time is never made up."

Thorne did not understand the general truth intended to be expressed, but supposed, at once, that the master of the shop meant to intimate that he would wrong him out of the lost hour, notwithstanding he had promised to make it up. He therefore turned an angry look upon him, and said—

"Do you mean to say that I would cheat you, sir ?"

The employer was a hasty man, and tenacious of his dignity as a master. He invariably discharged a journeyman who was in the least degree disrespectful in his language or manner towards him before the other workmen. Acting under the impulse that at once prompted him, he said:

"You are discharged ;" and instantly turned away.

As quickly did Henry Thorne turn and leave the shop. He took his way homeward, but he paused and lingered as he drew nearer and nearer his little cottage, for troubled thoughts had now taken the place of angry feelings. At length he was at the door, and lifting slowly the latch, he entered.

"Henry !" said Ellen, with a look and tone of surprise. Her face was paler and more care-worn than it was a year before ; and its calm expression had changed into a troubled one. She had a babe upon her lap, her first and only one. The room in which she sat, so far from indicating circumstances improved by the passage of a year, was far less tidy and comfortable ; and her own attire, though neat, was faded and unseasonable. Her husband replied not to her inquiring look, and surprised ejaculation, but seated himself in a chair, and burying his face in his hands, remained silent, until, unable to endure the suspense, Ellen went to him, and taking his hand, asked, so earnestly, and so tenderly, what it was that troubled him, that he could not resist her appeal.

"I am discharged!" said he, with bitter emphasis. "And there is no other establishment in the town, nor within fifty miles!"

"O, Henry! how did that happen?"

"I hardly know myself, Ellen, for it all seems like a dream. When I left home this morning, I did not go directly to the shop; I wanted to see a man at the upper end of the town, and when I got back it was an hour later than usual. Old Ballard took me to task before all the shop, and intimated that I was not disposed to act honestly towards him. This I cannot bear from any one; I answered him in anger, and was discharged on the spot. And now, what we are to do, heaven only knows! Winter is almost upon us, and we have not five dollars in the world."

"But something will turn up for us, Henry, I know it will," said Ellen, trying to smile encouragingly, although her heart was heavy in her bosom.

Her husband shook his head, doubtingly, and then all was gloomy and oppressive silence. For nearly an hour, no word was spoken by either. Each mind was

10*

busy with painful thoughts, and one with fearful fore-
bodings of evil.   At the end of that time, the husband
took up his hat and went out.   For a long, long time
fter, Ellen sat in dreamy, sad abstraction, holding her
oabe to her breast.   From this state, a sense of duty
roused her, and laying her infant on the bed,—for they
had not yet been able to spare money for a cradle,
—she began to busy herself in her domestic duties.
This brought some little relief.

About eleven o'clock Jane came in with her usual
cheerful, almost happy face, bringing in her hand a
stout bundle.   Her countenance changed in its expression to one of concern, the moment her eyes rested upon
her sister's face, and she laid her bundle on a chair
quickly, as if she half desired to keep it out of Ellen's sight.

"What is the matter, Ellen!" she asked, with tender
concern, the moment she had closed the door.

Ellen could not reply; her heart was too full.   But
she leaned her head upon her sister's shoulder, and, for
the first time since she had heard the sad news of the
morning, burst into tears.   Jane was surprised, and
filled with anxious concern.   She waited until this
ebullition of feeling in some degree abated, and then
said, in a tone still more tender than that in which she
had first spoken,—

"Ellen, dear sister! tell me what has happened?"

"I am foolish, sister," at length, said Ellen, looking up, and endeavoring to dry her tears. "But I cannot help it. Henry was discharged from the shop this morning; and now, what are we to do? We have nothing ahead, and I am afraid he will not be able to get anything to do here, or within many miles of the village."

"That is bad, Ellen," replied Jane, while a shadow fell upon her face, but a few moments before so glowing and happy. And that was nearly all she could say; for she did not wish to offer false consolation, and she could think of no genuine words of comfort. After a while, each grew more composed and less reserved; and then the whole matter was talked over, and all that Jane could say, that seemed likely to soothe and give hope to Ellen's mind, was said with earnestness and affection.

"What have you there?" at length asked Ellen, glancing towards the chair upon which Jane had laid her bundle.

Jane paused a moment, as if in self-communion, and then said—

"Only a pair of blankets, and a couple of calico dresses that I have been out buying."

"Let me look at them," said Ellen, in as cheerful a voice as she could assume.

A large heavy pair of blankets, for which Jane had paid five dollars, were now unrolled, and a couple of handsome chintz dresses, of dark rich colors, suitable for the winter season, displayed. It was with difficulty that Ellen could restrain a sigh, as she looked at these comfortable things, and thought of how much she needed, and of how little she had to hope for. Jane felt that such thoughts must pass through her sister's mind, and she also felt much pained that she had undesignedly thus added, by contrast, to Ellen's unhappy feelings. When she returned home, she put away her new dresses and her blankets. She had no heart to look at them, no heart to enjoy her own good things, while the sister she so much loved was denied like present comforts, and, worse than all, weighed down with a heart-sickening dread of the future.

We will not linger to contrast, in a series of domestic pictures, the effects of industry and idleness on the two married sisters and their families,—effects, the causes of which, neither aided materially in producing. Such contrasts, though useful, cannot but be painful to the mind, and we would, a thousand times, rather give pleasure than pain. But one more striking contrast we will give, as requisite to show the tendency of good or bad principles, united with good or bad habits.

Unable to get any employment in the village

Thorne, hearing that steady work could be obtained in
Charleston, South Carolina, sold off a portion of his
scanty effects, by wnich he received money enough to
remove there with his wife and child. Thus were the
sisters separated ; and in that separation, gradually
estranged from the tender and lively affection that
presence and constant intercourse had kept burning
with undiminished brightness. Each became more and
more absorbed, every day, in increasing cares and
duties ; yet to one those cares and duties were painful,
and to the other full of delight.

Ten years from the day on which they parted in
tears, Ellen sat, near the close of day, in a meanly
furnished room, in one of the southern cities, watching,
with a troubled countenance, the restless slumber of
her husband. Her face was very thin and pale, and it
had a fixed and strongly marked expression of suffering.
Two children, a boy and a girl, the one about six, and
the other a little over ten years of age, were seated
listlessly on the floor, which was uncarpeted. They
eemed to have no heart to play. Even the elasticity
of childhood had departed from them. From the
appearance of Thorne, it was plain that he was very
sick ; and from all the indications the room in which
he lay, afforded, it was plain that want and suffering
were its inmates. The habit of idleness he had

suffered to creep at a slow but steady pace upon him Idleness brought intemperance, and intemperance, reacting upon idleness, completed his ruin, and reduced his family to poverty in its most appalling form. Now he was sick with a southern fever, and his miserable dwelling afforded him no cordial, nor his wife and children the healthy food that nature required.

"Mother!" said the little boy, getting up from the floor, where he had been sitting for half an hour, as still as if he were sleeping, and coming to Ellen's side, he looked up earnestly and imploringly in her face.

"What, my child ?" the mother said, stooping down and kissing his forehead, while she parted with her fingers the golden hair that fell in tangled masses over it.

"Can't I have a piece of bread, mother ?"

Ellen did not reply, but rose slowly and went to the closet, from which she took part of a loaf, and cutting a slice from it, handed it to her hungry boy. It was her last loaf, and all their money was gone. The little fellow took it, and breaking a piece off for his sister, gave it to her ; the two children then sat down side by side, and ate in silence the morsel that was sweet to them.

With an instinctive feeling, that from nowhere but above could she look for aid and comfort, did Ellen lift her heart, and pray that she might not be forsaken in her extremity. And then she thought of her sister Jane, from whom she had not heard for a long, long time, and her heart yearned towards her with an eager and yearning desire to see her face once more.

And now let us look in upon Jane and her family. Her husband, by saving where Thorne spent in foolish trifles, and working when Thorne was idle, gradually laid by enough to purchase a little farm, upon which he had removed, and there industry and frugality brought its sure rewards. They had three children : little Ellen had grown to a lively, rosy-cheeked, merry-faced girl of eleven years ; and George, who had followed Ellen, was in his seventh year, and after him came the baby, now just completing the twelfth month of its innocent, happy life. It was in the season when the farmers' toil is rewarded, and William Moreland was among those whose labor had met an ample return.

How different was the scene, in his well established cottage, full to the brim of plenty and comfort, to that which was passing at the same hour of the day, a few weeks before, in the sad abode of Ellen, herself its saddest inmate.

The table was spread for the evening meal, always eaten before the sun hid his bright face, and George and Ellen, although the supper was not yet brought in, had taken their places; and Moreland, too, had drawn up with the baby on his knee, which he was amusing with an apple from a well filled basket, the product of is own orchard.

A hesitating rap drew the attention of the tidy maiden who assisted Mrs. Moreland in her duties.

"It is the poor old blind man," she said, in a tone of compassion, as she opened the door.

"Here is a shilling for him, Sally," said Moreland, handing her a piece of money. "The Lord has blessed us with plenty, and something to spare for his needy children."

The liberal meal upon the table, the mother sat down with the rest, and as she looked around upon each happy face, her heart blessed the hour that she had given her hand to William Moreland. Just as the meal was finished, a neighbor stopped at the door and said :

"Here's a letter for Mrs. Moreland; I saw it in the post-office, and brought it over for her, as I was coming this way."

"Come in, come in," said Moreland, with a hearty welcome in his voice.

"No, I thank you, I can't stop now. Good evening," replied the neighbor.

"Good evening," responded Moreland, turning from the door, and handing the letter to Jane.

"It must be from Ellen," Mrs. Moreland remarked, as she broke the seal. "It is a long time since we heard from them; I wonder how they are doing?"

She soon knew, for on opening the letter she read thus :—

SAVANNAH, September, 18—.

MY DEAR SISTER JANE :—Henry has just died. I am left here without a dollar, and know not where to get bread for myself and two children. I dare not tell you all I have suffered since I parted from you. I ——

My heart is too full; I cannot write. Heaven only knows what I shall do! Forgive me, sister, for troubling you; I have not done so before, because I did not wish to give you pain, and I only do so now, from an impulse that I cannot resist.

ELLEN.

Jane handed the letter to her husband, and sat down 'n a chair, her senses bewildered, and her heart sick.

"We have enough for Ellen, and her children, too, Jane," said Moreland, folding the letter after he had read it. "We must send for them at once: Poor Ellen! I fear she has suffered much."

"You are good, kind and noble-hearted, William!" exclaimed Jane, bursting into tears.

"I don't know that I am any better than anybody else, Jane. But I can't bear to see others suffering, and never will, if I can afford relief. And surely, if industry brought no other reward, the power it gives us to benefit and relieve others, is enough to make us ever active "

*   *   *   *   *

In one month from the time Ellen's letter was received, she, with her children, were inmates of Moreland's cottage. Gradually the light returned to her eye, and something of the former glow of health and contentment to her cheek. Her children in a few weeks, were as gay and happy as any. The delight that glowed in the heart of William Moreland, as he saw this pleasing change, was a double reward for the little he had sacrificed in making them happy. Nor did Ellen fall, with her children, an entire burden upon her sister and her husband ;—her activity and willingness found enough to do that needed doing. Jane often used to say to her husband—

"I don't know which is the gainer over the other, I or Ellen ; for I am sure I can't see how we could do without her."

GOOD-HEARTED PEOPLE.

THERE are two classes in the world : one acts from impulse, and the other from reason ; one consults the heart, and the other the head. Persons belonging to the former class are very much liked by the majority of those who come in contact with them : while those of the latter class make many enemies in their course through life. Still, the world owes as much to the latter as to the former—perhaps a great deal more.

Mr. Archibald May belonged to the former class ; he was known as a good-hearted man. He uttered the word " no" with great difficulty ; and was never known to have deliberately said that to another which he knew would hurt his feelings. If any one about him acted wrong, he could not find it in his heart to wound him by calling his attention to the fact. On one occasion, a clerk was detected in purloining money ; but it was all hushed up, and when Mr. May dismissed him, he gave him a certificate of good character.

"How could you do so?" asked a neighbor, to whom he mentioned the fact.

"How could I help doing it? The young man had a chance of getting a good place. It would have been cruel in me to have refused to aid him. A character was required, and I could do no less than give it. Poor, silly fellow! I am sure I wish him well. I always liked him."

"Suppose he robs his present employer?"

"He won't do that, I'm certain. He is too much ashamed of his conduct while in my store. It is a lesson to him. And, at any rate, I do not think a man should be hunted down for a single fault."

"No: of course not. But, when you endorse a man's character, you lead others to place confidence in him; a confidence that may be betrayed under very aggravated circumstances."

"Better that many suffer, than that one innocent man should be condemned and cast off."

"But there is no question about guilt or innocence. It was fully proved that this young man robbed you."

"Suppose it was. No doubt the temptation was very strong. I don't believe he will ever be guilty of such a thing again."

" You have the best evidence in the world that he will, in the fact that he has taken your money."

" O no, not at all.   It doesn't follow, by any means, that a fault like this will be repeated.   He was terribly mortified about it.   That has cured him, I am certain."

" I wouldn't trust to it."

" You are too uncharitable," replied Mr. May.   " For my part, I always look upon the best side of a man's character.   There is good in every one.   Some have their weaknesses—some are even led astray at times; but none are altogether bad.   If a man falls, help him up, and start him once more fair in the world—who can say that he will again trip ?   Not I.   The fact is, we are too hard with each other.   If you brand your fellow with infamy for one little act of indiscretion, or, say crime, what hope is there for him."

" You go rather too far, Mr. May," the neighbor said, " in your condemnation of the world.   No doubt there are many who are really uncharitable in their denunciations of their fellow man for a single fault But, on the other side, I am inclined to think, that there are just as many who are equally uncharitable, in loosely passing by, out of spurious kindness, what should mark a man with just suspicion, and cause a withholding of confidence.   Look at the case now before us.   You feel unwilling to keep a young man about you, because he has betrayed your trust, and yet, out of kind feelings, you give him a good character, and enable him to get a situation where he may seriously wrong an unsuspecting man."

"But I am sure he will not do so."

"But what is your guarantee?"

"The impression that my act has evidently made upon him. If I had, besides hushing up the whole matter, kept him still in my store, he might again have been tempted. But the comparatively light punishment of dismissing him with a good character, will prove a salutary check upon him."

"Don't you believe it."

"I will believe it, until I see evidence to the contrary. You are too suspicious—too uncharitable, my good friend. I am always inclined to think the best of every one. Give the poor fellow another chance for his life, say I."

"I hope it may all turn out right."

"I am sure it will," returned Mr. May. "Many and many a young man is driven to ruin by having all confidence withdrawn from him, after his first error. Depend upon it, such a course is not right."

"I perfectly agree with you, Mr. May, that we should not utterly condemn and cast off a man for a single fault. But, it is one thing to bear with a fault, and encourage a failing brother man to better courses, and another to give an individual whom we know to be dishonest, a certificate of good character."

"Yes, but I am not so sure the young man we are speaking about is dishonest."

"Didn't he rob you?"

"Don't say *rob*. That is too hard a word. He did take a little from me; but it wasn't much, and there were peculiar circumstances."

"Are you sure that under other peculiar circumstances, he would not have taken much more from you?"

"I don't believe he would."

"I wouldn't trust him."

"You are too suspicious—too uncharitable, as I have already said. I can't be so. I always try to think the best of every one."

Finding that it was no use to talk, the neighbor said but little more on the subject.

About a year afterwards the young man's new employer, who, on the faith of Mr. May's recommendation, ad placed great confidence in him, discovered that he ad been robbed of several thousand dollars. The robbery was clearly traced to this clerk, who was arrested, tried, and sentenced to three years imprisonment in the Penitentiary.

"It seems that all your charity was lost on that

voung scoundrel, Blake," said the individual whose conversation with Mr. May has just been given.

" Poor fellow!" was the pitying reply. "I am most grievously disappointed in him. I never believed that he would turn out so badly."

" You might have known it after he had swindled you. A man who will steal a sheep, needs only to be assured of impunity, to rob the mail. The principle is the same. A rogue is a rogue, whether it be for a pin or a pound."

" Well, well—people differ in these matters. I never look at the worst side only. How could Dayton find it in his heart to send that poor fellow to the State Prison! I wouldn't have done it, if he had taken all I possess. It was downright vindictiveness in him."

" It was simple justice. He could not have done otherwise. Blake had not only wronged him, but he had violated the laws, and to the laws he was bound to give him up."

" Give up a poor, erring young man, to the stern, unbending, unfeeling laws! No one is bound to do that. It is cruel, and no one is under the necessity of being cruel."

" It is simply just, Mr. May, as I view it. And, further, really more just to give up the culprit to the law he has knowingly and wilfully violated, than to let him escape its penalties."

Mr. May shook his head.

"I certainly cannot see the charity of locking up a young man for three or four years in prison, and utter-ly and forever disgracing him."

"It is a great evil to steal?" said the neighbor.

"O, certainly—a great sin."

"And the law made for its punishment is just?"

"Yes, I suppose so."

"Do you think that it really injures a thief to lock him up in prison, and prevent him from trespassing on the property of his neighbors?"

"That I suppose depends upon circumstances. If——"

"No, but my friend, we must fix the principle yea or nay. The law that punishes theft is a good law—you admit that—very well. If the law is good, it must be because its effect is good. A thief, will, under such a law, be really more benefitted by feeling its force than in escaping the penalty annexed to its infringement. No distinction can or ought to be made. The man who, in a sane mind, deliberately takes the property of another, should be punished by the law which forbids stealing. It will have at least one good effect, if none other, and that will be to make him less willing to run

11

similar risk, and thus leave to his neighbor the peaceable possession of his goods."

"Punishment, if ever administered, should look to he good of the offender. But, what good disgracing and imprisoning a young man who has all along borne a fair character, is going to have, is more than I can tell. Blake won't be able to hold up his head among respectable people when his term has expired."

"And will, in consequence, lose his power of injuring the honest and unsuspecting. He will be viewed in his own true light, and be cast off as unworthy by a community whose confidence he has most shamefully abused."

"And so you will give an erring brother no chance for his life ?"

"O yes. Every chance. But it would not be kindness to wink at his errors and leave him free to continue in the practice of them, to his own and others' injury. Having forfeited his right to the confidence of this community by trespassing upon it, let him pay the penalty of that trespass. It will be to him, doubtless, a salutary lesson. A few years of confinement in a prison will give him time for reflection and repentance; whereas, impunity in an evil course could only have strengthened his evil purposes. When he has paid the just penalty of his crime, let him go into another part

of the country, and among strangers live a virtuous
life, the sure reward of which is peace."

Mr. May shook his head negatively, at these
remarks.

"No one errs on the side of kindness," he said,
"while too, many, by an opposite course, drive to ruin
those whom leniency might have saved."

A short time after the occurrence of this little
interview, Mr. May, on returning home one evening,
found his wife in much apparent trouble.

"Has anything gone wrong, Ella!" he asked.

"Would you have believed it?" was Mrs. May's
quick and excited answer. "I caught Jane in my
drawer to-day, with a ten dollar bill in her hand which
she had just taken out of my pocket book, that was
still open."

"Why, Ella!"

"It is too true! I charged it at once upon her, and
she burst into tears, and owned that she was going to
take the money and keep it."

"That accounts, then, for the frequency with which
you have missed small sums of money for several
months past."

"Yes. That is all plain enough now. But what
shall we do! I cannot think of keeping Jane any
longer."

· "Perhaps she will never attempt such a thing again, now that she has been discovered."

"I cannot trust her. I should never feel safe a moment. To have a thief about the house! Oh, no. That would never answer. She will have to go."

"Well, Ella, you will have to do what you think best; but you mustn't be too hard on the poor creature. You mustn't think of exposing her, and thus blasting her character. It might drive her to ruin."

"But, is it right for me, knowing what she is, to let her go quietly into another family? It is a serious matter, husband."

"I don't know that you have anything to do with that. The safest thing, in my opinion, is for you to talk seriously to Jane, and warn her of the consequences of acts such as she has been guilty of. And then let her go, trusting that she will reform."

"But there is another fault that I have discovered within a week or two past. A fault that I suspected, but was not sure about. It is a very bad one."

"What is that, Ella?"

"I do not think she is kind to the baby."

"What?"

"I have good reason for believing that she is not kind to our dear little babe. I partly suspected this for some time. More than once I have came suddenly upon her, and found our sweet pet sobbing as if his heart would break. The expression in Jane's face I could not exactly understand. Light has gradually broken in upon me, and now I am satisfied that she has abused him shamefully."

" Ella ?"

"It is too true. Since my suspicions were fully aroused, I have asked Hannah about it, and she, unwillingly, has confirmed my own impressions."

" Unwillingly ! It was her duty to have let you know this voluntarily. Treat my little angel Charley unkindly ! The wretch ! She doesn't remain in this house a day longer."

" So I have fully determined. I am afraid that Jane has a wretched disposition. It is bad enough to steal, but to ill-treat a helpless, innocent babe, is fiend-like."

Jane was accordingly dismissed.

"Poor creature !" said Mrs. May, after Jane had left the house; "I feel sorry for her. She is, after all, the worst enemy to herself. I don't know what will become of her."

" She'll get a place somewhere."

"Yes, I suppose so. But, I hope she won't refer to me for her character. I don't know what I should say, if she did."

" If I couldn't say any good, I wouldn't say any

harm, Ella. It's rather a serious matter to break down the character of a poor girl."

"I know it is; for that is all they have to depend upon. I shall have to smooth it over some how, I suppose."

"Yes: put the best face you can upon it. I have no doubt but she will do better in another place."

On the next day, sure enough, a lady called to ask about the character of Jane.

" How long has she been with you ?" was one of the first questions asked.

" About six months," replied Mrs. May.

" In the capacity of nurse, I think she told me ?"

" Yes. She was my nurse."

" Was she faithful ?"

This was a trying question. But it had to be answered promptly, and it was so answered.

" Yes, I think I may call her quite a faithful nurse. She never refused to carry my little boy out; and always kept him very clean."

" She kept him nice, did she ? Well, that is a recommendation. And I want somebody who will not be above taking my baby into the street. But how is her temper ?"

" A little warm sometimes. But then, you know, perfection is not to be attained any where."

" No, that is very true. You think her a very good nurse ?"

" Yes, quite equal to the general run."

" I thank you very kindly," said the lady rising. " I hope I shall find, in Jane, a nurse to my liking."

" I certainly hope so," replied Mrs. May, as she attended her to the door.

" What do you think ?" said Mrs. May to her husband, when he returned in the evening.—" That Jane had the assurance to send a lady here to inquire about her character."

" She is a pretty cool piece of goods, I should say. But, I suppose she trusted to your known kind feelings, not to expose her."

" No doubt that was the reason. But, I can tell her that I was strongly tempted to speak out the plain truth. Indeed, I could hardly contain myself when the lady told me that she wanted her to nurse a little infant. I thought of dear Charley, and how she had neglected and abused him—the wretched creature! But I restrained myself, and gave her as good a character as I could."

" That was right. We should not let our indignant feelings govern us in matters of this kind. We can never err on the side of kindness."

" No, I am sure we cannot."

Mrs. Campbell, the lady who had called upon Mrs.
May, felt quite certain that, in obtaining Jane for a
nurse, she had been fortunate. She gave, confidently,
o her care, a babe seven months old.   At first, from a
mother's natural instinct, she kept her eye upon Jane;
but every thing going on right, she soon ceased to
observe her closely.   This was noted by the nurse, who
began to breathe with more freedom.   Up to this time,
the child placed in her charge had received the kindest
attentions.   Now, however, her natural indifference led
her to neglect him in various little ways, unnoticed by
the mother, but felt by the infant.   Temptations were
also thrown in her way by the thoughtless exposure of
money and jewelry.   Mrs. Campbell supposed, of
course, that she was honest, or she would have been
notified of the fact by Mrs. May, of whom she had
inquired Jane's character ; and, therefore, never thought
of being on her guard in this respect.   Occasionally she
could not help thinking that there ought to be more
money in her purse than there was.   But she did not
suffer this thought to rise into a suspicion of unfair
dealing against any one.   The loss of a costly breast
pin, the gift of a mother long since passed into the
invisible world, next worried her mind; but, even this
did not cause her to suspect that any thing was wrong
with her nurse.

Thus the time passed on, many little losses of money and valued articles disturbing and troubling the mind of Mrs. Campbell, until it became necessary to wean her babe. This duty was assigned to Jane, who took the infant to sleep with her. On the first night, it cried for several hours—in fact, did not permit Jane to get more than a few minutes' sleep at a time all night. Her patience was tried severely. Sometimes she would hold the distressed child with angry violence to her bosom, while it screamed with renewed energy; and then, finding that it still continued to cry, toss it from her upon the bed, and let it lie, still screaming, until fear lest its mother should be tempted to come to her distressed babe, would cause her again to take it to her arms. A hard time had that poor child of it on that first night of its most painful experience in the world. It was scolded, shaken, and even whipped by the unfeeling nurse, until, at last, worn out nature yielded, and sleep threw its protecting mantle over the wearied babe.

"How did you get along with Henry?" was the mother's eager question, as she entered Jane's room soon after daylight.

"O very well, ma'am," returned Jane.

"I heard him cry dreadfully in the night. Several times I thought I would come in and take him."

11*

" Yes, ma'am, he did scream once or twice very hard but he soon gave up, and has long slept as soundly as you now see him."

" Dear little fellow!" murmured the mother in a trembling voice. She stooped down and kissed him tenderly—tears were in her eyes.

On the next night, Henry screamed again for several hours. Jane, had she felt an affection for the child, and, from that affection been led to soothe it with tenderness, might easily have lulled it into quiet ; but her ill-nature disturbed the child. After worrying with it a long time, she threw it from her with violence, exclaiming as she did so—

" I'll fix you to-morrow night ! There'll be no more of this. They needn't think I'm going to worry out my life for their cross-grained brat."

She stopped. For the babe had suddenly ceased crying. Lifting it up, quickly, she perceived, by the light of the lamp, that its face was very white, and its lips blue. In alarm, she picked it up and sprang from the bed. A little water thrown into its face, soon revived it. But the child did not cry again, and soon fell away into sleep. For a long time Jane sat partly up in bed, leaning over on her arm, and looking into little Henry's face. He breathed freely, and seemed to be as well as ever. She did not wake until morning.

When she did, she found the mother bending over her, and gazing earnestly down into the face of her sleeping babe. The incident that had occurred in the night glanced through her mind, and caused her to rise up and look anxiously at the child. Its sweet, placid face, at once reassured her.

"He slept better last night," remarked Mrs. Campbell.

"O, yes. He didn't cry any at all, hardly."

"Heaven bless him!" murmured the mother, bending over and kissing him softly.

On the next morning, when she awoke, Mrs. Campbell felt a strange uneasiness about her child. Without waiting to dress herself, she went softly over to the room where Jane slept. It was only a little after daylight. She found both the child and nurse asleep. There was something in the atmosphere of the room that oppressed her lungs, and something peculiar in its odor. Without disturbing Jane, she stood for several minutes looking into the face of Henry. Something about it troubled her. It was not so calm as usual, nor had his skin that white transparency so peculiar to a babe.

"Jane," she at length said, laying her hand upon the nurse.

Jane roused up.

"How did Henry get along last night, Jane?"

"Very well, indeed, ma'am; he did not cry at all."

"Do you think he looks well?"

Jane turned her eyes to the face of the child, and egarded it for some time.

"O, yes, ma'am, he looks very well; he has been sleeping sound all night."

Thus assured, Mrs. Campbell regarded Henry for a few minutes longer, and then left the room. But her heart was not at ease. There was a weight upon it, and it labored in its office heavily.

"Still asleep," she said, about an hour after, coming into Jane's room. "It is not usual for him to sleep so long in the morning."

Jane turned away from the penetrating glance of the mother, and remarked, indifferently:

"He has been worried out for the last two nights. That is the reason, I suppose."

Mrs. Campbell said no more, but lifted the child in her arms, and carried it to her own chamber. There she endeavored to awaken it, but, to her alarm, she found that it still slept heavily in spite of all her efforts.

Running down into the parlor with it, where her husband sat reading the morning papers, she exclaimed:

"Oh, Henry! I'm afraid that Jane has been giving this child something to make him sleep. See! I cannot awake him. Something is wrong, depend upon it!"

Mr. Campbell took the babe and endeavored to arouse him, but without effect.

"Call her down here," he then said, in a quick, resolute voice.

Jane was called down.

"What have you given this child?" asked Mr. Campbell, peremptorily.

"Nothing," was the positive answer. "What could I have given him?"

"Call the waiter."

Jane left the room, and in a moment after the waiter entered.

"Go for Doctor B—— as fast as you can, and say to him I must see him immediately."

The waiter left the house in great haste. In about twenty minutes Dr. B—— arrived.

"Is there any thing wrong about this child?" Mr. Campbell asked, placing little Henry in the doctor's arms

"There is," was replied, after the lapse of about half a minute. "What have you been giving it."

"Nothing. But we are afraid the nurse has."

"Somebody has been giving it a powerful anodyne, that is certain. This is no natural sleep. Where is the nurse? let me see her."

Jane was sent for, but word was soon brought that she was not to be found. She had, in fact, bundled up her clothes, and hastily and quietly left the house. This confirmed the worst fears of both parents and physician. But, if any doubt remained, a vial of laudanum and a spoon, found in the washstand drawer in Jane's room, dispelled it.

The most prompt and active treatment was resorted to by Doctor B—— in the hope of saving the child. But his anxious efforts were in vain. The deadly narcotic had taken entire possession of the whole system; had, in fact, usurped the seat of life, and was poisoning its very fountain. At day dawn on the next morning the flickering lamp went out, and the sad parents looked their last look upon their living child.

"I have heard most dreadful news," Mrs. May said to her husband, on his return home that day.

"You have! What is it?"

"Jane has poisoned Mrs. Campbell's child!"

"Ella!" and Mr. May started from his chair.

"It is true. She had it to wean, and gave it such a dose of laudanum, that it died."

"Dreadful! What have they done with her?"

"She can't be found, I am told."

"You recommended her to Mrs. Campbell."

"Yes. But I didn't believe she was wicked enough for that."

"Though it is true she ill-treated little Charley, and ve knew it. I don't see how you can ever forgive your-elf. I am sure that I don't feel like ever again looking Mr. Campbell in the face."

"But, Mr. May, you know very well that you didn't want me to say any thing against Jane to hurt her character."

"True. And it is hard to injure a poor fellow crea-ture by blazoning her faults about. But I had no idea that Jane was such a wretch!"

"We knew that she would steal, and that she was unkind to children ; and yet, we agreed to recommend her to Mrs. Campbell."

"But it was purely out of kind feelings for the girl, Ella."

"Yes. But is that genuine kindness? Is it real charity? I fear not."

Mr. May was silent. The questions probed him to the quick. Let every one who is good-hearted in the sense that Mr. May was, ask seriously the same ques-tions.

"You D better take the whole case. These goods will sell as fast as they can be measured off."

The young man to whom this was said by the polite and active partner in a certain jobbing house in Philadelphia, shook his head and replied firmly—

"No, Mr. Johnson. Three pieces are enough for my sales. If they go off quickly, I can easily get more."

"I don't know about that, Mr. Watson," replied the jobber. "I shall be greatly mistaken if we have a case of these goods left by the end of a week. Every on who looks at them, buys. Miller bought two whole cases this morning. In the origina packages, we sell them at a half cent per yard lower than by the piece."

"If they are gone, I can buy something else," said the cautious purchaser.

"Then you won't let me sell you a case?"

" No, sir."

" You buy too cautiously," said Johnson.

" Do you think so ?"

" I know so.   The fact is, I can sell some of your neighbors as much in an hour as I can sell you in a week.   We jobbers would starve if there were no more active men in the_trade than you are, friend Watson."

Watson smiled in a quiet, self-satisfied way as he replied—

" The number of wholesale dealers might be diminished ; but failures among them would be of less frequent occurrence.   Slow and sure, is my motto."

" Slow and sure don't make much headway in these times.   Enterprise is the word.   A man has to be swift-footed to keep up with the general movement."

" I don't expect to get rich in a day," said Watson.

" You'll hardly be disappointed in your expectation," remarked Johnson, a little sarcastically.   His customer did not notice the feeling his tones expressed, but went on to select a piece or two of goods, here and there from various packages, as the styles happened to suit him.

" Five per cent off for cash, I suppose," said Watson, after completing his purchase.

" Oh, certainly," replied the dealer.   " Do you wish to cash the bill ?"

" Yes ; I wish to do a cash business as far as I can. It is rather slow work at first ; but it is safest, and sure to come out right in the end."

" You're behind the times, Watson," said Johnson, shaking his head. " Tell me—who can do the most profitable business, a man with a capital of five thousand dollars, or a man with twenty thousand ?"

" The latter, of course."

" Very well. Don't you understand that credit is capital ?"

" It isn't cash capital."

" What is the difference, pray, between the profit on ten thousand dollars' worth of goods purchased on time or purchased for cash ?"

" Just five hundred dollars," said Watson.

" How do you make that out ?" The jobber did not see the meaning of his customer.

" You discount five per cent. for cash, don't you ?" replied Watson, smiling.

" True. But, if you don't happen to have the ten thousand dollars cash, at the time you wish to make a purchase, don't you see what an advantage credit gives you ? Estimate the profit at twenty per cent. on a cash purchase, and your credit enables you to make fifteen per cent. where you would have made nothing."

" All very good theory," said Watson. " It looks

beautiful on paper. Thousands have figured themselves out rick in this way, but, alas! discovered themselves poor in the end. If all would work just right—if the thousands of dollars of goods bought on credit would invariably sell at good profit and in time to meet the purchase notes, then your credit business would be first rate. But, my little observation tells me that this isn't always the case—that your large credit men are forever on the street, money hunting, instead of in their stores looking after their business. Instead of getting discounts that add to their profits, they are constantly suffering discounts of the other kind; and, too often, these, and the accumulating stock of unsaleable goods —the consequence of credit temptations in purchasing —reduce the fifteen per cent. you speak of down to ten, and even five per cent. A large business makes large store-expenses; and these eat away a serious amount of small profits on large sales. Better sell twenty thousand dollars' worth of goods at twenty per cent. profit, than eighty thousand at five per cent. You can do it with less labor, less anxiety, and at less cost for rent and clerk hire. At least, Mr. Johnson, this is my mode of reasoning."

"Well, plod along," replied Johnson. "Little boats keep near the shore. But, let me tell you, my young friend, your mind is rather too limited for a merchant

of this day. There is Mortimer, who began business
about the time you did. How much do you think he
has made by a good credit ?"

"I'm sure I don't know."

"Fifty thousand dollars."

"And by the next turn of fortune's wheel, may lose
it all."

"Not he. Mortimer, though young, is too shrewd a
merchant for that. Do you know that he made ten
thousand by the late rise in cotton; and all without
touching a dollar in his business ?"

"I heard something of it. But, suppose prices had
receded instead of advancing ? What of this good
credit, then ?"

"You're too timid—too prudent, Watson," said the
merchant, "and will be left behind in the race for prosperity by men of half your ability."

"No matter; I will be content," was the reply of
Watson.

It happened, a short time after this little interchange
of views on business matters, that Watson met the
daughter of Mr. Johnson in a company where he
chanced to be. She was an accomplished and interesting young woman, and pleased Watson particularly; and it is but truth to say, that she was equally well
pleased with him.

The father, who was present, saw, with a slight feel·
ing of disapprobation, the lively conversation that
passed between the young man and his daughter ; and
when an occasion offered, a day or two afterwards,
made it a point to refer to him in a way to give the
impression that he held him in light estimation.
Flora, that was the daughter's name, did not appear to
notice his remark.   One evening, not long after this, as
the family of Mr. Johnson were about leaving the tea-
table, where they had remained later than usual, a
domestic announced that there was a gentleman in the
parlor.

"Who is it ?" inquired Flora.

"Mr. Mortimer," was answered.

An expression of dislike came into the face of Flora,
as she said—

"He didn't ask for me ?"

"Yes," was the servant's reply.

"Tell him that I'm engaged, Nancy."

"No, no !" said Mr. Johnson, quickly.   "This
would not be right.   *Are* you engaged ?"

"That means, father, that I don't wish to see him ;
and he will so understand me."

"Don't wish to see him ?   Why not ?"

"Because I don't like him."

"Don't like him?" Mr. Johnson's manner was slightly impatient. "Perhaps you don't know him."

The way in which her father spoke, rather embarrassed Flora. She cast down her eye and stood for a few moments.

"Tell Mr. Mortimer that I will see him in a little while," she then said, and, as the domestic retired to give the answer, she ascended to her chamber to make some slight additions to her toilet.

To meet the young man by constraint, as it were, was only to increase in Flora's mind the dislike she had expressed. So coldly and formally was Mortimer received, that he found his visit rather unpleasant than agreeable, and retired, after sitting an hour, somewhat puzzled as to the real estimation in which he was held by the lady, for whom he felt more than a slight preference.

Mr. Johnson was very much inclined to estimate others by a money-standard of valuation. A man was a man, in his eyes, when he possessed those qualities of mind that would enable him to make his way in the world—in other words, to get rich. It was this ability in Mortimer that elevated him in his regard, and produced a feeling of pleasure when he saw him inclined to pay attention to his daughter. And it was the apparent want of this ability in Watson, that caused him to be lightly esteemed.

Men like Mr. Johnson are never very wise in their estimates of character; nor do they usually adopt the best means of attaining their ends when they meet with opposition. This was illustrated in the present case. Mortimer was frequently referred to in the presence of Flora, and praised in the highest terms; while the bare mention of Watson's name was sure to occasion a series of disparaging remarks. The effect was just the opposite of what was intended. The more her father said in favor of the thrifty young merchant, the stronger was the repugnance felt towards him by Flora; and the more he had to say against Watson, the better she liked him. This went on until there came a formal application from Mortimer for the hand of Flora. It was made to Mr. Johnson first, who replied to the young man that if he could win the maiden's favor, he had his full approval. But to win the maiden's favor was not so easy a task, as the young man soon found. His offered hand was firmly declined.

"Am I to consider your present decision as final?" said the young man, in surprise and disappointment.

"I wish you to do so, Mr. Mortimer," said Flora.

"Your father approves my suit," said he. "I have his full consent to make you this offer of my hand."

"I cannot but feel flattered at your preference," returned Flora; "but, to accept your offer, would not be just either to you or myself. I, therefore, wish you to understand me as being entirely in earnest."

This closed the interview and definitely settled the question. When Mr. Johnson learned that the offer of Mortimer had been declined, he was very angry with his daughter, and, in the passionate excitement of his feelings, committed a piece of folly for which he felt an immediate sense of shame and regret.

The interview between Mr. Mortimer and Flora took place during the afternoon, and Mr. Johnson learned the result from a note received from the disappointed young man, just as he was about leaving his store to return home. Flora did not join the family at the tea-table, on that evening, for her mind was a good deal disturbed, and she wished to regain her calmness and self-possession before meeting her father.

Mr. Johnson was sitting in a moody and angry state of mind about an hour after supper, when a domestic came into the room and said that Mr. Watson was in the parlor.

"What does he want here?" asked Mr. Johnson, in a rough, excited voice.

"He asked for Miss Flora," returned the servant.

"Where is she?"

"In her room."

"Well, let her stay there. I'll see him myself."

And without taking time for reflection, Mr. Johnson descended to the parlor.

"Mr. Watson," said he, coldly, as the young man arose and advanced towards him.

His manner caused the visitor to pause, and let the hand he had extended fall to his side.

"Well, what is your wish?" asked Mr. Johnson. He looked with knit brows into Watson's face.

"I have called to see your daughter Flora," returned the young man, calmly.

"Then, I wish you to understand that your call is not agreeable," said the father of the young lady, with great rudeness of manner.

"Not agreeable to whom?" asked Watson, manifesting no excitement.

"Not agreeable to me," replied Mr. Johnson. "Nor greeable to any one in this house."

"Do you speak for your daughter?" inquired the young man.

"I have a right to speak for her, if any one has," was the evasive answer.

12

Watson bowed respectfully, and, without a word more, retired from the house.

The calm dignity with which he had received the rough treatment of Mr. Johnson, rebuked the latter, and added a feeling of shame to his other causes of mental disquietude.

On the next day Flora received a letter from Watson, in part in these words—

"I called, last evening, but was not so fortunate as to see you. Your father met me in the parlor, and on learning that my visit was to you, desired me not to come again. This circumstance makes it imperative on me to declare what might have been sometime longer delayed—my sincere regard for you. If you feel towards me as your father does, then I have not a word more to say; but I do not believe this, and, therefore, I cannot let his disapproval, in a matter so intimately concerning my happiness, and it may be yours, influence me to the formation of a hasty decision. I deeply regret your father's state of feeling. His full approval of my suit, next to yours, I feel to be in every way desirable.

"But, why need I multiply words? Again, I declare that I feel for you a sincere affection. If you can return this, say so with as little delay as possible; and if you cannot, be equally frank with me."

Watson did not err in his belief that Flora recipro-
cated his tender sentiments ; nor was he kept long in
suspense. She made an early reply, avowing her own
attachment, but urging him, for her sake, to do all in his
power to overcome her father's prejudices. But this
was no easy task. In the end, however, Mr. Johnson,
who saw, too plainly, that opposition on his part would
be of no avail, yielded a kind of forced consent that the
plodding, behind-the-age young merchant, should lead
Flora to the altar. That his daughter should be content
with such a man, was to him a source of deep mortification. His own expectations in regard to her had been
of a far higher character.

"He'll never set the world on fire ;" "A man of no
enterprise ;" "A dull plodder ;" with similar allusions
to his son-in-law, were overheard by Mr. Johnson on
the night of the wedding party, and added no little to
the ill-concealed chagrin from which he suffered. They
were made by individuals who belonged to the new
school of business men, of whom Mortimer was a
representative. He, too, was present. His disappointment in not obtaining the hand of Flora, had been
solaced in the favor of one whose social standing and
money-value was regarded as considerably above that
of the maiden who had declined the offer of his hand.
He saw Flora given to another without a feeling of regret.

A few months afterwards, he married the daughter of a gentleman who considered himself fortunate in obtaining a son-in-law that promised to be one of the richest men in the city.

It was with a very poor grace that Mr. Johnson bore his disappointment; so poor, that he scarcely treated the husband of his daughter with becoming respect. To add to his uncomfortable feelings by contrast, Mortimer built himself a splendid dwelling almost beside the modest residence of Mr. Watson, and after furnishing it in the most costly and elegant style, gave a grand entertainment. Invitations to this were not extended to either Mr. Johnson's family or to that of his son-in-law—an omission that was particularly galling to the former.

A few weeks subsequent to this, Mr. Johnson stood beside Mr. Watson in an auction room. To the latter a sample of new goods, just introduced, was knocked down, and when asked by the auctioneer how many cases he would take, he replied "Two."

"Say ten," whispered Mr. Johnson in his ear.

"Two cases are enough for my sales," quietly returned the young man.

"But they're a great bargain. You can sell them at an advance," urged Mr. Johnson

"Perhaps so. But I'd rather not go out of my regular line of business."

By this time, the auctioneer's repeated question of "Who'll take another case?" had been responded to by half a dozen voices, and the lot of goods was gone.

"You're too prudent," said Mr. Johnson, with some impatience in his manner.

"No," replied the young man, with his usual calm tone and quiet smile. "Slow and sure—that is my motto. I only buy the quantity of an article that I am pretty sure will sell. Then I get a certain profit, and am not troubled with paying for goods that are lying on my shelves and depreciating in value daily."

"But these wouldn't have lain on your shelves. You could have sold them at a quarter of a cent advance to-morrow, and thus cleared sixty or seventy dollars."

"That is mere speculation."

"Call it what you will; it makes no difference. The chance of making a good operation was before you, and you did not improve it. You will never get along at your snail's pace."

There was, in the voice of Mr. Johnson, a tone of contempt that stung Watson more than any previous remark or action of his father-in-law. Thrown, for a moment, off his guard, he replied with some warmth—

" You may be sure of one thing, at least."

" What ?"

" That I shall never embarrass you with any of my fine operations."

" What do you mean by that ?" asked Mr. Johnson.

" Time will explain the remark," replied Watson, turning away, and retiring from the auction room.

A coolness of some months was the consequence of this little interview.

Time proves all things. At the end of fifteen years, Mortimer, who had gone on in the way he had begun, was reputed to be worth two hundred thousand dollars. Every thing he touched turned to money; at least, so it appeared. His whole conversation was touching handsome operations in trade; and not a day passed in which he had not some story of gains to tell. Yet, with all his heavy accumulations, he was always engaged in money raising, and his line of discounts was enormous. Such a thing as proper attention to business was almost out of the question, for nearly his whole time was taken up in financiering—and some of his financial schemes were on a pretty grand scale. Watson, on the other hand, had kept plodding along in the old way, making his regular business purchases, and gradually extending his operations, as his profits, changing into capital, enabled him to do so. He was not anxious to get rich fast; at least, not so anxious as to suffer himself to be tempted from a safe and prudent course; and was, therefore, content to do well. By this time, his father-in-law began to understand him a little better than at first, and to appreciate him more highly. On more than one occasion, he had been in want of a few thousand dollars in an emergency, when the check of Watson promptly supplied the pressing need.

As to the real ability of Watson, few were apprised, for he never made a display for the sake of establishing a credit. But it was known to some, that he generally had a comfortable balance in the bank, and to others that he never exchanged notes, nor asked an endorser on his business paper. He always purchased for cash, and thus obtained his goods from five to seven per cent cheaper than his neighbors; and rarely put his business paper in bank for discount at a longer date than sixty days. Under this system, his profits were, usually, ten per cent. more than the profits of many who were engaged in the same branch of trade. His credit was so good, that the bank where he kept his account readily gave him all the money he asked on his regular paper, without requiring other endorsements; while many of his more dashing neighbors, who were

doing half as much business again, were often obliged
to go upon the street to raise money at from one to
two per cent. a month. Moreover, as he was always
to be found at his store, and ready to give his personal
attention to customers, he was able to make his own
discriminations and to form his own estimates of men
—and these were generally correct. The result of this
was, that he gradually attracted a class of dealers who
were substantial men ; and, in consequence, was little
troubled with bad sales.

Up to this time, there had been but few changes in
the external domestic arrangements of Mr. Watson.
He had moved twice, and, each time, into a larger
house. His increasing family made this necessary.
But, while all was comfortable and even elegant in his
dwelling, there was no display whatever.

One day, about this period, as Watson was walking
with his father-in-law, they both paused to look at a
handsome house that was going up in a fashionable
part of Walnut street. By the side of it was a larg
building lot.

"I have about made up my mind to buy this lot,"
remarked Watson.

"You ?" Mr. Johnson spoke in a tone of surprise.

"Yes. The price is ten thousand dollars. Rather
nigh ; but I like the location."

"What will you do with it?" inquired Mr. Johnson

"Build upon it."

"As an investment?"

"No. I want a dwelling for myself."

"Indeed! I was not aware that you had any such intentions."

"Oh, yes. I have always intended to build a house so soon as I felt able to do it according to m, own fancy."

Mr. Johnson felt a good deal surprised at this. No more was said, and the two men walked on.

"How's this? For sale!" said Mr. Johnson. They were opposite the elegant dwelling of Mr. Mortimer, upon which was posted a hand-bill setting forth that the property was for sale.

"So it seems," was Watson's quiet answer.

"Why should he sell out?" added Mr. Johnson. "Perhaps he is going to Europe to make a tour with his family," he suggested.

"It is more probable," said Watson, "that he has got to the end of his rope."

"What do you mean by that remark?"

"Is obliged to sell in order to save himself."

"Oh, no! Mortimer is rich."

"So it is said. But I never call a man rich whose

12*

paper is floating about by thousands on the street seeking purchasers at two per cent. a month."

Just then the carriage of Mortimer drove up to his loor, and Mrs. Mortimer descended to the pavement nd passed into the house. Her face was pale, and had a look of deep distress. It was several years since Mr. Johnson remembered to have seen her, and he was alr ... startled at the painful change which had taken place.

A little while afterwards he looked upon the cheerful, smiling face of his daughter Flora, and there arose in his heart, almost involuntarily, an emotion of thankfulness that she was not the wife of Mortimer. Could he have seen what passed a few hours afterwards, in the dwelling of the latter, he would have been more thankful than ever.

It was after eleven o'clock when Mortimer returned home that night. He had been away since morning. It was rarely that he dined with his family, but usually came home early in the evening. Since seven o'clock, he tea-table had been standing in the floor, awaiting nis return. At eight o'clock, as he was still absent, supper was served to the children, who, soon after, retired for the night. It was after eleven o'clock as we have said, before Mortimer returned. His face was pale and haggard. He entered quietly, by means of his night-key, and went noiselessly up to his chamber. He found his wife lying across the bed, where, wearied with watching, she had thrown herself and fallen asleep. For a few moments he stood looking at her, with a face in which agony and affection were blended. Then he clasped his hands suddenly against his temples, and groaned aloud. That groan penetrated the ears of his sleeping wife, who started up with an exclamation of alarm, as her eyes saw the gesture and expression of her husband.

"Oh, Henry! what is the matter? Where have you been? Why do you look so?" she eagerly inquired.

Mortimer did not reply; but continued standing like a statue of despair.

"Henry! Henry!" cried his wife, springing towards him, and laying her hands upon his arm. "Dear husband! what is the matter?"

"Ruined! Ruined!" now came hoarsely from the lips of Mortimer, and, with another deep groan, he threw himself on a sofa, and wrung his hands in uncontrollable anguish.

"Oh, Henry! speak! What does this mean?" said his wife, the tears now gushing from her eyes. "Tell me what has happened."

But, "Ruined! Ruined!" was all the wretched

man would say for a long time. At last, however, he
made a few vague explanations, to the effect that he
would be compelled to stop payment on the next day.

"I thought," said Mrs. Mortimer, "that the sale of
this house was to afford you all the money you
needed ?"

"It is not sold yet," was all his reply to this. He
did not explain that it was under a heavy mortgage,
and that, even if sold, the amount realized would be a
trifle compared with his need on the following day.

During the greater part of the night, Mortimer
walked the floor of his chamber; and, for a portion of
the time, his wife moved like a shadow by his side.
But few words passed between them.

When the day broke, Mrs. Mortimer was lying on
the bed, asleep. Tears were on her cheeks. In a crib,
beside her, was a fair-haired child, two years old,
breathing sweetly in his innocent slumber; and over
this crib bent the husband and father. His face was
now calm, but very pale, and its expression of sadness
as he gazed upon his sleeping child, was heart-touching.
For many minutes he stood over the unconscious slum-
berer; then stooping down, he touched its forehead
lightly with his lips, while a low sigh struggled up
from his bosom. Turning, then, his eyes upon his
wife, he gazed at her for some moments, with a sad,

pitying look. He was bending to kiss her, when a movement, as if she were about to awaken, caused him to step back, and stand holding his breath, as, if he feared the very sound would disturb her. She did not open her eyes, however, but turned over, with a low moan of suffering, and an indistinct murmur of his name.

Mortimer did not again approach the bed-side, but stepped noiselessly to the chamber door, and passed into the next room, where three children, who made up the full number of his household treasures, were buried in tranquil sleep. Long he did not linger here. A hurried glance was taken of each beloved face, and a kiss laid lightly upon the lips of each. Then he left the room, moving down the stairs with a step of fear. A moment or two more, and he was beyond the threshold of his dwelling.

When Mrs. Mortimer started up from unquiet slumber, as the first beams of the morning sun fell upon her face, she looked around, eagerly, for her husband. Not seeing him, she called his name. No answer was received, and she sprung from the bed. As she did so, a letter placed conspicuously on the bureau met her eyes. Eagerly breaking the seal, she read this brief sentence :

" Circumstances make it necessary for me to leave

the city by the earliest conveyance. Say not a word
of this to any one—not even to your father. My
safety depends on your silence. I will write to you in
a little while. May Heaven give you strength to bea
the trials through which you are about to pass !"

But for the instant fear for her husband, which this
communication brought into the mind of Mrs. Mortimer, the shock would have rendered her insensible.
He was in danger, and upon her discretion depended
his safety. This gave her strength for the moment.
Her first act was to destroy the note. Next she strove
to repress the wild throbbings of her heart, and to
assume a calm exterior. Vain efforts ! She was too
weak for the trial ; and who can wonder that she was !

Mr. Johnson was sitting in his store about half past
three o'clock that afternoon, when a man came in and
asked him for the payment of a note of five thousand
dollars. He was a Notary.

"A protest !" exclaimed Mr. Johnson, in astonish-
ment. " What does this mean ?"

" I don't understand this," said he, after a momen
or two. " I have no paper out for that amount falling
due to-day. Let me see it ?"

The note was handed to him.

"It's a forgery !" said he, promptly. " To whom is
it payable ?" he added. " To Mortimer, as I live !"

And he handed it back to the Notary, who departed.

Soon after he saw the father-in-law of Mortimer go hurriedly past his store. A glimpse of his countenance showed that he was strongly agitated.

"Have you heard the news?" asked his son-in-law, coming in, half an hour afterwards.

"What?" ˉ

"Mortimer has been detected in a forgery!"

"Upon whom?"

"His father-in-law."

"He has forged my name also."

"He has!"

"Yes. A note for five thousand dollars was presented to me by the Notary a little while ago."

"Is it possible? But this is no loss to you."

"If he has resorted to forgery to sustain himself," replied Mr. Johnson, looking serious, "his affairs are, of course, in a desperate condition."

"Of course."

"I am on his paper to at least twenty thousand dollars."

"You!"

"Such, I am sorry to say, is the case. And to meet that paper will try me severely. Oh, dear! How little I dreamed of this! I thought him one of the soundest men in the city."

"I am pained to hear that you are so deeply involved," said Mr. Watson. "But, do not let it trouble you too much. I will defer my building intentions to another time, and let you have whatever money you may need."

Mr. Johnson made no answer. His eyes were upon the floor, and his thoughts away back to the time when he had suffered the great disappointment of seeing his daughter marry the slow, plodding Watson, instead of becoming the wife of the enterprising Mortimer.

"I will try, my son," said he, at length, in a subdued voice, "to get through without drawing upon you too largely. Ah, me! How blind I have been."

"You may depend on me for at least twenty thousand dollars," replied Watson, cheerfully; "and for even more, if it is needed."

It was soon known that Mortimer had committed extensive forgeries upon various persons, and that he had left the city. Officers were immediately despatched for his arrest, and in a few days he was brought back as a criminal. In his ruin, many others were involved. Among these was his father-in-law, who was stripped of every dollar in his old age.

"Slow and sure—slow and sure. Yes, Watson was right." Thus mused Mr. Johnson, a few months afterwards, on hearing that Mortimer was arraigned before the criminal court, to stand his trial for forgery. "It is the safest and the best way, and certainly leads to prosperity. Ah, me! How are we drawn aside into false ways through our eagerness to obtain wealth by a nearer road than that of patient industry in legitimate trade. Where one is successful, a dozen are ruined by this error. Slow and sure! Yes, that is the true doctrine. Watson was right, as the result has proved. Happy for me that his was a better experiment than that of the envied Mortimer !"

THE SCHOOL GIRL.

"WHERE now?" said Frederick Williams to his friend Charles Lawson, on entering his own office and finding the latter, carpet-bag in hand, awaiting his arrival.

"Off for a day or two on a little business affair," replied Lawson.

"Business! What have you to do with business?"

"Not ordinary, vulgar business," returned Lawson with a slight toss of the head and an expression of contempt.

"Oh! It's of a peculiar nature?"

"It is—very peculiar; and, moreover, I want the good offices of a friend, to enable me the more certainly to accomplish my purposes."

"Come! sit down and explain yourself," said Williams.

"Havn't a moment to spare. The boat goes in half an hour."

"What boat ?"

"The New Haven boat. So come, go along with me to the slip, and we'll talk the matter over by th way."

"I'm all attention," said Williams, as the two young men stepped forth upon the pavement.

"Well, you must know," began Lawson, "that I have a first rate love affair on my hands."

"You !"

"Now don't smile ; but hear me."

"Go on—I'm all attention."

"You know old Everett ?"

"Thomas Everett, the silk importer ?"

"The same."

"I know something about him."

"You know, I presume, that he has a pretty fair looking daughter ?"

"And I know," replied Williams, "that when ' pret ty fair looking' is said, pretty much all is said in hei favor."

"Not by a great deal," was the decided answer of Lawson.

"Pray what is there beyond this that a man can call attractive ?"

"Her father's money."

"I didn't think of that."

"Didn't you?"

"No. But it would take the saving influence of a pretty large sum to give her a marriageable merit in my eyes."

"Gold hides a multitude of defects, you know, Fred."

"It does; but it has to be heaped up very high to cover a wife's defects, if they be as radical as those in Caroline Everett. Why, to speak out the plain, home-spun truth, the girl's a fool!"

"She isn't over bright, Fred, I know," replied Law-son. "But to call her a fool, is to use rather a broad assertion."

"She certainly hasn't good common sense. I would be ashamed of her in company a dozen times a day if she were any thing to me."

"She's young, you know, Fred."

"Yes, a young and silly girl."

"Just silly enough for my purpose. But, she will grow older and wiser, you know. Young and silly is a very good fault."

"Where is she now?"

"At a boarding school some thirty miles from New Haven. Do you know why her father sent her there?"

"No."

" She would meet me on her way to and from school while in the city, and the old gentleman had, I presume, some objections to me as a son-in-law."

" And not without reason," replied Williams.

" I could not have asked him to do a thing more consonant with my wishes," continued Lawson. " Caroline told me where she was going, and I was not long in making a visit to the neighborhood. Great attention is paid to physical development in the school, and the young ladies are required to walk, daily, in the open air, amid the beautiful, romantic, and secluded scenery by which the place is surrounded. They walk alone, or in company, as suits their fancies. Caroline chose to walk alone when I was near at hand ; and we met in a certain retired glen, where the sweet quiet of nature was broken only by the dreamy murmur of a silvery stream, and there we talked of love. It is not in the heart of a woman to withstand a scene like this. I told, in burning words, my passion, and she hearkened and was won " Lawson paused for some moments ; but, as Williams made no remark, he continued—

" It is hopeless to think of gaining her father's consent to a marriage. He is pence-proud, and I, as you know, am penniless."

" I do not think he would be likely to fancy you for a son-in-law," said Williams.

"I have the best of reasons for knowing that he would not. He has already spoken of me to his daughter in very severe terms."

"As she has informed you?"

"Yes. But, like a sensible girl, she prefers consulting her own taste in matters of the heart."

"A very sensible girl, certainly!"

"Isn't she! Well, as delays are dangerous, I have made up my mind to consummate this business as quickly as possible. You know how hard pressed I am in certain quarters, and how necessary it is that I should get my pecuniary matters in a more stable position. In a word, then, my business, on the present occasion, is to remove Caroline from school, it being my opinion that she has completed her education."

"Has she consented to this?"

"No; but she won't require any great persuasion. I'll manage all that. What I want you to do is, first, to engage me rooms at Howard's, and, second, to meet me at the boat, day after to-morrow, with a carriage."

"Where will you have the ceremony performed?"

"In this city. I have already engaged the Rev. Mr. B—— to do that little work for me. He will join us at the hotel immediately on our arrival, and in your presence, as a witness, the knot will be tied."

"All very nicely arranged," said Williams.

"Isn't it! And what is more, the whole thing will go off like clock work. Of course I can depend on you. You will meet us at the boat."

"I will, certainly."

"Then good by." They were by this time at the landing. The two young men shook hands, and Lawson sprung on board of the boat, while Williams returned thoughtfully to his office.

Charles Lawson was a young man having neither principle nor character. A connection with certain families in New York, added to a good address, polished manners, and an unblushing assurance, had given him access to society at certain points, and of this facility he had taken every advantage. Too idle and dissolute for useful effort in society, he looked with a cold, calculating baseness to marriage as the means whereby he was to gain the position at which he aspired. Possessing no attractive virtues—no personal merits of any kind, his prospects of a connection, such as he wished to form, through the medium of any honorable advan-s, were hopeless, and this he perfectly well understood. But, the conviction did not in the least abate the ardor of his purpose. And, in a mean and dastardly spirit, he approached one young school girl after another, until he found in Caroline Everett one weak enough to be flattered by his attentions. The father of Caroline, who was a man of some discrimination and force of mind, understood his daughter's character, and knowing the danger to which she was exposed, kept upon her a watchful eye. Caroline's meetings with Lawson were not continued long before he became aware of the fact, and he at once removed her to a school at a distance from the city. It would have been wiser had he taken her home altogether. Lawson could have desired no better arrangement, so far as his wishes were concerned.

On the day succeeding that on which Lawson left New York, Caroline was taking her morning walk with two or three companions. when she. noticed a mark on a certain tree, which she knew as a sign that her lover was in the neighborhood and awaiting her in the secluded glen, half a mile distant, where they had already met. Feigning to have forgotten something, she ran back, but as soon as she was out of sight of her companions, she glided off with rapid steps in the direction where she expected to find Lawson. And she was not disappointed.

"Dear Caroline!" he exclaimed, with affected tenderness, drawing his arm about her and kissing her cheek, as he met her. "How happy I am to see you again! Oh! it has seemed months since I looked upon your sweet young face."

"And yet it is only a week since you were here," returned Caroline, looking at him fondly.

"I cannot bear this separation. It makes me wretched," said Lawson.

"And I am miserable," responded Caroline, with a sigh, and her eyes fell to the ground. "Miserable," she repeated.

"I love you, tenderly, devotedly," said Lawson, as he tightly clasped the hand he had taken : "and it is my most ardent wish to make you happy. Oh ! why should a parent's mistaken will interpose between us and our dearest wishes ?"

Caroline leaned toward the young man, but did not reply.

"Is there any hope of his being induced to give his consent to—to—our—union ?"

"None, I fear," came from the lips of Caroline in a faint whisper.

"Is he so strongly prejudiced against me ?"

"Yes."

"Then, what are we to do ?"

Caroline sighed.

"To meet, hopelessly, is only to make us the more wretched," said Lawson. "Better part, and forever, than suffer a martyrdom of affection like this."

Still closer shrunk the weak and foolish girl to the

13

young man's side. She was like a bird in the magic circle of the charmer.

"Caroline," said Lawson, after another period of silence, and his voice was low, tender and penetrating—"Are you willing, for my sake, to brave your father's anger?"

"For your sake, Charles!" replied Caroline, with sudden enthusiasm. "Yes—yes. His anger would be light to the loss of your affection."

"Bless your true heart!" exclaimed Lawson. "I knew that I had not trusted it in vain. And now, my dear girl, let me speak freely of the nature of my present visit. With you, I believe, that all hope of your father's consent is vain. But, he is a man of tender feelings, and loves you as the apple of his eye."

Thus urged the tempter, and Caroline listened eagerly.

"If," he continued, "we precipitate a union—if we put the marriage rite between us and his strong opposition, that opposition will grow weak as a withering leaf. He cannot turn from you. He loves you too well."

Caroline did not answer; but, it needed no words to tell Lawson that he was not urging his wishes in vain.

"I am here," at length he said, boldly, "for the

purpose of taking you to New York. Will you go with me ?"

" For what end ?" she whispered.

" To become my wife."

There was no starting, shrinking, nor trembling at this proposal. Caroline was prepared for it; and, in the blindness of a mistaken love, ready to do as the tempter wished. Poor lamb! She was to be led to the slaughter, decked with ribbons and garlands. a victim by her own consent.

Frederick Williams, the friend of Lawson, was a young attorney, who had fallen into rather wild company, and strayed to some distance along the paths of dissipation. But, he had a young and lovely-minded sister, who possessed much influence over him. The very sphere of her purity kept him from debasing himself to any great extent, and ever drew him back from a total abandonment of himself in the hour of temptation. He had been thrown a good deal into the society of Lawson, who had many attractive points for young men about him, and who knew how to adapt himself to the characters of those with whom he associated. In some things he did not like Lawson, who, at times, manifested such an entire want of principle, that he felt shocked. On parting with Lawson at the boat, as we have seen, he walked

thoughtfully away.   His mind was far from approving
what he had heard, and the more he reflected upon it,
the less satisfied did he feel.   He knew enough of the
character of Lawson to be well satisfied that his
marriage with Caroline, who was an overgrown, weak-
minded school girl, would prove the wreck of her
future happiness, and the thought of becoming a party
to such a transaction troubled him.   On returning to
his office, he found his sister waiting for him, and, as
his eyes rested upon her innocent young countenance,
the idea of her being made the victim of so base a
marriage, flashed with a pang amid his thoughts.

.   " I will have no part nor lot in this matter," he said,
mentally.   And he was in earnest in this resolution.
But not long did his mind rest easy under his assumed
passive relation to a contemplated social wrong, that
one word from him might prevent.   From the thought
of betraying Lawson's confidence, his mind shrunk with
a certain instinct of honor ; while, at the same time,
pressed upon him the irresistible conviction that a
deeper dishonor would attach to him if he permitted
the marriage to take place.

The day passed with him uncomfortably enough.
The more he thought about the matter, the more he
felt troubled.   In the evening he met his sister again,
and the sight of her made him more deeply conscious

of the responsibility resting upon him. His oft repeated mental excuse—"It's none of my business," or, "I can't meddle in other men's affairs," did not satisfy certain convictions of right and duty that presented themselves with, to him, a strange distinctness. The thought of his own sister was instantly associated with the scheme of some false-hearted wretch, involving her happiness in the way that the happiness of Caroline Everett was to be involved ; and he felt that the man who knew that another was plotting against her, and did not apprize him of the fact, was little less than a villain at heart.

On the next day Williams learned that there was a writ out against the person of Charles Lawson on a charge of swindling, he having obtained a sum of money from a broker under circumstances construed by the laws into crime. This fact determined him to go at once to Mr. Everett, who, as it might be supposed, was deeply agitated at the painful intelligence he received. His first thought was to proceed immediately to New Haven, and there rescue his daughter from the hands of the young man ; but on learning the arrangements that had been made, he, after much reflection, concluded that it would be best to remain in New York, and meet them on their arrival.

In the mean time, the foolish girl, whom Lawson had

determined to sacrifice to his base cupidity, was half wild with delighted anticipation. Poor child! Passion-wrought romances, written by men and women who had neither right views of life, nor a purpose in literature beyond gain or reputation, had bewildered her half-formed reason, and filled her imagination with unreal pictures. All her ideas were false or exaggerated. She was a woman, with the mind of an inexperienced child; if to say this does not savor of contradiction. Without dreaming that there might be thorns to pierce her naked feet in the way she was about to enter, she moved forward with a joyful confidence.

On the day she had agreed to return with Lawson, she met him early in the afternoon, and started for New Haven, where they spent the night. On the following day they left in the steamboat for New York. All his arrangements for the marriage were fully explained to Caroline by Lawson, and most of the time that elapsed after leaving New Haven, was spent in settling their future action in regard to the family. Caroline was confident that all would be forgiven after the first outburst of anger on the part of her father, and that they would be taken home immediately. The cloud would quickly melt in tears, and then the sky would be purer and brighter than before.

When the boat touched the wharf, Lawson looked eagerly for the appearance of his friend Williams, and was disappointed, and no little troubled, at not seeing him. After most of the passengers had gone on shore he called a carriage, and was driven to Howard's, where he ordered a couple of rooms, after first enquiring whether a friend had not already performed this service for him. His next step was to write a note to the Rev. Mr. B——, desiring his immediate attendance, and, also, one to Williams, informing him of his arrival. Anxiously, and with a nervous fear lest some untoward circumstance might prevent the marriage he was about effecting with a silly heiress, did the young man await the response to these notes, and great was his relief, when informed, after the lapse of an hour, that the Reverend gentleman, whose attendance he had desired, was in the house.

A private parlor had been engaged, and in this the ceremony of marriage was to take place. This parlor adjoined a chamber, in which Caroline awaited, with trembling heart, the issue of events. It was now, fo the first time, as she was about taking the final and irretrievable step, that her resolution began to fail her. Her father's anger, the grief of her mother, the unknown state upon which she was about entering, all came pressing upon her thoughts with a sense of realization such as she had not known before.

Doubts as to the propriety of what she was about oing, came fast upon her mind. In the nearness of the approaching event, she could look upon it stripped of its halo of romance. During the two days that she had been with Lawson, she had seen him in states of absent thought, when the true quality of his mind wrote itself out upon his face so distinctly that even a dim-sighted one could read; and more than once she had felt an inward shrinking from him that was irrepressible. Weak and foolish as she was, she was yet pure-minded; and though in the beginning she did not, because her heart was overlaid with frivolity, perceive the sphere of his impurity, yet now, as the moment was near at hand when there was to be a marriage-conjunction, she began to feel this sphere as something that suffocated her spirit. At length, in the agitation of contending thoughts and emotions, the heart of the poor girl failed her, till, in the utter abandonment of feeling, she gave way to a flood of tears and commenced wringing her hands. At this moment, having arranged with the clergyman to begin the ceremony forthwith, Lawson enteied her room, and, to his surprise, saw her in tears.

"Oh, Charles!" she exclaimed, clasping her hands

and extending them towards him, " Take me home to my father ! Oh, take me home to my father !"

Lawson was confounded at such an unexpected change in Caroline. " You shall go to your father the moment the ceremony is over," he replied ; " Come ! Mr. B—— is all ready."

" Oh, no, no ! Take me now ! Take me now !" returned the poor girl in an imploring voice. And she sat before the man who had tempted her from the path of safety, weeping, and quivering like a leaf in the wind.

" Caroline ! What has come over you !" said Lawson, in deep perplexity. " This is only a weakness. Come ! Nerve your heart like a brave, good girl ! Come ! It will soon be over."

And he bent down and kissed her wet cheek, while she shrunk from him with an involuntary dread. But, he drew his arm around her waist, and almost forced her to rise.

" There now ! Dry your tears !" And he placed his handkerchief to her eyes. " It is but a moment of weakness, Caroline,—of natural weakness."

As he said this, he was pressing her forward towards the door of the apartment where the clergyman (such clergymen disgrace their profession) awaited their appearance.

13*

"Charles!" said Caroline, with a suddenly constrained calmness—"do you love me?"

"Better than my own life!" was instantly replied.

"Then take me to my father. I am too young—too weak—too inexperienced for this."

"The moment we are united you shall go home," returned Lawson. "I will not hold you back an instant."

"Let me go now, Charles! Oh, let me go now!"

"Are you mad, girl!" exclaimed the young man, losing his self-control. And, with a strong arm, he forced her into the next room. For a brief period, the clergyman hesitated, on seeing the distressed bride. Then he opened the book he held in his hand and began to read the service. As his voice, in tones of solemnity, filled the apartment, Caroline grew calmer. She felt like one driven forward by a destiny against which it was vain to contend. All the responses had been made by Lawson, and now the clergyman addressed her. Passively she was about uttering her assentation, when the door of the room was thrown open, and two men entered.

"Stop!" was instantly cried in a loud, agitated voice, which Caroline knew to be that of her father, and never did that voice come to her ears with a more welcome sound.

Lawson started, and moved from her side. While Caroline yet stood trembling and doubting, the man who had come in with Mr. Everett approached Lawson, and laying his hand upon him, said—"I arrest you on a charge of swindling!"

With a low cry of distress, Caroline sprung towards her father; but he held his hands out towards her as if to keep her off, saying, at the same time—

"Are you *his* wife?"

"No, thank Heaven!" fell from her lips.

In the next moment she was in her father's arms, and both were weeping.

Narrow indeed was the escape made by Caroline Everett; an escape which she did not fully comprehend until a few months afterwards, when the trial of Lawson took place, during which revelations of villany were made, the recital of which caused her heart to shudder. Yes, narrow had been her escape! Had her father been delayed a few moments longer, she would have become the wife of a man soon after condemned to expiate his crimes against society in the felon's cell!

May a vivid realization of what Caroline Everett escaped, warn other young girls, who bear a similar relation to society, of the danger that lurks in their way. Not once in a hundred instances, is a school girl approached with lover-like attentions, except by a man who is void of principle; and not once in a hundred instances do marriages entered upon clandestinely by such persons, prove other than an introduction to years of wretchedness.

UNREDEEMED PLEDGES.

Two men were walking along a public thoroughfare in New York. One of them was a young merchant—the other a man past the prime of life, and belonging to the community of Friends. They were in conversation, and the manner of the former, earnest and emphatic, was in marked contrast with the quiet and thoughtful air of the other.

"There is so much idleness and imposture among the poor," said the merchant, "that you never know when your alms are going to do harm or good. The beggar we just passed is able to work ; and that woman sitting at the corner with a sick child in her arms, would be far better off in the almshouse. No man is more willing to give than I am, if I only knew where and when to give."

"If we look around us carefully, Mr. Edwards," re-

turned the Quaker, " we need be at no loss on this subject.   Objects enough will present themselves.   Virtuous want is, in most cases, unobtrusive, and will suffer
rather than extend a hand for relief.   We must seek
or objects of benevolence in by-places.   We must
turn aside into untrodden walks."

"But even then," objected Mr. Edwards, "we cannot be certain that idleness and vice are not at the
basis of the destitution we find.   I have had my doubts
whether any who exercise the abilities which God has
given them, need want for the ordinary comforts of life
in this country.   In all cases of destitution, there is
something wrong, you may depend upon it."

"Perhaps there is," said the Quaker.   "Evil of
some kind is ever the cause of destitution and wretchedness.   Such bitter waters as these cannot flow from a
sweet fountain.   Still, many are brought to suffering
through the evil ways of others ; and many whose own
wrong doings have reacted upon them in unhappy consequences, deeply repent of the past, and earnestly desire to live better lives in future.   Both need kindness,
encouragement, and, it may be, assistance ; and it is the
duty of those who have enough and to spare, to stretch
forth their hands to aid, comfort and sustain them."

"Yes.   That is true.   But, how are we to know who
are the real objects of our benevolence ?"

"We have but to open our eyes and see, Mr. Edwards," said the Quaker. "The objects of benevolence are all around us."

"Show me a worthy object, and you will find me ready to relieve it," returned the merchant. "I am not so selfish as to be indifferent to human suffering. But I think it wrong to encourage idleness and vice; and for this reason, I never give unless I am certain that the object who presents himself is worthy."

"True benevolence does not always require us to give alms," said the Friend. "We may do much to aid, comfort and help on with their burdens our fellow travellers, and yet not bestow upon them what is called charity. Mere alms-giving, as thee has intimated, but too often encourages vice and idleness. But thee desires to find a worthy object of benevolence. Let us see if we cannot find one, What have we here?" And as the Quaker said this he paused before a building, from the door of which protruded a red flag, containing the words, "Auction this day." On a large card just beneath the flag was the announcement, "Positive sale of unredeemed pledges."

"Let us turn in here," said the Quaker. "No doubt we shall find enough to excite our sympathies."

Mr. Edwards thought this a strange proposal; but

he felt a little curious, and followed his companion with out hesitation.

The sale had already begun, and there was a smal company assembled. Among them, the merchant noticed a young woman whose face was partially veiled. She was sitting a little apart from the rest, and did not appear to take any interest in the bidding. But he noticed that, after an article was knocked off, she was all attention until the next was put up, and then, the moment it was named, relapsed into a sort of listlessness or abstraction.

The articles sold embraced a great variety of things useful and ornamental. In the main they were made up of watches, silver plate, jewellery and wearing apparel. There were garments of every kind, quality and condition, upon which money to about a fourth of their real value had been loaned ; and not having been redeemed, they were now to be sold for the benefit of the pawnbroker.

The company bid with animation, and article after article was sold off. The interest at first awakened by the scene, new to the young merchant, wore off in a little while, and turning to his companion he said—

" I don't see that much is to be gained by staying here."

" Wait a little longer, an l perhaps thee will think

differently," returned the Quaker, glancing towards the young woman who has been mentioned, as he spoke.

The words had scarcely passed his lips, when the auctioneer took up a small gold locket containing a miniature, and holding it up, asked for a bid.

"How much for this? How much for this beautiful gold locket and miniature! Give me a bid. Ten dollars! Eight dollars! Five dollars! Four dollars—why, gentlemen, it never cost less than fifty! Four dollars! Four dollars! Will no one give four dollars for this beautiful gold locket and miniature? It's thrown away at that price."

At the mention of the locket, the young woman came forward and looked up anxiously at the auctioneer. Mr. Edwards could see enough of her face to ascertain that it was an interesting and intelligent one, though very sad.

"Three dollars!" continued the auctioneer. But there was no bid. "Two dollars! One dollar!"

"One dollar," was the response from a man who stood just in front of the woman. Mr. Edwards, whose eyes were upon the latter, noticed that she became much agitated the moment this bid was made.

"One dollar we have! One dollar! Only one dollar!" cried the auctioneer. "Only one dollar for a gold locket and miniature worth forty. One dollar!"

"Nine shillings," said the young woman in a low timid voice.

"Nine shillings bid! Nine shillings! Nine shilings!"

"Ten shillings," said the first bidder.

"Ten shillings it is! Ten shillings, and thrown away. Ten shillings!"

"Eleven shillings," said the girl, beginning to grow excited. Mr. Edwards, who could not keep his eyes off of her face, from which the veil had entirely fallen, saw that she was trembling with eagerness and anxiety.

"Eleven shillings!" repeated the auctioneer, glancing at the first bidder, a coarse-looking man, and the only one who seemed disposed to bid against the young woman.

"Twelve shillings," said the man resolutely.

A paleness went over the face of the other bidder, and a quick tremor passed through her frame.

"Twelve shillings is bid. Twelve shillings is bid. Twelve shillings!" And the auctioneer now looked owards the young woman who, in a faint voice, said—

"Thirteen shillings."

By this time the merchant began to understand the meaning of what was passing before him. The miniature was that of a middle-aged lady; and it required no great strength of imagination to determine that the original was the mother of the young woman who seemed so anxious to possess the locket.

"But how came it here?" was the involuntary suggestion to the mind of Mr. Edwards. "Who pawned it? Did she?"

"Fourteen shillings," said the man who was bidding, breaking in upon the reflections of Mr. Edwards.

The veil that had been drawn aside, fell instantly over the face of the young woman, and she shrunk back from her prominent position, yet still remained in the room.

"Fourteen shillings is bid. Fourteen shillings! Are you all done? Fourteen shillings for a gold locket and miniature. Fourteen! Once!———"

The companion of Mr. Edwards glanced towards him with a meaning look. The merchant, for a moment bewildered, found his mind clear again.

"Twice!" screamed the auctioneer. "Once! Twice! Three———"

"Twenty shillings," dropped from the lips of Mr. Edwards.

"Twenty shillings! Twenty shillings!" cried the auctioneer with renewed animation. The man who had been bidding against the girl turned quickly to see what bold bidder was in the field: and most of the company turned with him. The young woman at the same time drew aside her veil and looked anxiously towards Mr. Edwards, who, as he obtained a fuller view of her face, was struck with it as familiar.

" Twenty-one shillings," was bid in opposition.

" Twenty-five," said the merchant, promptly.

The first bidder, seeing that Mr. Edwards was determined to run against him, and being a little afraid that he might be left with a ruinous bid on his hands, declined advancing, and the locket was assigned to the young merchant, who, as soon as he had received it, turned and presented it to the young woman, saying as he did so—

" It is yours."

The young woman caught hold of it with an eager gesture, and after gazing on it for a few moments, pressed it to her lips.

" I have not the money to pay for it," she said in a low sad voice, recovering herself in a few moments, and seeking to return the miniature.

" It is yours!" replied Mr. Edwards.   Then thrusting back the hand she had extended, and speaking with some emotion, he said—"Keep it—keep it, in Heaven's name !"

And saying this he hastily retired, for he became conscious that many eyes were upon him ; and he felt half ashamed to have betrayed his weakness before a

coarse, unfeeling crowd. For a few moments he lingered in the street; but his companion not appearing, he
went on his way, musing on the singular adventure he
had encountered. The more distinctly he recalled the
young woman's face, the more strangely familiar did it
seem.

About an hour afterwards, as Mr. Edwards sat reading a letter, the Quaker entered his store.

" Ah, how do you do? I am glad to see you," said
the merchant, his manner more than usually earnest.
" Did you see anything more of that young woman?"

" Yes," replied the Quaker. " I could not leave one
like her without knowing something of her past life and
present circumstances. I think even you will hardly be
disposed to regard her as an object unworthy of
interest."

" No, certainly I will not. Her appearance, and the
circumstances under which we found her, are all in her
favor."

" But we turned aside from the beaten path. We
ooked into a by-place to us; or we would not have
discovered her. She was not obtrusive. She asked no
aid; but, with the last few shillings that remained to
her in the world, had gone to recover, if possible, an
unredeemed pledge—the miniature of her mother, on
which she had obtained a small advance of money to

buy food and medicine for the dying original. This is but one of the thousand cases of real distress that are all around us. We could see them if we did but turn aside for a moment into ways unfamiliar to our feet."

"Did you learn who she was, and anything of her condition?" asked Mr. Edwards.

"Oh yes. To do so was but a common dictate of humanity. I would have felt it as a stain upon my conscience to have left one like her uncared for in the circumstances under which we found her."

"Did you accompany her home?"

"Yes; I went with her to the place she called her home—a room in which there was scarcely an article of comfort—and there learned the history of her past life and present condition. Does thee remember Belgrave, who carried on a large business in Maiden Lane some years ago?"

"Very well. But, surely this girl is not Mary Belgrave?"

"Yes. It was Mary Belgrave whom we met at th pawnbroker's sale."

"Mary Belgrave! Can it be possible? I knew the family had become poor; but not so poor as this!"

And Mr. Edwards, much disturbed in mind, walked uneasily about the floor. But soon pausing, he said—

"And so her mother is dead!"

"Yes. Her father died two years ago; and her mother, who has been sick ever since, died last week in abject poverty, leaving Mary friendless, in a world where the poor and needy are but little regarded. The miniature which Mary had secretly pawned in order to supply the last earthly need of her mother, she sought by her labor to redeem; but ere she had been able to save up enough for the purpose, the time for which the pledge had been taken, expired, and the pawn broker refused to renew it. Under the faint hope that she might be able to buy it in with the little pittance of money she had saved, she attended the sale where we found her."

The merchant had resumed his seat, and although he had listened attentively to the Quaker's brief history, he did not make any reply, but soon became lost in thought. From this he was interrupted by his visitor, who said, as he moved towards the door—

"I will bid thee good morning, friend Edwards."

"One moment, if you please," said the merchant, arousing himself, and speaking earnestly, "Where does Mary Belgrave live?"

The Friend answered the question, and, as Mr. Edwards did not seem inclined to ask any more, and besides fell back again into an abstract state, he wished him good morning and retired.

The poor girl was sitting alone in her room sewing,

late in the afternoon of the day on which the incident
at the auction room occurred, musing, as she had mused
for hours, upon the unexpected adventure. She did
not, in the excitement of the moment, know Mr.
Edwards when he first tendered her the miniature ; but
when he said with peculiar emphasis and earnestness,
turning away as he spoke—"Keep it, in Heaven's
name !" she recognized him fully. Since that moment,
she had not been able to keep the thought of him from
her mind. They had been intimate friends at one time;
but this was while they were both very young. Then
he had professed for her a boyish passion ; and she
had loved him with the childish fondness of a young
school-girl. As they grew older, circumstances separated them more ; and though no hearts were broken
in consequence, both often thought of the early days
of innocence and affection with pleasure.

Mary sat sewing, as we have said, late in the afternoon of the day on which the incident at the auction
room occurred, when there was a tap at her door. On
opening it, Mr. Edwards stood before her. She stepped
back a pace or two in instant surprise and confusion,
and he advanced into the desolate room. In a
moment, however, Mary recovered herself, and with as
much self-possession as, under the circumstances, she

could assume, asked her unexpected visitor to take a chair, which she offered him.

Mr. Edwards sat down, feeling much oppressed. Mary was so changed in everything, except in the purity and beauty of her countenance, since he had seen her years before, that his feelings were completely borne down. But he soon recovered himself enough to speak to her of what was in his mind. He had an old aunt, who had been a friend of Mary's mother, and from her he brought a message and an offer of a home. Her carriage was at the door—it had been sent for her —and he urged her to go with him immediately. Mary had no good reason for declining so kind an offer. It was a home that she most of all needed ; and she could not refuse one like this. *   *   *

" There is another unredeemed pledge," said Mr. Edwards, significantly, as he sat conversing with Mary about a year after she had found a home in the house of his aunt. Allusion had been made to the miniature f Mary's mother.

" Ah !" was the simple response.

" Yes. Don't you remember," and he took Mary's unresisting hand—" the pledge of this hand which you made me, I cannot tell how many years ago ?"

" That was a mere girlish pledge," ventured Mary with drooping eyes.

14

"But one that the woman will redeem," said Edwards confidently, raising the hand to his lips at the same time, and kissing it.

Mary leaned involuntarily towards him; and he perceiving the movement, drew his arm around her, and pressed his lips to her cheek.

It was no very long time afterwards before the pledge was redeemed.

⁻ DON'T MENTION IT.

"Don't mention it again for your life."

" No, of course not. The least said about such things the better."

" Don't for the world. I have told you in perfect confidence, and you are the only one to whom I have breathed it. I wouldn't have it get out for any consideration."

" Give yourself no uneasiness. I shall not allude to the subject."

" I merely told you because I knew you were a friend, and would let it go no farther. But would you have thought it ?"

" I certainly am very much surprised."

" So am I. But when things pass right before your eyes and ears, there is no gainsaying them."

"No. Seeing is said to be believing."

"Of course it is."

"But, Mrs. Grimes, are you very sure that you heard aright ?"

"I am positive, Mrs. Raynor. It occurred only an hour ago, and the whole thing is distinctly remembered. I called in to see Mrs. Comegys, and while I was there, the bundle of goods came home. I was present when she opened it, and she showed me the lawn dress it contained. There were twelve yards in it. 'I must see if there is good measure,' she said, and she got a yard-stick and measured it off. There were fifteen yaras instead of twelve. 'How is this ?' she remarked. 'I am sure I paid for only twelve yards, and here are fifteen.' The yard-stick was applied again. There was no mistake ; the lawn measured fifteen yards. 'What are you going to do with the surplus ?' I asked. 'Keep it, of course,' said Mrs. Comegys. 'There is just enough to make little Julia a frock. Won't she look sweet in it ?' I was so confounded that I could'nt say a word. Indeed, I could hardly look her in the face. At first I thought of calling her attention to the dishonesty of the act; but then I reflected that, as it was none of my business, I might get her ill-will for meddling in what didn't concern me."

" And you really think, then, that she meant to keep the three yards without paying for them ?"

" Oh, certainly ! But then I wouldn't say anything about it for the world. I wouldn't name it, on any consideration. Of course you will not repeat it."

" No. If I cannot find any good to tell of my friends, I try to refrain from saying anything evil."

" A most-excellent rule, Mrs. Raynor, and one that I always follow. I never speak evil of my friends, for it always does more harm than good. No one can say that I ever tried to injure another."

" I hope Mrs. Comegys thought better of the matter, upon reflection," said Mrs. Raynor.

" So do I. But I am afraid not. Two or three little things occur to me now, that I have seen in my intercourse with her, which go to satisfy my mind that her moral perceptions are not the best in the world. Mrs. Comegys is a pleasant friend, and much esteemed by every one. It could do no good to spread this matter abroad, but harm."

After repeating over and over again her injunction to Mrs. Raynor not to repeat a word of what she had told her, Mrs. Grimes bade this lady, upon whom she had called, good morning, and went on her way. Ten minutes after, she was in the parlor of an acquaintance, named Mrs. Florence, entertaining her with the gossip she had picked up since their last meeting. She had not been there long, before, lowering her voice, she said in a confidential way—

"I was at Mrs. Comegys' to-day, and saw something hat amazed me beyond every thing."

"Indeed !"

"Yes. You will be astonished when you hear it. Suppose you had purchased a dress and paid for a certain number of yards; and when the dress was sent home, you should find that the storekeeper had made a mistake and sent you three or four yards more than you had settled for. What would you do ?"

"Send it back, of course."

"Of course, so say I. To act differently would not be honest. Do you think so ?"

"It would not be honest for me."

"No, nor for any one. Now, would you have believed it ? Mrs. Comegys not only thinks but acts differently."

"You must be mistaken, certainly, Mrs. Grimes "

"Seeing is believing, Mrs. Florence."

"So it is said, but I could hardly believe my eyes against Mrs. Comegys' integrity of character. I think I ought to know her well, for we have been very intimate for years."

"And I thought I knew her, too. But it seems that I was mistaken."

Mrs. Grimes then repeated the story of the lawn dress.

"Gracious me! Can it be possible?" exclaimed Mrs. Florence. "I can hardly credit it."

"It occurred just as I tell you. But Mrs. Florence, you musn't tell it again for the world. I have mentioned it to you in the strictest confidence. But I neea hardly say this to you, for I know how discreet you are."

"I shall not mention it."

"It could do no good."

"None in the world."

"Isn't it surprising, that a woman who is so well off in the world as Mrs. Comegys, should stoop to a petty act like this?"

"It is, certainly."

"Perhaps there is something wrong here," and Mrs. Grimes placed her finger to her forehead and looked ber.

"How do you mean?" asked the friend.

"You've heard of people's having a dishonest monomania. Don't you remember the case of Mrs. Y——?"

"Very well."

"She had every thing that heart could desire. Her

husband was rich, and let her have as much money as
she wanted. I wish we could all say that, Mrs. Florence, don't you ?"

"It would be very pleasant, certainly, to have as
much money as we wanted."

"But, notwithstanding all this, Mrs. Y—— had such
a propensity to take things not her own, that she never
went into a dry goods store without purloining something, and rarely took tea with a friend without slip-
ping a teaspoon into her pocket. Mr. Y—— had a
great deal of trouble with her, and, in several cases,
paid handsomely to induce parties disposed to prose-
cute her for theft, to let the matter drop. Now do you
know that it has occurred to me that, perhaps, Mrs.
Comegys is afflicted in this way ? I shouldn't at all
wonder if it were so."

"Hardly."

"I'm afraid it is as I suspect. A number of suspicious circumstances have happened when she has been
about, that this would explain. But for your life, Mrs.
Florence, don't repeat this to any mortal !"

"I shall certainly not speak of it, Mrs. Grimes. It
is too serious a matter. I wish I had not heard of it,
for I can never feel toward Mrs. Comegys as I have
done. She is a very pleasant woman, and one with

whom it is always agreeable and profitable to spend an hour."

" It is a little matter, after all," remarked Mrs. Grimes, and, perhaps, we treat it too seriously."

" We should never think lightly of dishonest prac tices, Mrs. Grimes. Whoever is dishonest in little things, will be dishonest in great things, if a good opportunity offer. Mrs. Comegys can never be to me what she has been. That is impossible."

" Of course you will not speak of it again."

" You need have no fear of that."

A few days after, Mrs. Raynor made a call upon a friend, who said to her,

" Have you heard about Mrs. Comegys ?"

" What about her ?"

" I supposed you knew it. *I've* heard it from half a dozen persons. It is said that Perkins, through a mistake of one of his clerks, sent her home some fifteen or twenty yards of lawn more than she had paid for, and that, instead of sending it back, she kept it and made it up for her children. Did you ever hear of such a trick for an honest woman ?"

" I don't think any honest woman would be guilty of such an act. Yes, I heard of it a few days ago as a great secret, and have not mentioned it to a living soul."

14*

" Secret ? bless me ! it is no secret.   It is in every one's mouth."

" Is it possible ?   I must say that Mrs. Grimes has been very indiscreet."

" Mrs. Grimes !   Did it come from her in the first place ?"

" Yes.   She told me that she was present when the lawn came home, and saw Mrs. Comegys measure it, and heard her say that she meant to keep it."

" Which she has done.   For I saw her in the street, yesterday, with a beautiful new lawn, and her little Julia was with her, wearing one precisely like it."

" How any woman can do so is more than I can understand."

" So it is, Mrs. Raynor.   Just to think of dressing your child up in a frock as good as stolen !   Isn't it dreadful ?"

" It is, indeed !"

" Mrs. Comegys is not an honest woman.   That is clear.   I am told that this is not the first trick of the kind of which she has been guilty.   They say that she has a natural propensity to take things that are not her own."

" I can hardly believe that."

" Nor can I.   But it's no harder to believe this than to believe that she would cheat Perkins out of fifteen or twenty yards of lawn. It's a pity; for Mrs. Comegys, in every thing else, is certainly a very nice woman. In fact, I don't know any one I visit with so much pleasure."

Thus the circle of detraction widened, until there was scarcely a friend or acquaintance of Mrs. Comegys, near or remote, who had not heard of her having cheated a dry goods dealer out of several yards of lawn. Three, it had first been alleged; but the most common version of the story made it fifteen or twenty. Meantime, Mrs. Comegys remained in entire ignorance of what was alleged against her, although she noticed in two or three of her acquaintances, a trifling coldness that struck her as rather singular.

One day her husband, seeing that she looked quite sober, said—

"You seem quite dull to-day, dear. Don't you feel well?"

"Yes, I feel as well as usual, in body."

"But not in mind?"

"I do not feel quite comfortable in mind, certainly, though I don't know that I have any serious cause of uneasiness."

"Though a slight cause exists. May I ask what it is?"

"It is nothing more nor less than that I was coolly

cut by an old friend to-day, whom I met in a store on
Chesnut street. And as she is a woman that I highly
esteem, both for the excellence of her character, and
the agreeable qualities, as a friend, that she possesses.
I cannot but feel a little bad about it. If she were one
of that capricious class who get offended with you,
once a month, for no just cause whatever, I should not
care a fig. But Mrs. Markle is a woman of character,
good sense and good feeling, whose friendship I have
always prized."

"Was it Mrs. Markle?" said the husband, with
some surprise.

"Yes."

"What can possibly be the cause?"

"I cannot tell."

"Have you thought over every thing?"

"Yes, I have turned and turned the matter in my
mind, but can imagine no reason why she, of all others,
could treat me coolly."

"Have you never spoken of her in a way to have
your words misinterpreted by some evil-minded person—Mrs. Grimes, for instance—whose memory, or
moral sense, one or the other, is very dull?"

"I have never spoken of her to any one, except in
terms of praise. I could not do otherwise, for I look
upon her as one of the most faultless women I know."

"She has at least shown that she possesses one fault."

"What is that ?"

"If she has heard any thing against you of a character so serious as to make her wish to give up your acquaintance, she should at least have afforded you the chance of defending yourself before condemning you."

"I think that, myself."

"It may be that she did not see you," Mr. Comegys suggested.

"She looked me in the face, and nodded with cold formality."

"Perhaps her mind was abstracted."

"It might have been so. Mine would have been very abstracted, indeed, to keep me from a more cordial recognition of a friend."

"How would it do to call and see her ?"

"I have been thinking of that. But my feelings naturally oppose it. I am not conscious of having done any thing to merit a withdrawal of the friendly sentiments she has held towards me ; still, if she wishes to withdraw them, my pride says, let her do so."

"But pride, you know, is not always the best adviser."

"No. Perhaps the less regard we pay to its promptings, the better."

"I think so "

"It is rather awkward to go to a person and ask why you have been treated coldly."

"I know it is. But in a choice of evils, is it not always wisest to choose the least?"

"But is any one's bad opinion of you, if it be not correctly formed, an evil?"

"Certainly it is."

"I don't know. I have a kind of independence about me which says, 'Let people think what they please, so you are conscious of no wrong.'"

"Indifference to the world's good or bad opinion is all very well," replied the husband, "if the world will misjudge us. Still, as any thing that prejudices the minds of people against us, tends to destroy our usefulness, it is our duty to take all proper care of our reputations, even to the sacrifice of a little feeling in doing so."

Thus argued with by her husband, Mrs. Comegys, after turning the matter over in her mind, finally concluded to go and see Mrs. Markle. It was a pretty hard trial for her, but urged on by a sense of right, she called upon her two or three days after having been treated so coldly. She sent up her name by the servant. In about five minutes, Mrs. Markle descended to the parlor, where her visitor was awaiting her, and met her in a reserved and formal manner, that was alto gether unlike her former cordiality. It was as much as Mrs. Comegys could do to keep from retiring instantly, and without a word, from the house. But she compelled herself to go through with what she had begun Mrs. Markle did, indeed, offer her hand; or rather the tips of her fingers; which Mrs. Comegys, in mere reciprocation of the formality, accepted. Then came an embarrassing pause, after which the latter said—

"I see that I was not mistaken in supposing that there was a marked coldness in your manner at our last meeting."

Mrs. Markle inclined her head slightly.

"Of course there is a cause for this. May I, in justice to myself as well as others, inquire what it is ?"

"I did not suppose you would press an inquiry on the subject," replied Mrs. Markle. "But as you have done so, you are, of course, entitled to an answer."

There came another pause, after which, with a disturbed voice, Mrs. Markle said—

"For some time, I have heard a rumor in regard to you, that I could not credit. Of. late it has been so often repeated that I felt it to be my duty to ascertain its truth or falsehood. On tracing, with some labor, the report to its origin, I am grieved to find that it is too true."

"Please say what it is," said Mrs. Comegys, in a firm voice.

"It is said that you bought a dress at a dry goods store in this city, and that on its being sent home, there proved to be some yards more in the piece of goods than you paid for, and that instead of returning what was not your own, you kept it and had it made up for one of your children."

The face of Mrs. Comegys instantly became like crimson ; and she turned her head away to hide the confusion into which this unexpected allegation had thrown her. As soon as she could command her voice, she said—

"You will, of course, give me the author of this charge."

"You are entitled to know, I suppose," replied Mrs. Markle. "The person who originated this report is Mrs. Grimes. And she says that she was present when the dress was sent home. That you measured it in her presence, and that, finding there were several yards over, you declared your intention to keep it and make of it a frock for your little girl. And, moreover, that she saw Julia wearing a frock afterwards, exactly like the pattern of the one you had, which she well remembers. This seems to me pretty conclusive evidence. At least it was so to my mind, and I acted accordingly."

Mrs. Comegys sat for the full space of a minute with her eyes upon the floor, without speaking. When she looked up, the flush that had covered her face had gone. It was very pale, instead. Rising from her chair, she bowed formally, and without saying a word, withdrew.

"Ah me! Isn't it sad?" murmured Mrs. Markle, as she heard the street door close upon her visitor. "So much-that is agreeable and excellent, all dimmed by the want of principle. It seems hardly credible that a woman, with every thing she needs, could act dishonestly for so small a matter. A few yards of lawn against integrity and character! What a price to set upon virtue!"

Not more than half an hour after the departure of Mrs. Comegys, Mrs. Grimes called in to see Mrs. Markle.

"I hope," she said, shortly after she was seated, "that you won't say a word about what I told you a few days ago; I shouldn't have opened my lips on the subject if you hadn't asked me about it. I only mentioned it in the first place to a friend in whom I had the greatest confidence in the world. She has told some one, very improperly, for it was imparted to her as a secret, and in that way it has been spread abroad. I regret it exceedingly, for I would be the last person in the world to say a word to injure any one. I am particularly guarded in this."

" If it's the truth, Mrs. Grimes, I don't see that you
need be so anxious about keeping it a secret," returned
Mrs. Markle.

" The truth ! Do you think I would utter a word
that was not true ?"

" I did not mean to infer that you would. I believe
that what you said in regard to Mrs. Comegys was the
fact."

" It certainly was. But then, it will do no good to
make a disturbance about it. What has made me call
in to see you is this; some one told me that, in consequence of this matter, you had dropped the acquaintance of Mrs. Comegys."

" It is true; I cannot associate on intimate terms
with a woman who lacks honest principles."

" But don't you see that this will bring matters to a
head, and that I shall be placed in a very awkward
position ?"

" You are ready to adhere to your statement in regard to Mrs. Comegys ?"

" Oh, certainly ; I have told nothing but the truth.
But still, you can see that it will make me feel exceedingly unpleasant."

" Things of this kind are never very agreeable, I
know, Mrs. Grimes. Still we must act as we think
right, let what will follow. Mrs. Comegys has already

called upon me to ask an explanation of my conduct towards her."

"She has!" Mrs. Grimes seemed sadly distressed. "What did you say to her?"

"I told her just what I had heard."

"Did she ask your author?" Mrs. Grimes was almost pale with suspense.

"She did."

"Of course you did not mention my name?"

"She asked the author of the charge, and I named you."

"Oh dear, Mrs. Markle! I wish you hadn't done that. I shall be involved in a world of trouble, and get the reputation of a tattler and mischief-maker. What did she say?"

"Not one word."

"She didn't deny it?"

"No."

"Of course she could not. Well, that is some satisfaction at least. She might have denied it, and tried to make me out a liar, and there would have been plenty to believe her word against mine. I am glad she didn't deny it. She didn't say a word?"

"No."

"Did she look guilty?"

"You would have thought so, if you had seen her."

"What did she do?"

"She sat with her eyes upon the floor for some time, and then rose up, and without uttering a word, left the house."

"I wish she had said something. It would have been a satisfaction to know what she thought. But I suppose the poor woman was so confounded, that she didn't know what to say."

"So it appeared to me. She was completely stunned. I really pitied her from my heart. But want of principle should never be countenanced. If we are to have social integrity, we must mark with appropriate condemnation all deviations therefrom. It was exceedingly painful, but the path of duty was before me, and I walked in it without faltering."

Mrs. Grimes was neither so clear-sighted, nor so well satisfied with what she had done, as all this. She left the house of Mrs. Markle feeling very unhappy. Although she had been using her little unruly member against Mrs. Comegys with due industry, she was all the while on the most friendly terms with her, visiting at her house and being visited. It was only a few days before that she had taken tea and spent an evening with her. Not that Mrs. Grimes was deliberately hypocritical, but she had a free tongue, and, like too many in society, more cautious about what they said than she, much better pleased to see evil than good in a neighbour. There are very few of us, perhaps, who have not something of this fault—an exceedingly bad fault, by the way. It seems to arise from a consciousness of our own imperfections, and the pleasure we feel in making the discovery that others are as bad, if not worse than we are.

Two days after Mrs. Comegys had called on Mrs. Markle to ask for explanations, the latter received a note in the following words:

"MADAM.—I have no doubt you have acted according to your own views of right, in dropping as suddenly as you have done, the acquaintance of an old friend. Perhaps, if you had called upon me and asked explanations, you might have acted a little differently. My present object in addressing you is to ask, as a matter of justice, that you will call at my house to-morrow at twelve o'clock. I think that I am entitled to speak a word in my own defence. After you hav heard that, I shall not complain of any course you may think it right to pursue.   ANNA COMEGYS."

Mrs. Markle could do no less than call as she had been desired to. At twelve o'clock she rang the bell at Mrs. Comegy's door, and was shown into the parlor, where, to her no small surprise, she found about twenty ladies, most of them acquaintances, assembled, Mrs. Grimes among the number. In about ten minutes Mrs. Comegys came into the room, her countenance wearing a calm but sober aspect. She bowed slightly, but was not cordial toward, or familiar with, any one present. Without a pause she said—

"Ladies, I have learned within a few days, very greatly to my surprise and grief, that there is a report circulated among my friends, injurious to my character as a woman of honest principles. I have taken some pains to ascertain those with whom the report is familiar, and have invited all such to be here to-day. I learn from several sources, that the report originated with Mrs. Grimes, and that she has been very industrious in circulating it to my injury."

"Perhaps you wrong Mrs. Grimes there," spoke up Mrs. Markle. "She did not mention it to me until I inquired of her if the report was true. And then she told me that she had neve told it but to a single person, in confidence, and that she had inadvertently alluded to it, and thus it became a common report.— So I think that Mrs. Grimes cannot justly be charged with having sought to circulate the matter to your injury."

"Very well, we will see how far that statement is

correct," said Mrs. Comegys. "Did she mention the subject to you, Mrs. Raynor?"

"She did," replied Mrs. Raynor. "But in strict confidence, and enjoining it upon me not to mention it to any one, as she had no wish to injure you."

"Did you tell it to any one?"

"No. It was but a little while afterward that it was told to me by some one else."

"Was it mentioned to you, Mrs. Florence?" proceeded Mrs. Comegys, turning to another of the ladies present.

"It was, ma'am."

"By Mrs. Grimes?"

"Yes, ma'am."

"In confidence, I suppose?"

"I was requested to say nothing about it, for fear that it might create an unfavorable impression in regard to you."

"Very well; there are two already. How was it in your case, Mrs. Wheeler?"

This lady answered as the others had done. The question was then put to each lady in the room, when it appeared that out of the twenty, fifteen had received their information on the subject from Mrs. Grimes, and that upon every one secrecy had been enjoined, although not in every case maintained.

"So it seems, Mrs. Markle," said Mrs. Comegys, after she had finished her inquiries, "that Mrs. Grimes has, as I alleged, industriously circulated this matter to my injury."

"It certainly appears so," returned Mrs. Markle, coldly.

Thus brought into a corner, Mrs. Grimes bristled up like certain animals, which are good at running and skulking, but which, when fairly trapped, fight desperately.

"Telling it to a thousand is not half as bad as doing it, Mrs. Comegys," she said, angrily. "You needn't try to screen yourself from the consequences of your wrong doings, by raising a hue and cry against me. Go to the fact, madam! Go to the fact, and stand alongside of what you have done."

"I have no hesitation about doing that, Mrs. Grimes. Pray, what have I done?"

"It is very strange that you should ask, madam."

"But I am charged, I learn, with having committed a crime against society; and you are the author of the charge. What is the crime?"

"If it is any satisfaction to you, I will tell you. I was at your house when the pattern of the lawn dress you now have on was sent home. You measured it in my presence, and there were several yards in it more than you had bought and paid for"—

" How many ?"

Mrs. Grimes looked confused, and stammered out,

" I do not now exactly remember."

" How many did she tell you, Mrs. Raynor ?"

" She said there were three yards."

" And you, Mrs. Fisher ?"

" Six yards."

" And you, Mrs. Florence ?"

" Fifteen yards, I think."

" Oh, no, Mrs. Florence ; you are entirely mistaken. You misunderstood me," said Mrs. Grimes, in extreme perturbation.

" Perhaps so. But that is my present impression," replied Mrs. Florence.

" That will do," said Mrs. Comegys. " Mrs. Grimes can now go on with her answer to my inquiry. I will remark, however, that the overplus was just two yards."

" Then you admit that the lawn overran what you had paid for ?"

" Certainly I do. It overran just two yards."

" Very well. One yard or a dozen, the principle is just the same. I asked you what you meant to do with it, and you replied, ' keep it, of course.' Do you deny that ?"

15

"No. It is very likely that I did say so, for it was my intention to keep it."

"Without paying for it?" asked Mrs. Markle.

Mrs. Comegys looked steadily into the face of her nterrogator for some moments, a flush upon her cheek, an indignant light in her eye. Then, without replying to the question, she stepped to the wall and rang the parlor bell. In a few moments a servant came in.

"Ask the gentleman in the dining-room if he will be kind enough to step here." In a little while a step was heard along the passage, and then a young man entered.

"You are a clerk in Mr. Perkins' store?" said Mrs. Comegys.

"Yes, ma'am."

"You remember my buying this lawn dress at your store?"

"Very well, ma'am. I should forget a good many incidents before I forgot that."

"What impressed it upon your memory?"

"This circumstance. I was very much hurried at the time when you bought it, and in measuring it off, 'made a mistake against myself of two yards. There should have been four dresses in the piece. One had been sold previous to yours. Not long after your dress had been sent home, two ladies came into the store and chose each a dress from the pattern. On measuring the piece, I discovered that it was two yards short, and lost the sale of the dresses in consequence, as the ladies wished them alike. An hour afterward you called to say that I had made a mistake and sent you home two yards more than you had paid for; but that as you liked the pattern very much, you would keep it and buy two yards more for a dress for your little girl."

" Yes; that is exactly the truth in regard .to the dress. I am obliged to you, Mr. S———, for the trouble I have given you. I will not keep you any longer."

The young man bowed and withdrew.

The ladies immediately gathered around Mrs. Comegys, with a thousand apologies for having for a moment entertained the idea that she had been guilty of wrong, while Mrs. Grimes took refuge in a flood of tears.

" I have but one cause of complaint against you all," said the injured lady, " and it is this. A charge of so serious a nature should never have been made a subject of common report without my being offered a chance to defend myself. As for Mrs. Grimes, I can't readily understand how she fell into the error she did. But she never would have fallen into it if she had not been more willing to think evil than good of her friends. I do not say this to hurt her, but to state a truth that it may be well for her, and perhaps some of the rest of us, to lay to heart. It is a serious thing to speak evil of another, and should never be done except on the most unequivocal evidence. It never occurred to me to say to Mrs. Grimes that I would pay for the lawn; that I supposed she or any one else would have inferred, when I said I would keep it."

A great deal was said by all parties, and many apologies were made. Mrs. Grimes was particularly humble, and begged all present to forgive and forget what was past. She knew, she said, that she was apt to talk; it was a failing with her which she would try to correct. But that she didn't mean to do any one harm.

As to the latter averment, it can be believed or not as suits every one's fancy. All concerned in this affair felt that they had received a lesson they would not soon forget. And we doubt not, that some of our readers might lay it to heart with great advantage to themselves and benefit to others.

THE HEIRESS

KATE DARLINGTON was a belle and a beauty; and had, as might be supposed, not a few admirers. Some were attracted by her person; some by her winning manners, and not a few by the wealth of her family. But though sweet Kate was both a belle and a beauty, she was a shrewd, clear-seeing girl, and had far more penetration into character than belles and beauties are generally thought to possess. For the whole tribe of American dandies, with their disfiguring moustaches and imperials, she had a most hearty contempt. Hair never made up, with her, for the lack of brains.

But, as she was an heiress in expectancy, and moved in the most fashionable society, and was, with all, a gay and sprightly girl, Kate, as a natural consequence, drew around her the gilded moths of society, not a few of whom got their wings scorched, on approaching too near.

Many aspired to be lovers, and some, more ardent than the rest, boldly pressed forward and claimed her hand. But Kate did not believe in the doctrine that love begets love in all cases. Were this so, it was clear that she would have to love half a dozen, for at least that number came kneeling to her with their hearts in their hands.

Mr. Darlington was a merchant. Among his clerks was the son of an old friend, who, in dying some years before, had earnestly solicited him to have some care over the lad, who at his death would become friendless. In accordance with this last request, Mr. Darlington took the boy into his counting-room; and, in order that he might, with more fidelity, redeem his promise to the dying father, also received him into his family.

Edwin Lee proved himself not ungrateful for the kindness. In a few years he became one of Mr. Darlington's most active, trustworthy and intelligent clerks; while his kind, modest, gentlemanly deportmen at home, won the favor and confidence of all the family With Edwin, Kate grew up as with a brother. Their intercourse was of the most frank and confiding character.

But there came, at last, a change. Kate from a graceful sweet-tempered, affectionate girl, stepped forth, almost in a day, it seemed to Edwin, a full-grown, lovely woman, into whose eyes he could not look as steadily as before, and on whose beautiful face he could no longer gaze with the calmness of feeling he had until now enjoyed.

For awhile, Edwin could not understand the reason of this change. Kate was the same to him; and yet not the same. There was no distance—no reserve on her part; and yet, when he came into her presence, he felt his heart beat more quickly; and when she looked him steadily in the face, his eyes would droop, involuntarily, beneath her gaze.

Suddenly, Edwin awoke to a full realization of the fact that Kate was to him more than a gentle friend or a sweet sister. From that moment, he became reserved in his intercourse with her; and, after a short time, firmly made up his mind that it was his duty to retire from the family of his benefactor. The thought of endeavoring to win the heart of the beautiful girl, whom he had always loved as a sister, and now almost worshipped, was not for a moment entertained. To him there would have been so much of ingratitude in this, and so much that involved a base violation of Mr. Darlington's confidence, that he would have suffered anything rather than be guilty of such an act.

But he could not leave the home where he had been

so kindly regarded for years, without offering some reason that would be satisfactory. The true reason, he
could not, of course, give. After looking at the subject
in various lights, and debating it for a long time, Edwin
could see no way in which he could withdraw from the
family of Mr. Darlington, without betraying his secret,
unless he were to leave the city at the same time. He,
therefore, sought and obtained the situation of supercargo in a vessel loading for Valparaiso.

When Edwin announced this fact to Mr. Darlington,
the merchant was greatly surprised, and appeared hurt
that the young man should take such a step without a
word of consultation with him. Edwin tried to explain;
but, as he had to conceal the real truth, his explanation
rather tended to make things appear worse than better.

Kate heard the announcement with no less surprise
than her father. The thing was so sudden, so unlooked
for, and, moreover, so uncalled for, that she could not
understand it. In order to take away any pecuniary
reason for the step he was about to take, Mr. Darlington, after holding a long conversation with Edwin,
made him offers far more advantageous than his proposed expedition could be to him, viewed in any light.
But he made them in vain. Edwin acknowledged the
kindness, in the warmest terms, but remained firm in
his purpose to sail with the vessel.

"Why will you go away and leave us, Edwin?" said Kate, one evening when they happened to be alone, about two weeks before his expected departure. "I do think it very strange!"

Edwin had avoided, as much as possible, being alone with Kate, a fact which the observant maiden had not failed to notice. Their being alone now was from accident rather than design on his part.

"I think it right for me to go, Kate," the young man replied, as calmly as it was possible for him to speak under the circumstances. "And when I think it right to do a thing, I never hesitate or look back."

"You have a reason, for going, of course. Why, then, not tell it frankly? Are we not all your friends?"

Edwin was silent, and his eyes rested upon the floor, while a deeper flush than usual was upon his face. Kate looked at him fixedly. Suddenly a new thought flashed through her mind, and the color on her own cheeks grew warmer. Her voice from that moment was lower and more tender; and her eyes, as she conversed with the young man, were never a moment from his face. As for him, his embarrassment in her presence was never more complete, and he betrayed the secret that was in his heart even while he felt the most earnest to conceal it. Conscious of this, he excused himself and retired as soon as it was possible to do so.

Kate sat thoughtful for some time after he had left. Then rising up, she went, with a firm step to her father's room.

"I have found out," she said, speaking with great self-composure, "the reason why Edwin persists in going away."

"Ah! what is the reason, Kate? I would give much to know."

"He is in love," replied Kate, promptly.

"In love! How do you know that?"

"I made the discovery to-night."

"Love should keep him at home, not drive him away," said Mr. Darlington.

"But he loves hopelessly," returned the maiden. "He is poor, and the object of his regard belongs to a wealthy family."

"And her friends will have nothing to do with him."

"I am 'not so sure of that. But he formed an acquaintance with the young lady under circumstances that would make it mean, in his eyes, to urge any claims upon her regard."

"Then honor as well as love takes him away."

"Honor in fact; not love. Love would make him stay," replied the maiden with a sparkling eye, and something of proud elevation in the tones of her voice.

A faint suspicion of the truth now came stealing on the mind of Mr. Darlington.

"Does the lady know of his preference for her?" he asked.

"Not through any word or act of his, designed to communicate a knowledge of the fact," replied Kate, her eyes falling under the earnest look bent upon her by Mr. Darlington.

"Has he made you his confidante?"

"No, sir. I doubt if the secret has ever passed his lips." Kate's face was beginning to crimson, but she drove back the tell-tale blood with a strong effort of the will.

"Then how came you possessed of it," inquired the father.

"The blood came back to her face with a rush, and she bent her head so that her dark glossy curls fell over and partly concealed it. In a moment or two she had regained her self-possession, and looking up she answered,

"Secrets like this do not always need oral or written language to make them known. Enough, father, that I have discovered the fact that his heart is deeply imbued with a passion for one who knows well his virtues—his pure, true heart—his manly sense of honor—with a passion for one who has looked upon him til now as a brother, but who henceforth must regard him with a different and higher feeling."

Kate's voice trembled. As she uttered the last few words, she lost control of herself, and bent forward, and hid her face upon her father's arm.

Mr. Darlington, as might well be supposed, was taken altogether by surprise at so unexpected an announcement. The language used by his daughter needed no interpretation. She was the maiden beloved by his clerk.

"Kate," said he, after a moment or two of hurried reflection, "this is a very serious matter. Edwin is only a poor clerk, and you—"

"And I," said Kate, rising up, and taking the words from her father, "and I am the daughter of a man who can appreciate what is excellent in even those who are humblest in the eyes of the world. Father, is not Edwin far superior to the artificial men who flutter around every young lady who now makes her appearance in the circle where we move? Knowing him as you do, I am sure you will say yes."

"But, Kate——"

"Father, don't let us argue this point. Do you want Edwin to go away?" And the young girl laid her hand upon her parent, and looked him in the face with unresisting affection.

"No dear; I certainly don't wish him to go."

Nor do I," returned the maiden, as she leaned forward again, and laid her face upon his arm. In a little while she arose, and, with her countenance turned partly away, said—

"Tell him not to go, father——"

And with these words she retired from the room.

On the next evening, as Edwin was sitting alone in one of the drawing-rooms, thinking on the long night of absence that awaited him, Mr. Darlington came in, accompanied by Kate. They seated themselves near the young man, who showed some sense of embarrassment. There was no suspense, however, for Mr. Darlington said—

"Edwin, we none of us wish you to go away. You know that I have urged every consideration in my power, and now I have consented to unite with Kate in renewing a request for you to remain. Up to this time you have declined giving a satisfactory reason for your sudden resolution to leave; but a reason is due to us—to me in particular—and I now most earnestly conjure you to give it."

The young man at this became greatly agitated, but did not venture to make a reply.

"You are still silent on the subject," said Mr. Darlington.

"He will not go, father," said Kate, in a tender, appealing voice. "I know he will not go. We cannot let him go. Kinder friends he will not find anywhere than he has here. And we shall miss him from our .ome circle. There will be a vacant place at our board. Will you be happier away, Edwin?"

The last sentence was uttered in a tone of sisterly affection.

"Happier!" exclaimed the young man, thrown off his guard. "Happier! I shall be wretched while away."

"Then why go?" returned Kate, tenderly.

At this stage of affairs, Mr. Darlington got up, and retired; and we think we had as well retire with the reader.

The good ship "Leonora" sailed in about ten days. She had a supercargo on board; but his name was not Edwin Lee.

Fashionable people were greatly surprised when the beautiful Kate Darlington married her father's clerk; and moustached dandies curled their lip, but it mattered not to Kate. She had married a man in whose worth, affection, and manliness of character, she could repose a rational confidence. If not a fashionable, she was a happy wife.